THE

THREE

MRS. GREYS

Also by Shelly Ellis

The Branch Avenue Boys series
In These Streets
Know Your Place
The Final Play

Chesterton Scandal series
Best Kept Secrets
Bed of Lies
Lust & Loyalty
To Love & Betray

Gibbons Gold Digger series
Can't Stand the Heat
The Player & the Game
Another Woman's Man
The Best She Ever Had

THE

THREE

MRS. GREYS

SHELLY ELLIS

www.kensingtonbooks.com

DAFINA BOOKS are published by

Kensington Publishing Corp.
119 West 40th Street
New York, NY 10018

All Kensington titles, imprints, and distributed lines are available at special quantity discounts for bulk purchases for sales promotion, premiums, fund-raising, and educational or institutional use.

Special book excerpts or customized printings can also be created to fit specific needs. For details, write or phone the office of the Kensington Sales Manager: Kensington Publishing Corp., 119 West 40th Street, New York, NY 10018. Attn. Sales Department. Phone: 1-800-221-2647.

The Dafina logo is a trademark of Kensington Publishing Corp.

ISBN-13: 978-1-4967-3131-9
ISBN-10: 1-4967-3131-X
First Kensington Trade Paperback Printing: April 2021

ISBN-13: 978-1-4967-3132-6 (ebook)
ISBN-10: 1-4967-3132-8 (ebook)
First Kensington Electronic Edition: April 2021

10 9 8 7 6 5 4 3 2 1

Printed in the United States of America

To Andrew and Chloe,
my compass, my conscience, my solace, and my heart . . .

Monday

Chapter 1

Vanessa

Vanessa Grey pushed herself up to her elbows and squinted in the dark of her bedroom as her cell phone continued to buzz like a persistent bee that refused to fly away. She reached out and turned on her night table desk lamp. She grabbed her cell and checked the screen. When she saw the message and who it was from, she grumbled.

BILAL: Gotta see you today. Won't take no for an answer

She wished Bilal would stop texting her. She'd already told him the last time they saw each other that enough was enough. She couldn't do this anymore.

VANESSA: NO!!!

She pressed send and was about to press the button to delete the entire message string, erasing all traces of it and Bilal from her phone and, hopefully, her life, when she saw another message appear within seconds.

BILAL: PLEASE! Won't take long. Got something to tell you

She huffed and glanced at the closed bathroom door.

It was just after dawn, and her husband Cyrus was getting ready for work in there, making more noise in their bathroom than any of the passing garbage trucks. But whenever he woke up, he always walked around like some Jolly Green Giant who was trying to scare off villagers—stomping his feet, snorting to clear his nose, and generally, making a lot of racket.

Cy was running water now. He was probably brushing his teeth, which meant he would come out of the bathroom soon. He'd ask her who she was texting this early and she'd have to make up some excuse. Vanessa was getting so tired of excuses. She wished Bilal would just go away.

VANESSA: Why do you need to see me? Say whatever you've gotta say now!

She saw the three little blinking dots appear that showed he was typing back a message.

BILAL: FINE! I love you. I want you. Leave him!

"Good God," Vanessa murmured before she grimaced.

If she'd known two months ago that a tryst with her eldest son's new soccer coach would mushroom into this, she never would've done it.

It had seemed innocent at first. Well, meeting up with a twenty-four-year-old to hook up two to three times a week wasn't *innocent*, per se, but Vanessa hadn't planned for the affair to ever get back to Cy or to impact their marriage. She definitely would never consider leaving her husband for Bilal.

Bilal was just meant to be a temporary side piece—a short-lived fling.

He was the sexy, charming younger man of her late-night fantasies—a milk chocolate delight who wore tight white Under Armour shirts and blue basketball shorts that showed off his ass and that he never skipped leg day. More than half the moms who showed up for practices and sat in the stands while the boys played soccer had whispered about how fine Bilal was.

Vanessa never partook in those whispers, keeping her

lustful thoughts to herself. But she'd noticed how Bilal had looked at her when she asked him questions about the game schedule and uniforms. She'd wondered if it was her imagination when he'd held her hand a lot longer than necessary whenever he shook it.

Years ago, before Vanessa had married Cy and had kids, men had flirted with her all the time. She'd had her pick of boyfriends, getting whatever she wanted out of them—money, clothes, cars, and getaway vacations. But those days were over. Vanessa had tried to keep herself up with her workout routines and monthly facials, but her breasts were admittedly not as buoyant now that they'd nursed three babies. Her thighs and butt had a lot more dimples. And she could spot more gray hairs on her head and *down there* than she could a decade ago, but Bilal didn't seem to mind any of that. He'd told her the first time they were alone, while they stood under the shade of her SUV's hatchback, away from the kids and the prying eyes of other parents, that she was the most beautiful woman he'd ever seen.

"Are you joking?" she'd asked him with a laugh, pausing from unloading the fruit snacks and Gatorade from her car, caught off guard by his admission.

"No," he'd said with a slow shake of the head, "I wouldn't joke about somethin' like that."

The flirting had only escalated from there.

When he asked her if she'd like to meet up for lunch one day at a Tex-Mex restaurant in a neighboring county, she didn't tell him no, or that his invitation was inappropriate because she was a married woman. She liked his compliments and his handsome smile.

It's just lunch, she'd convinced herself after saying yes. *Nothing wrong with that!*

Vanessa could blame the two margaritas at their lunch for being so tipsy that she hadn't felt comfortable driving, and instead climbed into Bilal's car for a ride back home when he offered. But she couldn't blame the drinks alone on how she'd ended up having sex with him in the back-seat of said car at a nearby public park soon after. The truth was, Bilal made her feel sexy and special, like the tummy tuck and breast lift she'd been considering weren't necessary. And he fulfilled her basic sexual needs. Was it her fault that she felt a sharp increase in her libido just when her husband seemed to lose almost all sexual interest in her? It was like she'd been set up to start cheating.

But that first hookup in his car had bloomed into about two dozen more, and now it was getting out of hand. The sex was good—*damn* good, but obviously Bilal was getting confused about their little arrangement. Vanessa had to set him straight. She began typing again.

VANESSA: I'm not leaving him but I would like you to leave me the hell alone. Stop texting. Stop calling here!

He'd called the house only yesterday. Luckily, Cy Jr. had answered the phone, not his father.

"Coach said he needs to speak with you, Mom," Cy Jr. had lisped through his braces, holding out the cordless phone in their kitchen to her.

"Tell him I'm busy and I'll call him back later," she'd said.

Cy Jr. had nodded and relayed the message. But Vanessa hadn't called Bilal back like she'd promised, which was probably why he was texting her with this nonsense.

BILAL: Well, maybe your husband will leave you if I tell him what's been going on

Reading those words, her stomach dropped.

Bilal wouldn't do that, would he? He wouldn't tell Cy about their affair. He wouldn't ruin their family so recklessly. He wasn't *that* stupid. Cy would kill him if he found out.

BILAL: Think I won't? I will! TRY ME. If you want me to keep my mouth shut, meet me today

Vanessa took a panicked glance at the bathroom door. Cy was no longer running water. He was about to come back into their bedroom. She was sure of it. She could imagine her husband strolling into the room, glancing over her shoulder, and seeing the string of texts. She couldn't let that happen. Her fingers flew over the screen.

VANESSA: Where? WHEN?

BILAL: My place. 12:30

She hated going to his place. It was too risky. She worried about nosy neighbors or if anyone around there would spot her walking into his apartment in the middle of the day and recognize her, but it didn't sound like she had much of a choice now that Cy was opening the bathroom door. She didn't have time to argue. Instead, she deleted the message string, set down her phone, sat upright, and pretended to stretch.

"Good morning, baby," she said with a grin to her husband, who strolled into the bedroom with a towel wrapped around his waist.

Cyrus Grey was a big man. His muscles weren't as defined and carefully sculpted as Bilal's, but Cy was still tall and solid. He could be a model for the folk hero John Henry with his wide shoulders, big arms, imposing height, thick beard, and bald head. When she'd seen him in the club more than a decade ago, she could remember thinking as she looked him up and down at the bar, "Now that is a dude nobody's gonna fuck with." He was a man who could lend protection and security, and that was exactly what he'd done for the past eleven years.

Cy worked hard as a financial consultant, putting in long hours and lots of business travel for his job, but he made sure he brought all that money home to his family. He took care of them by setting them up with a four-thousand-square-foot colonial in the picturesque Maryland suburbs with a pool, a basketball court, and a three-car garage. He drove a silver BMW while Vanessa zipped around town in a black Mercedes SUV with personalized plates that said "MOM4EVA". The kids all went to a private academy where all the children wore blazers with the school's insignia on the breast pocket and toted violin cases, tennis rackets, and lacrosse sticks along with their backpacks. The tuition cost the same as some colleges.

Cy was a loving, if sometimes absent, husband and a doting father. And how had she repaid him for all of this?

By cheating on him, she thought guiltily, kicking herself for agreeing to meet up with Bilal later.

"Mornin', baby," Cy rumbled in his heavy baritone as he leaned down and gave her a kiss on the cheek.

She rose from their California king and reached for her silk robe as he dropped his towel to the floor, opened one of his dresser drawers, and began to dress. The morning light piercing the blinds played on his back and legs, creating gold bands on skin as dark as coffee, sans milk.

"When do you have to leave today?" she asked, shoving her arms into the robe's sleeves. "Got enough time for breakfast?"

He chuckled as he stepped into his boxer briefs. "You're really gonna cook me breakfast?"

"Why do you sound so surprised?" She laughed too. "I cook you breakfast all the time!"

"Not lately."

"Well, I am today!" She walked across the bedroom, stood on the balls of her feet, wrapped her arms around him, and gave him a lip-smacking kiss. "I know how to take care of my man. You want your eggs over easy or scrambled?"

"Scrambled. Thanks, baby," he said, before giving her a pat on the bottom. He then resumed dressing while she walked into the hall to wake up their kids for the school day and start cooking that bacon and scrambled eggs.

* * *

More than four hours later, Vanessa lowered dark shades over her eyes before climbing out of her SUV. She looped the strap of her designer handbag over her arm and took a surreptitious glance around her before slamming the car door shut and walking swiftly along the curb and past the gate to Bilal's garden apartment on the first floor of the complex.

She wore her hair in a ponytail under an old baseball cap and had zippered her black Versace hoodie all the way up to the collar even though it was a particularly humid day in May, and almost eighty degrees outside. She felt like a secret agent, trying so hard not to be noticed, hoping no one recognized her. But it looked like her efforts weren't necessary. The block was mostly empty save for a mailman unloading his truck, a jogger, and one old man walking his dog—a nervous, pint-sized terrier who kept tugging at his zip leash and yipping frantically.

She walked the short distance to Bilal's front door and knocked. Within seconds, the door opened, and Bilal stood in the doorway in a tank top and pair of sweats.

"What's up?" he said with a smirk.

"Don't 'what's up' me," she snapped, shoving her way past him into his apartment. As he closed the door behind her, she yanked off her sunglasses and glared around her.

Bilal's apartment was what you would expect of a twenty-something bachelor. The only adornment on the bare white walls was his mounted flat screen TV. Next to his sofa was a weight bench along with a series of weights on the floor and a video game console and stack of game cartridges. She knew from past experience that his bedroom was just as bare and underwhelming—a mattress with a box spring and no headboard, surrounded by a series of tennis shoes and discarded dirty socks and T-shirts.

She turned her withering gaze back to him.

Vanessa couldn't believe this little boy actually thought she would leave Cy and their life together for this.

He must be crazy, she thought, sucking her teeth.

Bilal's smirk disappeared. "You really gonna come in here with attitude?"

"What did you expect? You threatened to tell my husband what we've been doing! You thought I was gonna bring you flowers?" she asked, cocking an eyebrow.

"You didn't have to bring me flowers, bae." He reached out and roughly dragged her against him so that she landed hard against his chest. The gesture caught her off guard. "Just bringing your fine ass over here was enough."

He leaned down to kiss her, but she turned her mouth away. She tried to ease out of his embrace but wasn't as successful. "Bilal, I told you that I'm done with this shit."

"No, you're not. I don't know why you keep saying that lie like somebody's gonna believe it."

Instead of trying to kiss her mouth again, he went for her neck—her weak spot. He dipped his head and licked the skin behind her ear then nibbled her ear lobe, making her close her eyes, despite herself.

"Don't fight it," he whispered as he reached up and lowered the zipper of her jacket, revealing the lace bra underneath. He then began to fondle her breast through the bra.

She should've pushed his hand away, but she didn't. Instead she fell under the spell she always did when she was with Bilal. Her brain was no longer in control; her vagina gave all he orders. She let him ease her back against the living room wall, tug the down her bra cup, and rub his thumb over the nipple until it hardened against the palm of his hand and she moaned. The entire time he left a trail of kisses along her neck, collar bone, and chin.

"Don't keep denying it," he panted. "You know you want this. You know what we've got . . . that we belong together."

That was a badly needed bucket of cold water on the moment.

Vanessa's eyes flashed open and she shoved his hand away. She stepped away from the wall and lifted her bra back into place. "*What we've got?* What we've got is a few weeks of screwin'! Why do you keep trying to make this more than what it is?"

"Are you really gonna stand there and act like you aren't in love with me?"

"I'm *not* in love with you!" she shouted as she raised the zipper of her jacket. "I just want you to leave me the hell alone! I came here to tell you that. I want you to get it through your head! I have a life, Bilal. Don't you get that? A life that's important to me. I've got a husband and—"

"And that's the problem," Bilal finished for her. "Your goddamn husband! You don't wanna be with him, Nessa. You don't love that dude. You're just with him for the shit he can buy you. I know what's up! But if you divorce him, you can *still* keep the money, bae. You and me can share it!"

She was certain of it now—Bilal was delusional.

"I'm not getting a divorce. But if you keep harassing me, I *am* going to get a restraining order against your ass."

He barked out a laugh. "Yeah, try explaining that to your man."

She knew Bilal probably wouldn't believe her when she said that, but she had to try. She had to say something to finally convince him it was over. Rather than back off the lie, she decided to double down.

"I will do it if I have to! If you call me again, I swear to God I'm going right to the Sheriff's Office and I'm filing that restraining order! You just try *me*," she said icily, echoing his own words from his earlier text back to him.

Vanessa put back on her sunglasses and walked toward the front door, but stopped in her tracks when Bilal grabbed her forearm. She tried to yank her arm away, but his vice-like grip only tightened.

"Get your hands off of me! Are you crazy?"

She glowered up at him, but the glower disappeared when she saw his face had changed. That cynical, cocky air he usually had had disappeared. Pure fury replaced it. For a few seconds, she wondered if he really had gone crazy. Her throat went dry and for the first time she was frightened, not angry.

"You walk out of that door right now, Nessa, and you're gonna regret this. I promise you. I'll make sure of that shit."

Vanessa tugged her arm again. This time she got free of him. Instead of walking, she almost ran to the door and outside of the apartment. She didn't look back. She bee-lined to her Mercedes and pulled off, driving so fast through the parking lot that her tires squealed.

As she drove and mile after mile was put between her and Bilal, she began to calm down. It was easier than she thought it would be to push him out of her mind; Bilal didn't text or call her again all day. Perhaps her message had finally sunken in this time, despite his threat. She could go back to the way things were before this whole fiasco. She could return to being a boring but harried, stay-at-home mom.

Vanessa did her errands for the day, going to the grocery store, picking up the dry cleaning, and getting her daughter, Zoe's, inhaler from the drug store.

Her cell phone rang and she rolled her eyes, certain it was Bilal.

But it was a hospital.

Cyrus had been shot.

Chapter 2

Noelle

It was a miracle that Noelle had made it to the hospital in one piece. Her nerves had been frayed thinner than cheap charmeuse during the drive from her store, Azure, in Northern Virginia, to the hospital fifty-five miles away in Maryland. But for the entire hour and half, she had chanted out loud and in her head, "I hope he's okay. I hope he's okay. Dear God, let him be okay!"

It was like a mantra. It had helped her focus and kept her from driving through stoplights or veering off the road even as her heart raced, her hands shook, and she was blinded by her tears.

Noelle still didn't know why the hospital hadn't called her to tell her that he'd been shot. She was his wife for God's sake. Thankfully, a nurse in the ER used to be a regular customer and had recognized Noelle's husband when they'd wheeled him in on a stretcher. "Noelle, you need to get down here right away," she'd whispered into her cell phone. "Your husband's been shot. They've called in the trauma team."

"*He's been shot?*" Noelle had exclaimed while she'd sat

in the back office. Through the office door, she could hear two of her salesgirls talking and laughing over the music playing in the boutique. "What? When? Who would . . . who would—"

"I don't know the details. I just know it's bad. *Really* bad! Just get here! Get here as fast as you can," the nurse said.

So now Noelle was racing across the hospital parking lot to the ER entrance, trying not to fall in her snakeskin pumps. She usually switched to flats when she was out of the boutique, but she'd forgotten to do it this time around. Her husband's welfare was more important to her than comfortable footwear.

As she approached the automatic doors, they slid open with a soft hush. It was hot outside but all the perspiration on her body was quickly wicked away when she stepped into the freezing waiting room where people sat in the more than forty plastic chairs assembled in rows in the center of the room and along the walls. One woman nearest to the door groaned as she squirmed in her seat, like she was trying her best to get comfortable, but was not succeeding. A baby let out strangled wails on the other side of the waiting room. His round face was flushed bright red and covered with spots that looked like chicken pox. An elderly man stood near one of the bathroom doors, yelling for the person inside to come out. Noelle went straight to the information desk, where a nurse sat, flipping casually through paperwork, either ignoring or just blissfully unaware of all the chaos around her.

"Hi. Uh, hi," Noelle said to the nurse's bowed head, barely able to articulate words. She adjusted her purse on her shoulder. "I wanted to . . . check on the status of m-m-my husband." She stuttered between gulping breaths as the nurse looked up at her. "He was sh-shot. I was . . . I was told he was t-t-taken to the ER about an hour ago."

The nurse nodded. "Can I have a name, please?"

"Cyrus . . . Cyrus Grey."

The nurse nodded again and typed his name into a nearby desk computer.

While Noelle waited, she anxiously glanced around her. "Please let him be okay," she whispered yet again. "Please let him be okay."

The nurse squinted at the computer screen.

"*What?*" Noelle asked, panic tightening her throat as her eyes shifted from the nurse's brown face to the computer screen and back again. "What's wrong?"

"Your husband is no longer in the ER. He's now in surgery, ma'am."

"Umm, OK, where is that?"

"Upstairs. Seventh floor. You can wait up there. The doctor can give you more information on the patient."

Noelle stepped off the steel elevator a few minutes later and looked around her. She quickly spotted yet another waiting room, though it was filled with a lot less people and the atmosphere was certainly much calmer than the ER waiting room seven floors below. This one looked more like a dentist's office with its upholstered armchairs, end tables, and a flat screen TV where a segment on how to live with diabetes now showed. She noticed an elderly woman in one chair near a large fichus plant staring off into space. Across the waiting area, three people sat—an older man and two younger women. In the far-off corner was a woman in a black track suit, loudly talking on her cell phone.

"No, Mama, I haven't gotten any updates yet," the light-skinned woman said, tossing her long dark ponytail over her shoulder. "I spoke to some cops earlier, but I'm still waiting for the doctor to come out . . . Did you pick up the kids like I asked?"

Noelle took the seat on the other side of the waiting room, facing the woman. When she sat down, she dropped her purse onto her lap and loudly exhaled. She adjusted the front of her silk wrap dress, realizing belatedly that her bra was showing.

Noelle felt like she had run around a stadium track about a half dozen times. The adrenaline spurred on by fear from earlier had finally worn off, and now she just felt exhausted and worried. She had no idea who would want to harm her husband. Was it a robbery gone wrong? Did the person shoot him on purpose? What the hell was he even doing in Baltimore? She thought he was on a business trip in Los Angeles.

And worse than the questions of why the shooting had happened, was what the aftermath of all this would be. What if Cyrus didn't make it through his surgery? What if he died?

Tears welled in Noelle's eyes again at the thought. She sniffed, wishing desperately that she had brought some tissues with her.

She regretted that her last words to Cy had been words of anger. Five nights ago, before he'd left for his trip, they'd had another one of their arguments. They seemed have them all the time nowadays. She had begged him to finally go to the fertility specialist with her to find out why she wasn't getting pregnant.

"We've been at this for a year and a half, Cy," she'd pled over dinner. "We *have* to do this!"

Cy had continued to eat his dinner at the other end of the table, slicing into his steak and taking a bite like he hadn't heard her, infuriating Noelle even more.

"Are you listening to me?" she'd shouted, pounding her fist on the table, making her wineglass topple over and spill a stream of Moscato across the glass tabletop.

He'd finally looked up at her. "Yes, baby! Damn, I hear you," Cy had said.

"You need to go to the doctor to get tested." She'd righted the wineglass again and dabbed with her dinner napkin at the spilled wine, halfheartedly cleaning it up. "They already tested me. I'm fine! Everything checked out. So the only person left is you. It's *your turn*, Cy."

She'd watched as he began to slice into his steak again. "No."

"No? Why the hell not?"

"Because I ain't jerking off into a cup in some doctor's office to prove my soldiers still work. Nothing is wrong with my sperm. Okay?"

"But how do you know? How the hell do you know for sure? Why not just get tested?" she'd cried.

He hadn't answered her but instead, silently continued eating. She'd closed her eyes.

"Cy, please! *Please*, do this for me!"

"Why are you so obsessed with having a baby? Would it be the end of the world if we didn't? Are you saying we aren't enough?"

"Of course we are! But we could be *so* much more if we had our own family."

He'd sat back in his chair and wiped his mouth with his dinner napkin. "Are you sure you're even ready to have a baby right now?"

"What the hell does that mean? Why wouldn't I be?"

"I mean are you stable, Noelle? Is your mind right?" He'd tapped his brow with his index finger. "Babies are stressful, sweetheart. I'd hate for you to . . . you know . . . have another one of your episodes with a baby around."

That's when she'd lost it.

How dare Cyrus use her mental health against her for something like this? He'd known how much having a child meant to her and how she saw it as righting the wrongs of her own messed-up childhood—the very childhood that had helped cause her depression. She had explained to him the abscess in her heart she'd felt for years, and how she believed it could only be filled with a baby.

But now he was acting like none of that mattered, that her long-held hopes and desires were silly and unimportant. He'd done that with the boutique too. She knew her husband's visits to Azure weren't social ones; Cy simply wanted to check up on her and his financial investment, which she suspected he still thought was a waste of money. The shop was just a little indulgence meant to keep his barren wife busy and distract her from the baby she kept begging him for, lest she fall into another one of her dark moods.

Did what she wanted even matter to him—or had he just been patronizing her this whole time?

"Fuck you, Cy," she'd whispered before slapping her napkin onto the dinner table, shoving back her chair, and walking out of the dining room. She'd stalked straight upstairs before slamming the door to their master suite shut behind her.

Now Noelle wished she had called Cy. She wished she'd told him that even though he'd hurt her with his flippant attitude about having a baby and so many other things that were important to her, she still cared for him. She just wanted to get back to the loving place where they used to be, where they hadn't been in quite a while. Now they may never get that chance.

Noelle clutched her hands in front of her and bowed her head in silent prayer. Even though she wasn't alone in the waiting room, she felt like she was. She wished someone were there to hold her hand and reassure her that everything would be okay, that Cy would be alright.

Tariq would do it if he were here. He was Cy's business

partner. His right-hand man. When Cy was traveling for his financial consultancy company, it was Tariq who would stop by their townhome to check on her and see if she needed anything. She never knew if he did it because Cy had asked him to, but Noelle appreciated Tariq's attention and company all the same.

She had called him on the way to the hospital to ask what had happened to Cyrus.

"What do you mean?" Tariq had asked. "What happened to Cy?"

"The nurse said he was shot! He was taken to Johns Hopkins in Baltimore. I didn't even know he was back home in the DMV! I thought he was on a business trip with you," she'd said.

Tariq had gone quiet on the other end of the line. In fact, he was quiet for so long she'd thought maybe the call had dropped, but then he'd suddenly said, "Uh, no . . . no, Cy had to . . . uh . . . he had to leave the trip early."

"*What?* So why didn't he come—"

"Don't worry," Tariq had interrupted, cutting her off. "I'll take the first flight home. Okay, Noelle? Just stay calm. I'll be there in a few hours . . . by this evening."

"But—"

"Stay strong! I'll see you soon."

Now she wondered why hadn't Cyrus called her to tell her that he'd left his business trip early? Why hadn't he come straight home instead of going to Baltimore for some reason, and what had he been doing when he was shot?

Noelle slowly looked up when one of the doctors, a short Asian man in a white coat and green scrubs, walked into the waiting room. Several eyes zeroed in on him simultaneously. They were all eager to hear news about their loved ones.

"Mama, I'll call you back," the woman across from

Noelle whispered into her cell phone before hanging up and dropping it into her purse.

Noelle sat upright in her chair as the doctor came to a stop in the middle of the waiting room. She braced herself.

"Mrs. Grey?" he called out.

"*Yes?*" Noelle and the woman answered simultaneously. Their eyes snapped to one another in surprise.

The doctor cleared his throat. "This would be the wife of Cyrus Grey."

"Yes, that's me," Noelle said, just as the woman answered, "Yeah, Cy's my husband."

This time their dual looks of surprise morphed into confusion.

"Is there . . . is there more than one Cyrus Grey at this hospital?" Noelle asked, hoping that would explain the mix up.

"Uh, not that I'm aware of," the doctor said, looking uneasily between the two women. "There could be though. I can have one of the nurses pull the patient's birth date or social if that helps to—"

"Look, my husband, Cyrus Grey, was shot today and rushed to this hospital this afternoon," the woman said, raising her voice.

"So was mine," Noelle answered tightly.

"I don't know who the hell this lady is," the woman shouted, shooting to her feet and giving a dismissive wave at Noelle, "but I'm here to hear news about Cyrus *William* Grey! My husband of eleven damn years!"

A sinking feeling settled into Noelle's stomach again— this time for a very different reason. Her mouth went dry. "Did you . . . did you say Cyrus William Grey?"

"Yes!" the woman replied.

"Cyrus William Grey is . . . that's my husband's name too," Noelle whispered, barely able to choke out the words.

Chapter 3

Diamond

Diamond sat upright in her hospital bed, rubbing absently at the bandage on her forearm. She wondered if the nurse had wrapped it too tightly.

She only felt a lingering soreness from her wound, thanks to the painkillers the hospital had given her. The bullet had only grazed her anyway. It wouldn't leave more than a scar that she could mask with makeup—if it even came to that. But the wounds Cyrus had suffered weren't superficial. The bullets that had pierced her husband's body had left him bloody and limp in her arms as she'd waited for the ambulance to arrive.

Cy had surprised her a half hour before the shooting by meeting her at The Seneca, the restaurant where she worked as a hostess. He'd strolled to the reservation desk with a gift in his hand—a robin's-egg-blue Birkin bag that she'd been lusting after for months, made of leather smoother than the skin on her bare legs. She'd gushed her thanks, and he'd whispered in her ear that she could show him just how grateful she was by coming home with him to enjoy an afternoon quickie. She hadn't been able to resist and made up an excuse to the floor manager, explaining that a family emergency had come up and she had to leave. She and Cy had sneaked away like two giggling teenagers.

They had been walking down the hall to their luxury condo when it happened. He'd wrapped his arm around her and had just leaned down to kiss her and open their door when the door leading to the stairwell at the end of the hall had opened.

Even now, when Diamond closed her eyes, she could still see the shooting replay in slow motion.

Diamond had looked over Cy's shoulder and seen the masked gunman before her husband had. She'd screamed and Cyrus had whipped around to look in the direction she'd been staring. He hadn't had the chance to run before the gunman fired.

He'd shouted, "No! This ain't right!" and shoved her inside the apartment as the first shot sounded.

She'd landed sprawled, face down on the foyer's hardwood floor, and stayed there whimpering in fear while she'd listened to the other gun shots. When everything finally went silent, she'd raised her head and turned to find Cy partially slumped against the foyer wall and their front door with his eyes closed, bleeding from three gunshot wounds to his chest. She'd rushed toward him, screaming all over again. Somehow in all the chaos, the gunman had fled.

That's how the paramedics and police had found them—her screaming and weeping, with Cy braced against her chest, both of them covered in his blood. Diamond had been barely able to answer their questions, instead asking them over and over again if her husband was going to be okay. She'd watched in a daze as they performed CPR, which in her hysteria, she hadn't thought to do herself. She'd watched as they loaded him onto a stretcher and sailed him down the hall to a waiting elevator.

Now the cops were questioning her again—this time, it was two plainclothes detectives who had given her their names, but she hadn't bothered to remember them. They were asking her stuff, like she knew more than what she'd already told the patrol cops. She wished they would finish their damn questioning so she could go check and see how Cyrus was doing. She was desperate to get an update about him. He wasn't dead—at least, not yet. She knew that much. But she would like to talk to his doctor to hear her husband's chances of survival from this.

"So you're saying the perp wore a ski mask?" the cop in the gray suit asked.

He was white with a grizzled face carved by wrinkles and a bald head that glistened under the hospital room lights.

Diamond gradually nodded, still absently rubbing the bandage on her arm. She tossed her long braids over her shoulder. "Yeah, it was black mask. I . . . I couldn't see his face."

"Did he say anything before he fired?" the black detective asked her.

He was shorter than the white cop and wearing a navy-blue suit. He also wore gold cufflinks and a chunky gold watch. He had a "big dick swinging" attitude about him, reminding her of a couple of her regulars from the old days.

"No. The only thing he said after he shot him was something like . . . like . . . 'You deserve this shit,' or 'You're gettin' what you deserve.'" She grimaced, struggling to recall the shooters exact words. "I couldn't hear it clearly. My head was down on the floor and his voice was kinda muffled because of the ski mask."

"What was he wearing? What else do you remember?" the white cop asked.

She closed her eyes, replaying the moment yet again.

Each time, her eyes locked with the shooter's dark irises. Her focus zeroed in on his handgun and then followed the path up his arm. "He had a . . . a tattoo right here," she said, gesturing to the inside of her forearm, remembering the gothic lettering. "It had a six . . . no . . . a nine. I remember that."

"Uh-huh. You remember the tattoo. Do you remember what he was wearing? A white shirt or a black shirt? Jeans or sweats?" the white cop persisted.

"I think it was a white shirt, but it could've been gray. Maybe light gray. I'm not sure."

The two cops exchanged a look.

"*What?*" she said, getting irritated. "Look, I would tell you if I could remember what he looked like. Trust me! I want y'all to find that son of a bitch so I can beat him with my bare hands for what he did to my husband. Cy is all that I have!"

"*Your husband?*" the black cop cried before he began to laugh. The white cop started to laugh too, and they exchanged yet another conspiratorial look, like naughty schoolgirls in a classroom when the teacher turned to face the chalkboard.

Watching them snicker, Diamond was no longer irritated. Now she was starting to get pissed off.

"What the hell is so funny?" she snapped.

"Being a wifey doesn't make you a wife, honey," the black cop said. "Pretty hard for you two to be married when he's already married to someone else."

Diamond blinked in amazement. "What are you talking about? Cy isn't married to someone else!"

The white cop laughed again. "You really expect us to believe you didn't know Cyrus Grey is married? Not a street-smart girl like you."

"Yeah, we did some research on you before we even came in here," the black cop said. "Ran your name through the database. This ain't the first time you've been a witness to a shooting, and it definitely isn't the first time you've had a run-in with the law."

The cop kept talking after that, but Diamond didn't hear a word he said. Everything from the cop's voice to the room faded into the background as her mind focused on one single thought: Cyrus was married to someone else.

That couldn't be true. *Could it?*

Sure, she had always wondered about what went on during his extended absences and business trips. She'd suspected a virile man like Cyrus might see other women on the side occasionally, but as long as his heart and his allegiance remained with her, Diamond didn't care. After all, *she* was the one with the ring on her finger, she constantly told herself. It wasn't like the old days, in another relationship, when she'd had to share her man with a half dozen other girls all jostling for superiority and the highest rank in his eyes. That's what it had been like with Julian, her ex and former pimp. One moment he could make her feel like the most important girl in the world, and the next, like she was lower than the gum stuck to the heel of his shoe.

When she and Cy had exchanged vows during a surprise trip to Las Vegas months ago, Diamond was sure things were different this time around. She had embraced her wedding ring as a physical representation . . . a twenty-four-karat-gold symbol that showed the world she meant more to Cy than any other woman in his life. But if another woman also wore his ring, what did that say about their relationship? What did that say about her? She'd thought she had moved on from that old life, but if what the cops said were true, she was still just another chick scratching and shoving at the competition, struggling to be her man's bottom bitch.

"It's funny that you always seem to be around when a

shooting goes on, but you have no clue what happened. You're always so fuzzy on the details . . . so confused," the black cop continued, drawing her attention and snapping her out of her malaise. "You said the same about your friend Julian Mason four years ago. Had no idea how that drug dealer ended up dead though the investigators knew your ass had to be there when Julian shot him."

"Either you need to see a doctor to get that memory of yours checked, Diamond," the white cop continued, "or you're full of shit and—"

"And suspicious as hell!" the black cop finished for him.

"What are you saying? That *I* know who shot Cyrus?" she asked with disbelief.

"We suspect that not only did you know who shot him, but you also arranged the whole thing," the black cop said. "So stop lying and come clean about that shit!"

"*What?* Why would I want Cyrus killed? Why would I want to hurt him at all? I love him!"

"I'm sure you did at some point," the white cop muttered sarcastically, "but not anymore. Now the other guy is back in the picture, I wouldn't be surprised that you're ready to end it . . . that you both wanted Cyrus gone. That's why you tried to have him taken out today, isn't it?"

She swore the detectives were speaking English. So why couldn't she understand a damn thing they were saying? It was like they were talking in riddles.

"*Who's* back in the picture?" she yelled. "What the hell are you talking about?"

"You know who, Diamond," the black cop replied. "Your ex, Julian! He got out of the pen three days ago."

"He gets out of jail and your sweetheart Cyrus gets shot three days later. Interesting coincidence, don't you think?" the white cop asked.

Diamond didn't respond. She was too stunned to speak.

Chapter 4

Vanessa

Vanessa stared at the woman sitting in front of her in the hospital waiting room.

Why the hell was this crazy woman claiming to be Cyrus's wife? Why would she say something so bizarre?

Vanessa wanted to believe the woman was either drunk or high, but she looked sober. In fact, with exception of her red-rimmed eyes and puffy nose, she looked like she had just strutted out of a Neiman Marcus catalog with her snakeskin pumps, royal purple silk wrap dress, and gold jewelry. Meanwhile, Vanessa was the one who looked tired, frazzled, and yes—maybe even a little bit crazy—in her haphazard ponytail and black tracksuit.

Vanessa felt like she was glaring at her exact antithesis—her image flipped in reverse. The woman claiming to be Cy's wife was tall and lean, whereas Vanessa was petite and curvy. Vanessa prided herself on her long hair and her fat curls that perfectly framed her heart-shaped face, while the woman in front of her had a short bob that was as sleek as her high cheekbones. The woman had skin like dark chocolate whereas Vanessa, who was always insecure about how pale she was, had to sunbathe for hours just to get a healthy toffee color.

Considering how different they were, the very idea that this woman could also be involved with Cyrus seemed impossible—downright preposterous.

She's not even his type, Vanessa thought with disgust, slowly looking the woman up and down.

Nevertheless, she had obviously come here to see Cy. She knew who he was.

"So . . . you're his side chick. Is that what this is about?" Vanessa asked with a sneer. "You thought you could lie and say you were his wife so that they would let you in to see him?"

She had never believed Cyrus would ever cheat on her, but then again, she never would've believed she would ever cheat on him either. So it turns out they were both harboring secrets.

The woman had the nerve to look taken aback by her question at first, then outright insulted. "No, I am *not* his side chick!" she cried indignantly as she stood. She held up her hand, showing off an emerald-cut diamond on her ring finger that was big enough to choke a squirrel. "Like I said before, I'm Cyrus's *wife!* My name is Noelle Grey and I am married to Cyrus William Grey. We were married in a private ceremony in New York City four years ago last month."

"Yeah, well, like *I* said," Vanessa countered, also brandishing her wedding ring—square cut, four carats, "I've been married to Cyrus for more than a damn decade, and I've never heard of you! I don't know who the hell you are or this wedding you claimed you two had, but I know one thing . . . I'm not up to dealing with this bullshit today!" She pointed up to Noelle. "I'll handle your ass later!" Vanessa then rounded again on the doctor. "I want to see my goddamn husband, and I want to see him now! Where is he?"

All eyes in the waiting room were focused on them. Vanessa wondered if the nosy family of three huddled across the room in the line of leather chairs was going to break out a bucket of popcorn to watch the show. The doctor seemed conscious of their intense gazes too. He didn't seem to appreciate all the attention though. He took a nervous glance around him, like he was searching for the nearest exit door.

"Ma'am, I'm going to have to ask you to keep your voice down." The doctor held up a hand. "This is a hospital."

"I know what the hell it is!" Vanessa bellowed. "This is clearly a waiting room. You're a doctor! I don't need you to tell me that! My husband is being treated here, and I want to know if he's okay. Can you at least tell me if he's alive? Can you answer that question?"

The doctor hesitated then gradually nodded.

"Good!" Vanessa exhaled with relief. She turned around and grabbed her purse that was sitting in her chair. She threw the handle over the crook of her arm. "If that's the case, I should be able to see him." She gestured to the doctor. "Lead the way."

"Ma'am, unfortunately, we can't let either of you see him until we sort this out."

"But Cy can tell you I'm his wife. He can say it himself!"

"No, he can't," the doctor said tightly. "Mr. Grey isn't conscious right now. He's in an induced coma. I'm sorry, but in order for either of you to see him, we have to determine which one of you is really Cyrus Grey's wife. I don't know if there's documentation either of you can provide that can—"

"*Documentation?*" Vanessa squeaked. Her mouth twisted

with outrage. "So I'm supposed to dig out my damn I.D. and marriage license for this . . . this bullshit? Just so I can see my goddamn husband?"

"You claim you and Cy have been married for more than a decade. Then bring your marriage license or some other form of evidence that shows it! It shouldn't be that hard, should it?" the woman who Vanessa now knew was named Noelle, challenged as she raised her chin. "I, on the other hand, have no problem providing any documentation you require if it means I can finally see my husband, Doctor."

Vanessa glared up at Noelle.

So this Big Bird bitch is actually trying to buck to me? Oh, she's gonna regret that shit, Vanessa thought.

She took a menacing step toward Noelle then another. "I said I'd handle your ass later," she said as she tugged off one of her hoop earrings, "but I can do it right now."

"You don't scare me!"

"You better be scared, you—"

"No! *No!* Security!" the doctor shouted just as Vanessa lunged forward, reaching for Noelle's scrawny neck. He stepped between the two women in a clumsy effort to intervene. "Security! I need help here!"

Two hulking guards in navy blue uniforms suddenly appeared in the waiting room. Vanessa didn't get a chance to catch her bearings—or to snatch Noelle—before one guard grabbed her around the waist and roughly yanked her back and off her feet.

"Let go of me! Let me at that skinny bitch!" she yelled. "I'll show her who the fuck I am!"

The other one grabbed onto Noelle's wrist, pulling her in the opposite direction. "Get off of me! I didn't do anything! I just . . . I just wanted to see my husband!" Noelle shouted as the two women were escorted to separate elevators.

* * *

Vanessa sat in the driver's seat of her Mercedes a half hour later, barely aware of where she was going. The roadway, storefronts, houses, and traffic were all a blur of streaming colors and shapes. She might have even run a stop sign or two during her drive, but she couldn't say for sure. She was too blinded by her rage.

Cyrus had cheated on her, but he hadn't had a one-night stand or gotten a mistress like any normal philandering husband. He had married someone else. He had been supposedly married to that bitch . . . that woman Noelle for four years.

How was that even possible? How had he managed to juggle two wives and households all this time? Why hadn't Vanessa had any inkling that he'd been cheating on her? Shouldn't she have gotten some hint that her husband was leading a double life?

As she drove, Vanessa began to replay their past together, all those questions she'd had about her husband, but had shoved aside . . . all those last-minute "business trips" she had naively accepted and even changed her schedule to work around.

"That son of a bitch," she mumbled as she turned her steering wheel to pull onto her street. "That son of a bitch!"

Cy was lucky he was already laid up in the hospital from gunshot wounds, because he'd be in the hospital right now if she could get her hands on that man. And to think, she had felt guilty that she might have been the cause of him getting shot in the first place.

Vanessa pulled into her driveway, gritting her teeth so hard that her jaw hurt. When she released the steering wheel and turned off the engine, she saw that she had left imprints in the leather because she had been squeezing the wheel in a death grip. She had to pull herself together. Her children would see all the emotions on her face and know something was wrong.

"Shit!" she spat in frustration, slapping the dashboard. "Shit! What am I gonna say?"

They were waiting to hear news about their father, but how the hell was she going to explain that she hadn't been able to go into the hospital room to see Cyrus because some other woman claiming to be his wife was also there?

Vanessa shoved open her door, climbed onto the asphalt, and slammed the door shut. She marched up the driveway, up the brick stairs that led to the front door of their colonial and paused before going inside. She glanced over her shoulder at the manicured front lawn, at the bike Cy Jr. had left leaning against one of the garage doors, and the rose bushes and line of pink and magenta peonies that had just come into bloom that were adjacent to the portico.

It was the best-looking house on the entire block, maybe even the entire neighborhood. It had even been commended by the homeowners' association with a plaque. She and Cy had renovated the exterior only two years ago and once a week, a gardening crew came to maintain the grounds so not a stray leaf littered the lawn or patch of weeds strangled her precious flowers. Vanessa had taken so much pride in her home, her marriage, and her life. Now it all felt like a farce. A big fat joke.

Vanessa unlocked the front door and stepped inside her airy foyer. She found her family in the living room. A children's cartoon played on their wall-mounted flat screen TV. Her daughter Zoe, the reigning princess of the household, lay on her belly on the area rug, gazing up at the television and singing along to the theme music. Cy Jr. reclined on their leather sofa in his usual butt groove, wearing headphones and staring down at the handheld computer that he seemed addicted to nowadays. Their middle child, Bryson, sat beside his grandmother—Vanessa's mother—on the leather sectional, snuggled against the older woman's side. He'd been a snuggler since he was a baby, always burrowing into the crook of either Vanessa's, Cy's, or her mother's shoulder. When Vanessa shut the front door behind her, her mother and Bryson turned and stared.

"Mom! Mommy," Bryson cried, leaping up from the cushion, "you're home!"

He ran straight to her with skinny arms outstretched. When he reached her, he slammed into her stomach and thighs, knocking the air out of her. He wrapped his arms around her waist.

"Is Daddy okay?" he asked. "Grandma said he had an accident. He didn't smash up his car, did he?"

Her two other children and her mother all rose from their perches and walked toward her, gazing at her, waiting eagerly for an answer.

An accident . . . so that was the lie her mother had told the children. Still, it was nothing compared to the lies Cyrus had been telling them all for years, it seemed.

Looking into her son's big brown eyes and their expectant faces, the anger quickly seeped out of Vanessa. She opened her mouth to answer but instead, burst into tears.

"Oh, no!" Zoe yelled. Her round little face crumbled. "Daddy died, didn't he? My daddy died!"

Now everyone was crying. The living room was filled with wails and hiccups. Vanessa's mother, Carol, tried frantically to comfort the children while Vanessa wiped her eyes, forcing herself to end her tears.

"No! No, babies, Daddy isn't dead," she said. "Daddy isn't dead! He's alive! He's alive, okay?"

The wailing abruptly halted. They all stared at her again in surprise.

"Then . . . then why were you crying?" Cy Jr. asked between sniffs, wiping his nose on the sleeve of his T-shirt.

Vanessa opened her mouth to answer but couldn't find the words. Instead, she locked eyes with her mother. A silent exchange occurred between the two women, one they had done many times in the past. After a few seconds, Carol gave a barely discernable nod and wrapped her arm around Cy Jr.'s shoulder. She squeezed him gently.

"Junior, honey," the older woman cooed, "why don't you take your brother and sister upstairs for a bit so me and your mama can talk?"

Cy Jr. frowned. "Talk about what, Grandma? I thought she was going to tell us about Dad. Is he okay?"

"She will," his grandmother assured, nodding her gray head. "Don't worry! But let me and your mama talk, okay? Head upstairs with your brother and sister now, like I said." She clutched his chin. Her dark eyes went hard. "I'm not gonna ask you again."

Cy Jr. bit down on his bottom lip. "Yes, Grandma," he mumbled, just as Carol let go of his face. "Come on, y'all," he said to his little brother and sister, inclining his head toward the stairs.

Bryson and Zoe looked unsure. The little boy's arms were still wrapped around his mother and he didn't seem like he wanted to let her go, clinging to her tighter than a suctioned Garfield cat to a car window.

Vanessa wiped at her wet cheeks with the backs of her hands. She gently, but firmly, pried Bryson's hands from around her waist. "Go with your brother," she managed to whisper. She leaned down and kissed his brow. "Watch TV in your rooms. I'll be upstairs soon."

A minute later, Vanessa heard the last of the children's footsteps on the top floor along with the sound of a door shutting and then their televisions. When she did, she turned to her mother.

"What happened?" Carol whispered, steering her daughter across the living room. They both sat down on the sofa, pushing aside one of the children's action figures to make a spot on the cushion. "What did you find out at the hospital? Is Cy alright?"

Vanessa dropped her face into her hands. "I think he's in a coma, but I really don't know. They wouldn't let me see him."

"*They wouldn't let you see him?*" Carol's brows drew together. "Why not?"

Vanessa lowered her hands from her face. That's when she unloaded and told her mother everything—how she met Noelle in the hospital waiting room, how Noelle had also claimed to be Cyrus's wife and the near brawl that had happened after.

"Four years, Mama!" Vanessa said, clenching her hands into fists. Her eyes flooded with angry tears again. "He's been married to this bitch for *four goddamn years* and I didn't even know she existed!"

"No, he is *not* married to her. You're his wife, according to the eyes of the law. You married him first. It doesn't matter what vows he made to that woman, Nessa . . . *if* he even made them, like she claims. You're Mrs. Cyrus Grey—not her."

"But how could Cy do this to me? Why would he do it? I loved him so much, Mama! Bilal even wanted me to leave Cy to be with him, and I told him no. I'm starting to wonder if I should've now!"

Carol crossed her legs and leaned back against the sofa arm.

"So, you still haven't ended things with that young

man?" Carol sniffed. "The one with a small apartment and no money? You two are still carrying on?"

Vanessa couldn't keep any secrets from her mother. The older woman knew a few of the details of her affair with Bilal and how Vanessa had been trying for weeks to break it off.

Vanessa groaned and stared down at her clenched hands. "We aren't carrying on anymore, but he won't leave me alone." She looked up at her mother again. "I went to see him today so I could talk some sense into him and . . . and he threatened me. He told me I would regret it."

"What does that mean? That you'll regret it?"

"I don't know! I wondered though if it had something to do with . . . you know . . . what happened to Cy today. If maybe . . . maybe . . ." Her words drifted off.

"If maybe your little boytoy shot your husband?" Carol finished for her.

Vanessa hesitated then nodded.

"Well, from what you told me about him, he seems like he's all talk, but you never know with men like that. Pushed far enough and any man is capable of doing something rash, something stupid. That's how they are!" Carol loudly exhaled. "If he did shoot your husband and it gets back to the police that you were having an affair with this boy, it won't look too good for you, Nessa, especially if Cyrus doesn't survive."

Vanessa winced. Even though she was angry at Cyrus, she hated that her mother was talking about his possible death with such detachment. But that's how her mother saw men. That's how she approached her relationships with them—in a cold, calculating way, with an almost clinical detachment like a scientist observing mice in a lab experiment.

Carol was darker than her daughter by several shades, but they were the same height and build. She could still attract her share of men even at the ripe age of sixty-five, and did on occasion—when she had use for one. But Carol Walters hadn't needed a man for quite a while. Her previous husbands had left her a wealthy widow.

She had always encouraged Vanessa to have the same attitude, and Vanessa had for many years, until she met and fell in love with Cyrus Grey. She suspected her mother still hadn't forgiven her for that slip up.

"That darling husband of yours might be a bigamist," Carol continued dryly, "but you're still supposed to be the dutiful wife no matter what, Nessa. If the police can connect you to this shooting through your affair, you could stand to lose a lot more than alimony in a divorce even if he does make it through this. You could lose your freedom, too. You better hope that boy doesn't hold a grudge and lie on you. You could go to jail too, honey." She slowly shook her head and clucked her tongue. "I told you about wasting your time with the pretty broke ones. They might be good in bed, but they aren't worth the trouble."

Vanessa winced again. "Mama, all this talk about divorce, alimony, and jail time . . . aren't we leaping ahead a bit here? I mean . . . I don't even know if Bilal did it! I don't even know if he shot Cy!"

"Then I guess you better find out before the cops do, and you better do it quick." Her mother dropped her hand to her knee and gave it a quick pat. "Now in the meantime, go upstairs and talk to your children. Don't tell them about that other woman, or that they wouldn't let you see Cyrus. Make up a lie if you have to."

Vanessa took a deep breath. "Yes, Mama."

The older woman then rose to her feet and pointed down at her. Her eyes went hard again. "And don't you ever . . . *ever* break down in front of those kids like that again. You hear me? You are my daughter and you are not weak. Understood?"

Vanessa lowered her gaze to the floor. "Yes, Mama."

"Good," Carol said before turning to the stairs. She took a few steps out of the living room then glanced over her shoulder at Vanessa. "You coming?"

Vanessa stood from the sofa, pushed back her shoulders, and wiped the last of the remaining tears from her face. "Right behind you," she said, before following her mother upstairs.

Chapter 5

Noelle

Noelle downed what was left in her wineglass and licked the briny taste off her lips. Even though it was her second glass, her hands were still shaking. Her nerves were still frayed. She eyed the bottle of Moscato on her marble island, wondering if she should have a third glass.

"To hell with it," she murmured, before reaching for the bottle and pouring what was left into her glass.

If she couldn't calm her nerves, at least she could get drunk.

Noelle glanced at her cell phone, which was buzzing on the counter. Her phone had been ringing off and on for the past three hours, since she'd arrived home from the hospital. She saw Cyrus's business partner, Tariq's name flash on the phone screen a few times along with the number to the shop. It was likely Miranda, her boutique's assistant manager, calling her, trying to get an update on Cy. But Noelle hadn't answered any of the calls. She didn't want to talk to anyone right now. If she spoke, she didn't know what would come out. Incoherent ranting. Maybe uncontrollable sobs.

I can't believe this is happening, she thought, wanting to wake up from this nightmare.

In one day, she'd found out that the man she loved and trusted was on the brink of death—and married to another woman. A woman so crass and tacky with her loud, foul mouth and gold and black Versace tracksuit that Noelle couldn't believe Cyrus had dated her, let alone been married to her for more than a decade.

What other secrets had Cyrus kept from Noelle? What other lies had he told? How had she been so stupid, so trusting?

"Because I loved him," she whispered, shaking her head ruefully before taking another sip from her glass.

Love made you a fool, and she had certainly been one for Cyrus Grey for the past five years, since the moment she'd met him on the sidewalk on Fifth Avenue in New York. She had just come from a casting for a runway show and been rejected, after being rejected by designers at every casting call that week.

Being twenty-five (practically an octogenarian by runway modeling standards), Noelle's agent had already warned her earlier that season that her modeling days were likely behind her and she'd been lucky to last way longer than most. Noelle was coming to terms with that reality when Cyrus had stopped her and asked her for her name. He'd told her that he recognized her from somewhere. Down and disappointed, she'd tried to brush him off, not in the mood for a weak come-on or flirting with a stranger.

"Just smile for me, please? *Please?*" he'd begged. "It'll only take a couple seconds. I bet that'll help me remember."

She'd given him almost a maniacal, Joker-like smile, hoping it would scare him off and make him go away. Instead, he'd snapped his fingers.

"Now I remember you! You did that tooth whitening

commercial." Cyrus had chuckled. "You know I bought three boxes of those whitening strips because of that pretty smile of yours, and those things didn't work worth a damn!"

She couldn't help it. She'd burst into laughter. Noelle had remembered filming the commercial he was talking about two years earlier.

"I threw those strips away after a couple months, you know. Couldn't get my money back either."

She'd inclined her head, still laughing. "I'm sorry to hear that."

"Well, if you're really sorry, you can make it up to me by having a cup of coffee with me." He'd glanced over his shoulder at the line of shops along the block. "I was just about to stain my teeth at the one up the street."

"You want to have coffee? I don't even know your name!"

"I'm Cyrus . . . Cyrus Grey. But most of my friends call me Cy." He'd then extended his hand to her.

Noelle had given him points for creativity. Most men just told her she was beautiful or sexy or striking and asked her out to dinner. Cyrus had at least been original in his approach. And under closer inspection, he wasn't bad looking either. He was tall—taller than her even in her three-inch heels, and broad shouldered, with sexy brown eyes, glowing dark skin, and a nice smile of his own. He looked to be in his late thirties, which was a little older than she usually went for back then. But she'd been willing to make an exception for him. He could distract her from her latest rejection, and besides, she had nothing else to do that morning.

"Sure, Cy. Why not? I'm Noelle, by the way," she'd said, shaking his hand.

She'd liked the warmth of his strong, weathered hand, and his sturdy grip.

That forty-five-minute, impromptu coffee date had turned into dinner and theater tickets the next night and a helicopter ride overlooking Manhattan a week later. By the fourth date, Noelle had been firmly smitten with Cyrus. No, she hadn't known a lot about him. She realized now how vague he had been on the details of his life and his financial consultancy business in the beginning, but she'd been too charmed by him to notice at the time. Now, she recognized it though, all the missing pieces . . . all the nagging questions about Cy that were still left unanswered.

She'd detected some of the holes in the story early on—like, for instance, why did a financial advisor need to travel so much? Couldn't he do most of his work by phone or email? She had even asked him about it once, and he'd told her he was hustling for his company, that he had high-touch, wealthy clients who wouldn't be satisfied with just phone calls, emails, and video conferencing. But now she suspected all that time Cyrus was "traveling for the company", he was really with his other wife.

"Lie after lie after lie," she now murmured, drumming her nails against their marble island.

She was tired of the lies. She wanted the truth.

Noelle raised her glass back to her lips, but paused when she heard the doorbell chime. She set the glass down on the counter, walked out of the kitchen and through the living room to her townhome's front door. She saw a shadowy figure pacing in front of the window on the stone walkway. She knew instantly from the tall height, sinewy build, and tense body posture who it was. She didn't even have to look at the video panel to see his face. Noelle unlocked the front door and swung it open.

Tariq was wearing a suit and tie. She couldn't remember the last time she'd ever seen him in just a T-shirt and jeans. Tariq was younger than his business partner, Cyrus, by about a decade or so, closer in age to her than to him, and he looked it. She suspected that his caramel-hued face would look even younger if it weren't for his goatee—hence the nickname Cy used for him behind his back, Mr. Baby Face.

"That was a quick flight," she deadpanned as Tariq came to a halt on her Welcome mat. She leaned against the door frame. "Made it all the way from Cali in less than five hours?"

Tariq blinked. He opened his mouth then closed it. He ran his hand over his closely cropped head. "I knew it was important to get here so I grabbed a . . . a direct flight. The . . . the weather back was good. Made the ride quicker, I guess."

"Uh-huh." She slowly looked him up and down in the fading evening light.

She could tell Tariq was lying through his teeth. Nevertheless, Noelle gestured for him to come inside. She strolled back to the kitchen. She knew if she was finally going to get any answers, Tariq would be the one to give them.

"I went to the hospital to see Cy," he said, stepping inside the house and closing the front door behind him. He trailed behind her. "I tried to find you, but you weren't there. I tried calling and texting but—"

"So how was San Francisco?" she interrupted. "Did you guys get everything done there that you needed to do before Cy left early?"

Tariq stilled, looking taken aback by her question. "Uh, yeah . . . yeah, we got it all done."

She grabbed her wineglass and gulped down what was left. She dropped it back to the counter with a clink. "Cut the bullshit, Tariq."

"Huh?"

"Cy told me you guys were going *to* L.A., not San Francisco!" She crossed her arms over her chest. "Did you even go on a business trip? Was he out there *at all*?"

Tariq opened his mouth to answer then stopped himself, like he thought better of it. A pained expression crossed his face. He dropped his eyes. "No. There was no business trip."

"How many times has he done this? How many times did Cy make up shit and just . . . just *lie* to me? And what's this stuff about him being married to someone else? She said they've been married for more than ten years! Was that woman telling the truth?"

Tariq's eyes shot up from the floor. He stared at her, looking as shocked as she felt three hours ago. "You spoke to Vanessa?"

"Oh, so you even know her name? Yes, I spoke to her! I ran into her today when I went to the hospital to find out if my husband was going to die! I wasn't expecting to find another goddamn woman who says she's Cy's wife waiting there. The bitch wanted to fight me!"

He grimaced. "I'm so sorry, Noelle. I told Cy that he should've—"

"No! No, I don't want to hear apologies or excuses!" She pointed at him. "You knew about this! You knew about this the whole time and didn't say *a word* to me!"

"It wasn't my place!" he boomed, making her suck her teeth. "I tried! Damnit, don't you think I tried with Cy . . . to get him to do the right thing? I told him to break it off with you in the beginning if he wasn't going to leave Vanessa. When he met you, I didn't know y'all were gonna get that serious. He made it sound like a fling! I didn't know he was gonna ask you to marry him!"

"But he did," she croaked with tears streaming down her cheeks, "and I said yes. And you didn't stop me. You didn't stop it from happening!"

"How could I have stopped it, Noelle?" He threw up his hands. "What the hell was I supposed to do?"

He was right. She knew he was right. It wasn't his job

to intervene in her and Cy's relationship. He was Cy's business partner and friend—that's it. But she had considered him a friend too. He had been a confidante and sounding board for her when she first moved from Manhattan to the sleepy Northern Virginia suburbs, soon after she and Cy got married. Her modeling career was on life support. It seemed like a good time in her life to make a change . . . to start over with her new husband, but the change in scenery and lifestyle had taken some time to get accustomed to. She had no friends here, no family. When Cy was off doing his thing and she felt lonely, depressed, and isolated, Tariq had stopped by the house to cheer her up and take her mind off things. He was the one who had encouraged her to find a way to fulfill herself, to open a business that played to her strengths and her fashion background. She'd thought Tariq liked her. She'd thought he cared.

Maybe he didn't care as much as I thought he did, she now reflected. Maybe Tariq had just been babysitting her like Cyrus wanted, keeping her occupied while Cy lived his other life. Tariq didn't give a damn about her beyond what Cyrus had asked of him, like she'd always suspected. It was clear where his loyalty truly lay.

"Nothing," she said coldly, wiping at her tears and licking her lips. "You didn't have to do anything, Tariq. You're right. It wasn't your job." She grabbed her wineglass and carried it toward the sink, turning her back to him. "Thanks for stopping by, but if you'll excuse me . . . I'm tired, and I have to—"

"Don't do that," he said, shaking his head. "Don't do that shit! Don't act like I'm the one who hurt you when I came here to be with you. I came running all the way here, driving like a bat out of hell on the highway because you called me crying and I—"

"You came because your business partner was shot!

You came to protect your own coin! It didn't have a damn thing to do with me!" She took a deep, shuddering breath. "Just admit it. It never did. It never had anything to do with me!"

The kitchen fell silent as they looked at one another. Finally, Tariq threw up his hands again like he was surrendering.

"Fine," he said. "Fine. I get it. You're pissed off at your man, but he was shot and now he's laid up in the hospital and you still need a punching bag, so I guess I'm it. Huh?"

She didn't answer him. She was too wounded to respond; she stayed stubbornly silent.

"Yeah, okay." He turned and walked out of the kitchen and back to her front door. He swung it open and paused to turn and look at her.

"By the way," he said, "you and Vanessa aren't his only wives. He has a third one. Her name is Diamond. He married her this year."

Noelle's stomach plummeted to her bare feet all over again. Her knees went weak. She gripped the edge of the counter to steady herself. "Wh-what?" she whispered helplessly. "H-he has *another one*?"

"And being married to three women ain't the only secret Cy has. If you really wanna know who your husband is, I'll tell you. The truth and nothin' but the truth. Just be prepared for what you're about to hear. Hit me up when you're ready," he called to her before walking out the front door and slamming it shut behind him.

Chapter 6

Diamond

"Hello, ma'am. I'm Nurse Simmons but you can call me Sally! I'll be escorting you downstairs," a perky voice called out. "Do you have everything? Are we all set?"

Diamond turned to find a smiling, white-haired nurse waiting at the entrance of her hospital room. An empty wheelchair sat in front of her. Nurse Sally leaned down and patted the wheelchair's seat, gesturing for Diamond to climb inside so she could transport her out of the hospital room and downstairs to the automatic doors. Diamond would be deposited on the curb in her hospital gown and flimsy robe since her clothes were covered in Cyrus's blood. She'd be left to wait for an Uber.

It wasn't a graceful exit, but the truth was, Diamond was desperate to get out of this place. After being here for hours, after being poked and prodded, Diamond was finally being discharged. She was exhausted and ready to leave. She wanted to sleep for twelve straight hours, and yet, she couldn't imagine getting a minute of shuteye back at her condo. Every time she closed her eyes, she would see the gunman charging toward her, pointing his handgun and firing. She would see Cyrus's bloody body slumped on the floor, against her front door. She would probably never get those red-tinged images out of her mind.

Diamond still couldn't believe that the cops thought she had something to do with the shooting, that she would actually set up her husband to be killed. They'd tried their best to get her to confess to something, but the only thing they had managed to do was shock and frighten her. They told her they would stay in touch, that they would keep an eye on her, and frankly, she wasn't sure that was a bad thing. Her life was probably at risk now that her former pimp, Julian, was out of jail.

She'd thought he was serving an eight-year sentence. How the hell had he gotten out so early and did he have anything to do with Cyrus's shooting?

I wouldn't put it past him, she now thought.

Julian had no problem conveying to her that *she* was easily replaceable.

"I could have any bitch I want," Julian had once said to her. "All I gotta do is snap my fingers and I could get another chick in here who will do whatever the fuck I tell her to do. Don't ever forget that, baby."

He refused to believe she could find a man to replace him. He'd let men rent her for the day or evening, but by dawn, she still had to come home to him and give him all the money she'd earned. He'd told her that she was his, that he would never let her go. Maybe he'd meant it. Maybe he was angry that she had married Cy and decided to kill him or her—or them both.

"Do you need a little more time, sweetheart?" Nurse Sally asked, noticing her hesitation and looking at Diamond worriedly. "Should I come back?"

"I still haven't seen my husband," Diamond whispered, rubbing the bandage on her arm. "He was shot too. I think he's in the ICU. I want to see my husband!"

She started to weep softly and the nurse's wrinkled face crumbled. She stepped around the wheelchair and walked into the room. She placed a hand on Diamond's shoulder then her arm then her shoulder again like she wasn't quite sure how comfort her. "Oh, you poor dear! It's okay. It's going to be all right, honey."

"And I'm here all alone! I've been . . . I've been stuck in this room. They wouldn't let me see him." She sniffed and gazed into Nurse Sally's big blue eyes. "Can you take me to him? I'd like to see him before I leave the hospital. Just once."

Nurse Sally seemed to hesitate. She glanced over her shoulder at the opened doorway where a doctor and a few other people walked by. She looked back at Diamond again. She took a deep breath in then loudly exhaled, making her shoulders rise then fall. "I have orders to take you straight down, but I think we can work in a quick detour."

"Thank you," Diamond said, grabbing her hand. "Thank you!"

Ten minutes later, Diamond was wheeled off the metal elevator onto the ICU ward. It was around eight o'clock, but it felt later than that because it was so silent and dark on the floor: a dozen or so rooms stuck in permanent night. Nurse Sally began to push her past the hexagonal desk where several other nurses stood and were seated, but paused when one of them looked up, narrowed her eyes at them, and said, "Hey, what are you doing? Where are you taking that patient?"

Diamond was put off by her question and tone, but Nurse Sally didn't seem to mind.

"Oh, I was just taking her to see her husband. He's in room 3023. Cyrus Grey. The poor thing hasn't had a chance to see him today. They were separated when he was taken into surgery."

"Cyrus Grey, you said?" The other nurse looked at Diamond, who was trying her best to seem meek, like the concerned wife that she was. The nurse frowned and reached for one of the desk phones. She raised the receiver to her ear. "Dr. Chang told me there was some issue with that patient's visitors earlier today. I should page him to make sure I can—"

"Please," Diamond interrupted. "I just want to see my husband. That's all! I haven't seen him since the paramedics took him away."

"Yes, I understand, ma'am. But the doctor said—"

"I don't care what he said! Look, I'm being discharged. I'm tired and I just want to go home, but before I do, I want to see my husband. Please don't make me have to wait for the doctor, too. *Please?*"

The seated nurse's finger hovered over the phone's keypad. Slowly, she lowered the receiver from her ear and placed it back into its cradle. Her eyes shifted from Diamond to Nurse Sally and back again. "Okay. You can see him. But make it quick!"

Nurse Sally nodded and steered the wheelchair toward the left.

"Thank you," Diamond whispered.

The other nurse sighed and nodded as well.

Diamond rode down the hall, listening to the wheels of the chair squeak and the beep of monitors in the hospital rooms as she went. She caught a glimpse of herself in the reflective surface of the glass walls along each room: her round, tired face that had lost almost all traces of makeup, her puffy brown eyes, and long box braids that now partially hung in her face, but she didn't have the energy to push them away. Sitting in a wheelchair, in her hospital gown and robe, she looked closer to thirty-three, not her actual twenty-three years at that moment. She wished she could look better for her husband. She always went to great lengths to be the glamorous, sexy girl she knew he adored, but this would have to do.

She tried her best to brace herself for what she was about to see in his hospital room, but she knew she couldn't. This was Cyrus. Her man. Her rock. He'd helped change her life for the better. Yes, the life he gave her may have been mostly a lie if the cops were to be believed, but she wouldn't be surprised that they made up that story about Cy having another wife just to get a reaction out of her, to get her to confess to a crime she didn't commit. And even if it were true, she still loved her husband despite the hurt. She didn't know what she would do if she ever lost Cy.

When she and Nurse Sally finally arrived at room 3023, she breathed in audibly. She cringed. Her eyes flooded with tears yet again.

Cyrus lay in bed with his eyes closed. A breathing tube was attached to his mouth. Monitors were connected to his arms and hands. He was flanked on both sides by pieces of hospital equipment, steel bars, and saline bags.

Nurse Sally pushed her inside the room, closer to the bed, and Diamond reached out to touch his hand. Cy had big hands, strong ones that he used to massage her feet at night and to bring her close to him for an embrace or a kiss. Now they were dry and limp. They were no better than paperweights.

"This ain't right!" he'd shouted before the shooting.

She agreed. It wasn't right what had happened to him.

"I'm so sorry, baby," she croaked, blinking through her tears.

Only the beep of the heart monitor responded and the soft hush from his ventilator.

Diamond had thought she'd put her past behind her. She hadn't even told Cy about Julian, about her old life. Why should she? She was a new woman—a sexy hostess at an upscale restaurant near the Inner Harbor with a snazzy condo that her man paid for. She was a blissful newlywed. Her new life—their life together—had held so much promise. Now all in one day, it had been wiped away.

"I'm gonna find out who did this to you. *Okay?* I promise, Cy."

Diamond would find out if her ex had anything to do with the shooting, and if not him, who else had harmed her man—and she would make them pay. She didn't know how, but she would do it.

Tuesday

Chapter 7

Noelle

Noelle opened her eyes and immediately regretted it. She raised her hand to cover them, scowling at the blinding morning light. It took a few seconds for her to orient herself. Where was she?

Not in her bedroom, it looked like. Her back rested against a velvet cushion that was propped behind her. Her two bare feet were splayed under her art deco-style coffee table. One snakeskin pump sat discarded on her faux cowhide rug. She realized, belatedly, that she was in her living room, slumped on the floor next to her sofa. She peered down at herself and saw she was still in the clothes she'd worn to the boutique yesterday—her purple silk wrap dress—but now it was wrinkled and stained with wine.

Why the hell hadn't she gone to bed? Why hadn't she changed into her PJ's?

She shifted and sat upright, wincing at the pain in her back and neck and the pounding in her head. Her eyes landed on the empty wineglass on the coffee table that sat on its side, spilling white wine unto the glass tabletop and area rug beneath it. She saw three smashed, framed photos of her and Cyrus lying on the floor next to the chrome bookshelf. The broken glass glittered in the sunlight.

Now she remembered why she was down here. She'd had her rage and sob-fest soon after Tariq had left. That's how the pictures had ended up broken. She'd collapsed to the floor when she was done with her tirade and cried herself to sleep. But the waking nightmare still wasn't over. Her surroundings bore witness to that. She was still stuck in it, but now she had the added burden of being sore and hungover.

Noelle cringed as she slowly pushed herself to her feet and the pounding in her head only got worse. She looked around her and took a quick inventory of the room . . . of her life.

Her husband was still in the hospital in a medically induced coma after being shot, and now she knew he had not one, but *two* other wives besides herself.

She'd heard of stories like her own. Noelle vaguely remembered a news segment about a woman in Louisiana who had been married to two men for three years, and got caught when she paid for a getaway vacation with one husband by using the credit card of the other. She remembered reading about a man who was arrested for bigamy and fraud when it turned out he was married to *six* women, all in different states, and had conned half of them out of their life savings.

Noelle could recall wondering as she'd read these stories online and watched them on the evening news, "How could someone pull that off?" How could a woman be married to two men or a man be married to six women and not get caught? How could their spouses be so stupid? Now she was in the same position—well, sort of. Cyrus hadn't stolen her money, but he'd certainly broken her heart and made her feel like a gullible idiot. And the worst part was that her sister wives weren't the only secrets her husband harbored, according to Tariq. It sounded like he had quite a few more.

"Bastard," she muttered.

She hated Tariq for dangling the truth about Cy in front of her face like a carrot then walking out. But based on his ominous warning, "Just be prepared for what you're about to hear," she was starting to wonder if she really did want to know the full truth of who her husband was. What else would Tariq tell her? What other skeletons would come tumbling out of Cy's closet?

Clutching her forehead, Noelle staggered out of her living room and toward the stairs. She gripped the metal handrail and kept her head bowed as she climbed to the second floor, deciding to focus on taking a shower and calming her headache at the moment, rather than the disaster her life had become.

Noelle emerged from the shower twenty minutes later, clean but still worse for the wear. She managed to get dressed, tugging on a tank top and a pair of silk drawstring pants, but she had a feeling that was the most she would accomplish this morning. She glanced at the clock on her night table. Scratch that—it was no longer morning. According to the clock, it was almost noon.

There was no way she was going to the boutique today. Not with this hangover. She couldn't make the drive and certainly couldn't withstand seven to nine hours of talking to customers, answering phone calls, handling shipments, and reviewing online orders and inventory. She would call Miranda and tell her she wasn't coming in. She'd finally update her on what had happened yesterday. Well, Noelle would tell Miranda *most* of what had happened—leaving out the bit about Cyrus's other wives. But before Noelle called anyone, she had to take her meds.

She walked from the bedroom back into her bathroom.

The mirror over her vanity and double sinks was covered in steam from her shower, but Noelle didn't have to glance at it to know she probably looked like a hot mess. She certainly felt that way.

She opened her medicine cabinet and removed a bottle of aspirin and her prescription bottle of Zoloft but paused when she thought she heard the doorbell ring downstairs. Noelle glanced over her shoulder and frowned. There it was, more bell chimes followed by a loud pounding, like someone was trying to beat her front door down.

"What is it now?" she muttered to herself as she turned away from the cabinet, still holding the bottles.

Trying not to stumble and ignoring her headache, Noelle rushed out of the bedroom and down the stairs to the first floor. The banging was even louder now. She set the bottles down on her coffee table, approached the door, and gazed at the video monitor on the nearby console. She saw two men—one white, the other black—in suits, standing outside. The white one almost had his face pressed against one of the front windows with his hands cupped around his eyes, like he was trying to peek through the blinds. The black one raised his fist to knock again just as she unlocked the front door and swung it open.

"*Yes?* Can I help you?" she asked, eyeing them.

The black man smiled. "Good Morning, ma'am! I'm Detective Derrick Turner." He flipped open his wallet to show identification, revealing that he was with the Baltimore Police Department, then pointed over his shoulder to the white guy walking up beside him. "And this is my partner, Detective Louis Macy." He tucked his wallet back into his jacket's inner pocket. "Are you Noelle Grey?"

So they were cops? She guessed, with her husband being shot, she should have expected a visit from them at some point. But seeing them on her doorstep now, Noelle was apprehensive for some reason, though she didn't know why. Maybe it was the cultural response of many black people when they saw someone with a badge, whether they'd done something wrong or not. Cops weren't always there to serve and protect. Cops sometimes couldn't be trusted. Nevertheless, it wouldn't pay to act hostile toward them.

"Yes. Yes, I am! How can I help you, detectives?"

Detective Turner gestured toward the house. "May we come inside, ma'am?"

"We'd like to ask you a few questions," Detective Macy chimed in.

"*Questions?*" She looked between the two. "Questions about what?"

"Just about your husband and what happened yesterday. We understand there were some . . . well . . . interesting revelations . . . some that could possibly impact our investigation. We want to make sure we aren't missing anything."

"Yes, I see," Noelle said, loudly swallowing. "You can come in."

They stepped into the home and she shut the door behind them. "Can I get you anything, detectives? Would you like some . . ."

Her voice faded when she saw that Detective Macy's blue eyes had zeroed in on the living room. His gaze lingered on the turned over wineglass and the shattered pictures. He turned to her, grinning.

"Guess things got wild last night, huh?" Macy asked.

Noelle rushed into the living room. She had planned to clean this up after she took her headache medicine. She hadn't meant for the detectives to see this. "Sorry. This was a . . . uh . . . an accident," she lied, putting the cushion back onto the sofa and grabbing the over-turned wineglass. "I fell asleep before I could clean it all up. I was just about to . . . uh . . . sweep up the rest of this."

She took the wineglass into the kitchen and set it in the sink. She walked to her pantry closet to retrieve a broom and dustpan. Just as she reached for both, she caught out of the corner of her eye, Detective Turner looking at her Zoloft bottle, reading the label. Watching him do it, her cheeks grew hot. Her chest warmed under her tank top. She angrily strode out of the kitchen and across the living room and yanked the bottle out of his hand. "*Excuse me?* Do you mind?"

"That's an antidepressant, ain't it?" he asked. Detective Turner's affable smile didn't budge. "I think my sister takes that."

"Is that the question you came all the way here to ask me? If I take antidepressants?"

"Actually, no," Detective Macy said, butting in, "we wanted to ask you about what happened at the hospital yesterday with you and the other Mrs. Grey. We understand that you both showed up claiming to be Cyrus Grey's wife and there was an altercation."

"I wasn't *claiming* to be his wife," Noelle corrected, dropping the pill bottle into her pants pocket. "Cyrus and I *are* married. And it wasn't an altercation. That woman tried to attack me! I was just defending myself."

"From what we heard from the hospital staff, you *both* were behaving badly yesterday. It wasn't just her," Detective Turner said.

"Emotions were high," she insisted. "I'd just gotten word that Cyrus was shot, and I show up there and some other woman says she's married to my husband. I'm allowed to be upset!"

"When did you discover this information?" Macy asked, stepping toward her. "That your husband was married to someone else?"

"Yesterday . . . when I came to the hospital, like I said."

"So, you're saying you've been married to this man for

years and you didn't know he was married to someone else?" Turner asked, sounding incredulous. "In all that time?"

Noelle crossed her arms over her chest. "If I was aware of it, I never would've married Cy in the first place, Detective."

Macy tilted his head. "Did you ever suspect your husband may be cheating on you though?"

Noelle stilled, confused by the question and its directness. Why was the detective asking her this?

Yes, in her weaker moments, she had wondered if Cyrus was having an affair. Sometimes, she thought she caught the whiff of a woman's perfume on his clothes or a stray hair on one of his suits that wasn't hers. She'd even questioned a few times if all his late nights and trips were business-related like he'd claimed, but she'd always tamped down those worries and fears. She'd told herself that Cy loved her and was loyal to her. She'd berated herself for questioning him. Now she knew that her secret fears had been right all along, and the truth about her husband was even worse than she'd imagined.

"Maybe," she finally murmured. "Doesn't every wife?"

Detective Macy stared down at his feet. He pushed aside the broken picture frames and the glass still littering the living room hardwood. "I don't know. Mine might. I know if she thought I was cheating on her she'd be mad enough to take a cleaver to me." He looked up at Noelle again. "She'd be mad enough to shoot me."

"Bet you wanted to shoot your husband, too, when you found out he was cheating on you," Turner said. "Or have someone else do it if you couldn't do it yourself, huh?"

The living room went still as the detective's question fell like a ton of bricks. Noelle finally realized what was happening, what they were asking her. They were really trying to pin Cyrus's shooting on her. They were really insinuating that she wanted to kill her husband, that she was behind what had happened to him.

Noelle stared at both men in bewilderment. They were looking right back at her like she was a mouse trapped in a cage. And she did feel trapped, standing here in the living room with them. Her pulse began to race. Her palms went damp with sweat. Her hangover headache was starting to get worse again, making her wince. She should've insisted she had a lawyer present when they started asking these questions, but she'd thought they would ask innocuous queries. She had no idea she might be the focus of their police investigation.

"I wouldn't know, Detective. I don't like to speculate about those kinds of things," she said, trying to sound casual. She walked around the detectives toward her front door. "Now if you'll excuse me, gentlemen, I have some cleaning to do—as you can see." She gestured to the floor and coffee table. "And I'd like to get to it."

She opened her front door and stood beside it. The sound of her neighborhood suddenly filled her living room: a passing UPS truck, the buzz of a lawnmower, and a dog barking. The two detectives looked at each other before walking toward her.

"You have a good day, ma'am," Macy said with a nod. "We'll keep in touch."

"Yes, you know where to reach me," she said as he stepped onto the stone walkway.

Turner began to walk out the door as well, but paused just before he did and stood in front of her. He was shorter than her, which wasn't that odd considering Noelle stood at a model height of five feet, eleven inches without heels. But she'd always had bad experiences with short men. They seemed to want to intimidate her, to prove that they could dominate her with their manliness, if not their stature.

"Before we go, just one more question, Mrs. Grey," he said.

"Yes?" she asked, keeping her hand gripped around the door handle, ready to slam the door closed as soon as he left.

"The last time the police were here . . . when you pulled that knife on your husband and threatened to kill him and yourself, did you do it because you thought he was having an affair?"

Noelle blinked. Her mouth fell open in shock and a sound came out that sounded like a soft grunt. It was the sound you made when you took a hit to the chest, which is what she felt like she had taken right now.

"I'm sorry. What did you say?" Turner persisted, taking a step closer to her so that they were mere inches apart. He cupped his hand over his ear for exaggeration. "I didn't hear you."

How had they found out about that night? No charges had been filed. Cyrus had insisted that she not be arrested.

I guess there's still the police report, she thought vaguely, now fighting fear and panic.

It had happened about three years ago, a year after she first moved to Virginia, before a psychiatrist had diagnosed her and put her on her meds. She hadn't really wanted to hurt Cy—only herself, and luckily, she hadn't hurt either of them, because he'd wrenched the butcher knife away from her before she could do it. He'd taken a few slaps to the face in the process. The neighbors had overheard their altercation and been alarmed by her screams and sobs. They'd called the cops.

Noelle wished she could take it all back. She wished she could have seen the alarm signs of her depression and loneliness before it had gotten that bad, but she hadn't. The loss of her modeling career and the isolation she felt in Virginia were worse than she'd been willing to admit, not to mention the issues from her childhood she still hadn't faced or dealt with. That's how police officers had ended up at their home one night and almost put her in handcuffs before her husband intervened and said he wouldn't press any charges for the assault, that he would take her to a doctor right away to have her evaluated. That's why this detective was asking her about it now, probably using it to support his theory for why she would have tried to kill her husband.

"No, I didn't think Cy was having an affair," she said, clearing her throat. "I was . . . I was having a depressive episode, but it's all under control now."

"Is it?"

"I've been on medication for years. Y-you . . . you saw the bottle," she stuttered. "I-I take them every d-d-day. I'm better now!"

Turner looked again at the shattered pictures. "Uh-huh," he said slowly, not sounding convinced. But he didn't comment further. Instead, he walked toward his partner and they walked along the sidewalk to the parking lot where a blue Ford Taurus awaited them.

Noelle stood in her doorway, watching them until they pulled away. When she finally shut the front door, she was shaking.

They thought she was responsible for the shooting. She could end up in jail.

No, you won't, a voice in her head countered. *You won't go to jail because you haven't done anything wrong.*

She laughed at the thought, almost hysterically. This was America in 2020. Innocent people were found guilty all the time. She'd watched the news. She'd seen the true crime shows. It didn't matter that she had nothing to do with Cyrus's shooting. She could end up charged with attempted murder or conspiracy to commit murder and go to prison for a long time.

Noelle staggered to her sofa and sat down. She finally took two aspirins and her Zoloft, swallowing them whole with no water. She sat silently and waited for the medicine to kick in, for her headache and her borderline hysteria to wane. When both finally did, she took a calming breath.

She hadn't tried to kill Cyrus, but someone obviously had, and based on the way the police were behaving, something made them suspect the shooting wasn't random. So who could've done it? Who would want to kill her husband?

Tariq said Cyrus had many secrets. She wondered if that included a few secret enemies. She had to talk to Tariq, to follow him up on his offer to find out the truth about her husband, even if she feared what he might say.

She had no choice now.

Chapter 8

Vanessa

Vanessa glared out her SUV windshield at the building in front of her, muttering under her breath. He was really going to make her do this, wasn't he? He was going to make her come in there.

After the children had gone to bed the night before, Vanessa had called Bilal and sent him several text messages. She had taken her mother's advice and tried to find out before the cops did if her lover had anything to do with her husband's shooting. If she could get Bilal to confess to something, maybe she could even hand over the evidence to the authorities.

"See," she'd say, brandishing his incriminating text, "I had nothing to do with it, officers! He just went crazy. He's obsessed with me!"

But Bilal hadn't given her a confession. He hadn't responded to her at all; all her phone calls and texts went unanswered. For a man who had been so hot and heavy only yesterday, making it seem like he couldn't live without her, like he'd fight an army to be with her, she wondered why he had abruptly turned lukewarm.

Maybe it's because you threatened to file a restraining order against him, a voice in her head chided.

That could be the reason. Another possibility was that Bilal wasn't speaking to her because he really was the one who had shot Cyrus, and wanted to keep his distance from her so as not to draw attention to himself. He didn't want to raise the cops' suspicions.

Was he innocent or was he guilty? The not knowing was eating away at Vanessa. She just couldn't take it anymore.

She'd left the kids with her mother a half hour ago and decided to try to track down Bilal so that she could speak to him in person. She knew he was likely at the Get-It-In Gym on Tuesdays, serving as assistant manager and one of the trainers. His uncle, who owned the gym, had given him the job after Bilal figured out, after being fired a half dozen times, that a traditional nine-to-five office job "just didn't work for a dude like me." If she wanted to speak with Bilal, she would have to do it here.

Vanessa tugged her key out of the ignition, threw open the door, and adjusted her leopard-print sundress around her hips and breasts. She slammed the door shut and strode across the sleepy shopping center parking lot to the gym's entrance and stepped inside.

Though it was the middle of a weekday, the gym still had a decent number of people on the treadmills and the elliptical machines. The room smelled vaguely of sweat, burnt rubber, and the sharp antiseptic scent of the spray they used to sanitize the exercise equipment.

"Can I help you, ma'am?" the guy in dreads sitting at the front desk asked.

"No. No, thank you," Vanessa said. "I just came to speak to someone."

She quickly spotted Bilal toward the back of the gym, among the weight machines, wearing one of his signature tight white tees and standing behind a young woman who was doing squats with a barbell braced on her shoulders.

Vanessa removed her sunglasses and walked through the maze of equipment toward them.

The young woman was wearing a bright pink halter top that barely contained her ample bosom and black booty shorts that looked closer to underwear than exercise clothing. She was letting out exaggerated moans and whimpers with each squat, like she and Bilal were doing a lot more than weightlifting.

"That's it, Keisha," he urged softly, bracing her upper back. "Do those deep knee bends, but keep those shoulders and that back straight."

As Vanessa approached, he looked up and locked eyes with her in the wall-to-ceiling mirrors.

"I need to speak with you *now*," Vanessa mouthed silently to him.

Bilal didn't reply. Instead, he licked his lips and dropped his hand a little lower on the young woman's back so that he almost cupped her waist.

"You've just got five more," he said. "You can do it. Bring it on home."

Keisha's moans and whimpers got even louder, sounding almost orgasmic. Finally, she did the last squat and lowered the barbell to the floor.

"Good job," he said, clapping. "I'm proud of you."

"Thank you, baby. Couldn't have done it without you," the young woman said. He gave her a hug and she giggled, hugging him back even tighter and whispering something in his ear that Vanessa didn't catch, but it made him laugh.

Vanessa rolled her eyes as she watched the couple.

She hoped he wasn't trying to make her jealous. If he was, it wasn't working. She just wanted to ask him her damn questions and be on her way.

He finally released his client and looked at Vanessa

again. "Keisha, why don't you climb on the stepper for a little bit? I gotta talk to my friend over here right quick. It won't take too long."

"*What friend?*" Keisha turned, for the first time, realizing Vanessa had been standing behind them for the past five minutes. When her eyes landed on Vanessa, she slowly looked her up and down. She let a loud gust of air through her flared nostrils. "Oh, well, I guess I can let you visit with your auntie."

Vanessa frowned. *Auntie? Why this little heffa . . .*

She was older than Bilal, but in no way did she look old enough to be his aunt—or did she?

"Just remember you're still on the clock though, baby," Keisha said to him, tapping an imaginary watch on her bare wrist. She tugged her booty shorts out of the crack of her ass as she strutted away. "I want my full hour!"

"I know," he said with a chuckle. "I'll be right back. Don't worry."

"I gotta admit . . . I'm surprised to see you in here," Bilal said a minute later, opening the door to his office.

Vanessa shut the door behind her and dropped her purse into the plastic chair facing his desk that clients usually sat in. "I don't know why you're surprised. I've texted and called you at least ten damn times!"

"Yeah. I was wondering about that too, since the last time we talked to one another, you basically told me you'd call the cops if I didn't keep my ass a hundred feet away from you." She watched as he sat down in his office chair, leaned back, and propped his scuffed Nikes on the lone empty spot of his cluttered desk. "I thought you were trying to set my ass up."

"No, I wasn't setting you up. Like I said, we need to talk."

"Okay, I'm listenin'." He raised his brows. "So, talk."

She eyed him, wondering why he was acting so blasé. The last time she saw him, he had been angry, almost furious, at her for rejecting him, and now he was acting like he couldn't be bothered with her one way or the other. Where did this sudden mood flip come from?

Vanessa thought again about Keisha and her tiny halter top and booty shorts. She thought about the young woman's perfect little medically enhanced twenty-something body.

I bet she has implants, Vanessa thought derisively. *I bet that ass ain't real either.*

But none of that would matter much to a guy like Bilal, as long as it felt and looked real. Was he hooked up with Keisha now? Had he really moved on to another woman that quickly? Was Vanessa that easily replaceable to the men in her life?

Damn it, she thought, now annoyed.

She hated to admit it, but maybe she was starting to feel the first pangs of jealousy. She couldn't focus on it right now though. She had come here for a reason and it wasn't to find out what other women her lover may be screwing. She needed to know if he'd shot her husband.

"Something happened yesterday," she began. "Something bad. Cyrus was shot. He's alive, but he's still in the hospital."

She watched his face for a reaction. Shock, guilt, or maybe even a smugness, but his face remained impassive.

"Did you hear me?" she cried. "I said he was shot!"

"Yeah, I heard you. The nigga got shot." He shrugged. "*And?* So what? You said he's alive. What you freaking out for? Why the hell are you telling me?"

"Because the cops don't know who shot him. I thought . . . I thought you might."

"Why would I know?"

She stared at him, wondering if he was playing stupid or if he really was this dense. Bilal wasn't going to make her say it out loud, was he? As the silence in his office stretched on, she realized that she would have to ask him plainly.

"Did you try to kill him, Bilal? Did you shoot my husband?"

"*What?*" Bilal slowly lowered his feet back to the linoleum-tiled floor. His eyes went wide as he pointed at his chest. "Why do you think *I* shot him?"

"Well, you said I would regret it! I don't know if that's what you meant. And then, I just told you he was shot, and you sat there like I told you it was sunny outside!"

He rose from his chair and stalked toward her. "When I said you'd regret it, I didn't mean I was gonna shoot him!"

She studied his face, trying to decipher the truth.

"Nessa, I swear to you, I ain't shoot that man! I just meant I was gonna put your ass on blast! I was gonna send him texts you sent me. Maybe pictures. That's all."

She gaped. "*That's all?* That's all? You could've ruined my marriage!"

"So? I don't give a fuck! I was pissed off and hurt! What the hell did you expect? I didn't give a shit if your husband wanted to divorce you. I still don't! And I didn't shoot him, but I wouldn't give a shit if someone killed his ass. Good! You'd finally be rid of him. You shouldn't be married to him no way. It's not a real marriage. You don't even love that nigga!"

"I do love him! But . . . but . . ."

"But what?"

She grimaced. "You're right. It's not a real marriage." She closed her eyes as they flooded with tears. "That's the other thing I found out yesterday. Cyrus isn't just married to me. He's married to another woman, too. He's been lying to me!"

"*Another woman?* How . . . how can he do that? You can't marry two people. That's—"

"I know! But he did it anyway! And now I don't know what to do with myself. I just wanna hurt him! I wanna hurt him so bad! I want to hurt him like he hurt me!"

She opened her eyes when she felt Bilal's warm hand against her cheek. He was gazing down at her, in that intense way of his, like he wanted to swallow her whole.

"So, you were hoping I *had* shot him because of what he did to you?"

"No!" she cried instantly. "Of . . . of course not."

He cocked an eyebrow. "You don't sound convincing. Tell the truth. You hoped I did it, didn't you? You *wanted* me to take him out."

"No! No! Stop saying that! I didn't want you to kill my husband, Bilal. Don't even joke about that! He's still the father of my children! That marriage may have been a lie, but I was in it for eleven years!"

Which made his betrayal even more cruel and devastating, but she didn't want her husband dead. Vanessa wanted to beat him to a pulp. She'd probably pretend she was going to run him over with her car to put a little fear into his heart, only to just clip him with her SUV. But kill him? No, that seemed a bit much.

"Fine. Y'all had years together. But don't tell me you still love him now—not after you found out the truth."

Vanessa couldn't answer that question. Her emotions were still too raw.

Bilal raised his other hand to cup her face. "I told you he wasn't the right man for you, and I meant it. I'm the one you should be with, Nessa. How can you not see that shit, especially after all this? I love you, bae! And I'll always take care of you."

Vanessa wasn't so sure of that. She was a mother of three, a woman with an expensive lifestyle. How was Bilal going to fulfill that with his assistant gym manager salary and volunteering for Little League soccer teams? At twenty-four, how could he be the doting father to her children, pay for their school tuition, and buy them all the things they wanted and needed? Say what you will about Cyrus, but he had never fallen short of those obligations.

She didn't get a chance to challenge Bilal though. He abruptly lowered his mouth to hers and dropped his hands from her face to her bottom. He tugged her against him possessively, pressing his groin against hers, rubbing it against her inner thigh. Like clockwork, he was already getting hard. But that was the one thing she'd always loved about him: it didn't take much to get him going, and he always lasted as long as she needed.

As Bilal slipped his tongue inside her mouth, she felt a tingle that started at her core and radiated outward to every region of her body. Her pulse raced. Her nipples became two pebbles straining against her bra cups. When he turned and pressed her against his desk, she didn't push him away. When he yanked the straps of her sundress and her bra straps off her shoulders, baring her breasts to the cool office air, she didn't tell him to stop or cover herself. Instead, she reached for the waistband of his drawstring shorts and yanked them down his hips. She pulled down his boxer briefs too, wrapped her hand around his dick, and began to stroke him right there in his office, taking him from half-mast to rock hard. He groaned against her lips, making her chuckle.

"Uh-oh," she whispered saucily, "looks like Miss Keisha might have to wait longer than she expected. Guess she won't get her hours' worth after all."

Bilal grinned and nibbled her lips. He pulled her hand away and hoisted up her dress. He roughly yanked her panties over her hips and down her thighs. They fell to her ankles and she quickly stepped out of them before kicking them aside, making them land in a lacy ball near his closed office door. Bilal hoisted her up on the edge of the desk, pushing aside papers and folders, a cup filled with one of his protein shakes and an apple. It all landed on the floor.

"You got any condoms in here?" she panted against his mouth, hoping they wouldn't have to stop.

"Hell yeah!" He opened one of the desk drawers and revealed about a half dozen condom packets amid a pile of rubber bands, pens, and boxes of staplers.

She watched Bilal as he ripped one of the packets open with his teeth and quickly put on the condom.

Why the hell did he have so many in his desk drawer? Was he bringing other women in here?

She didn't get to ask him. He was kissing and rubbing her between her legs again, making her wet, making her forget about the condom packets and Keisha and all the others that he may have also humped on his desk. Vanessa spread her legs wide and he centered himself between her thighs, cupping one of her breasts and toying with nipple as he plunged forward and inside her. She cried out and he grunted.

She wanted this. She *needed* it. All the revelations around Cyrus had not only made Vanessa question her marriage, but also her desirability as a woman. So her husband thought he could treat her like she was the member of some harem. He thought he could easily exchange her for another woman, switching her out for a new one, like the tie around his neck.

I'll show you, you son of a bitch, she thought as Bilal plunged into her over and over, and she tightened her hold around the younger man's back. She met Bilal stroke for stroke, all the while thinking about Cyrus, imagining that he could see her right now. She pretended he was sitting in the plastic chair facing the desk, forced to watched as another man made her moan and beg for more.

"Harder, baby," she urged breathlessly. "Do it harder."

Bilal followed her command. He shifted her legs and plunged even deeper, pounding into her, making her squeal in delight.

They both knew they were in an office and even the sounds in the gym might not mask all the noise they were making, but neither seemed to care. They had sex with abandon, getting their fill of one another until the orgasms rocked their bodies and they collapsed back onto his desk.

Chapter 9

Diamond

Diamond pulled into the reserved parking space in her condominium's parking garage, turned off her Aston Martin's Vantage V8 engine, and slumped back against her leather headrest, thoroughly exhausted.

She'd checked out of her hotel a half hour ago, after an uncomfortable night of tossing and turning in one of two double beds, and constantly being woken up by night terrors. She'd slept there because the cops had been in her condo last night when she'd arrived home from the hospital. They had been strolling in and out her front door, still collecting evidence. They'd escorted her to her own bedroom, monitoring her as she collected clothes, clean underwear, toothpaste, a toothbrush, and other sundry items for her overnight stay elsewhere. When she'd left, she had to step over the bloody spot where Cyrus had fallen, while some technician stood nearby taking pictures.

She hoped that they were gone now. She hoped she could finally have her condo back.

Five minutes later, Diamond stepped into the front lobby and walked straight to the line of gilded mailboxes to pick up the mail that had accumulated over the past two days.

When she and Cy had moved in ten months ago, she had been astounded by how grand the lobby was. It had a two-story, white, coffered ceiling, marble floors, and a starburst of chandeliers that looked like glowing dandelions dangling from the heavens. It was all plush velvet banquettes and expensive-looking rugs. She'd known then if their condo was anything close to as nice as the lobby, it was a steep climb up from the two-bedroom apartment in Elkridge she'd shared with her roommate after starting a new life in Baltimore.

The only selling point the leasing office had boasted about to them about that apartment when they moved in was that the view from their balcony faced the parking lot, not the dumpsters. But there were no views of parking lots *or* dumpsters in her brand-new home with Cy.

"It's beautiful," Diamond could remember gushing as they walked through the condo's lobby to the elevators. She'd looked around her, thunderstruck.

Diamond had felt like Cinderella right after her fairy godmother had waved her magic wand and made her rags into a ball gown and a pumpkin and mice into a horse-drawn carriage.

"Only the best for my baby," Cyrus had whispered to her before giving her a kiss.

Now she barely noticed the lobby as she closed her mailbox and dropped the stack of envelopes into her purse. Her eyes were instead trained on the elevators which would take her up nine floors to her home. The day-time security guard, who sat at the ebony front desk staring at his cell phone, glanced up at her. He dropped his phone to the counter with a clatter when he saw her approach. He straightened up in his chair and adjusted the bill of his black cap.

"Oh, hey! Hey, Mrs. Grey," he said as she approached.

"Hey, Richard," she murmured.

"I heard what happened to Mr. Grey, ma'am."

She was just about to pass his desk, but slowed to a stop to turn to look at him.

"I'm sorry?" she asked, barely aware of what he was saying.

She didn't want to talk to anyone. She didn't want to say a single word if she could avoid it. She just wanted to take a warm bath, curl up in bed, sleep a hundred years, and then head back to the hospital to be by Cyrus's side.

"I said I heard what happened to your husband. The cops were asking me if I saw anybody come in that was unusual, if I saw anyone running out, but I swear I didn't see anything, Mrs. Grey. Nobody ran in. Nobody ran out. Maybe the guy took a back door or something, but he didn't pass this desk. I wouldn't lie about that. I swear it!"

Diamond scanned her eyes over his pale face. Richard was maybe twenty-one . . . twenty-two, only a couple years younger than herself. He had that earnest, stereotypical All-American look about him, like he had lived on a farm and decided to move to the big city. He had bright green eyes, even had freckles. He was a grown-up Opie Taylor from the Andy Griffith show. She doubted he would lie to her. He was probably offended at the mere suggestion that he would lie.

"I believe you, Richard."

"Thank you, ma'am."

She started to turn to head to the elevators again, but paused when he stood and said, "I told them that the only thing unusual I remember happening was the day before the shooting. This repair guy came in here, asking if he could go to the ninth floor and do some work in one of the units. I told him I had to clear it with the tenant first, and have someone escort him up there. I asked him for his name and the company name. But he started to get all aggressive with me. He started to argue. His language got pretty blue and he threatened . . . well . . . he threatened to 'take care of my ass,'" he said in an embarrassed whisper, like he hated uttering the word "ass." "I told him if he didn't leave, I was gonna call the cops, but then he just walked out after that. I didn't have to."

"He threatened you?"

"Yep! And I knew something wasn't right about him the minute he walked in. He wasn't even wearing a uniform! He just came in regular clothes and he was covered in tattoos on his neck and arms. He even had one on his face. What repair guy looks like that?"

"*Tattoos?*" Now he had her full interest. "Do you remember any of them?"

"Well, he had a woman's lips tattooed on his neck, I think. And there was the flag on his arm and—"

"Do you remember a tattoo of a nine? Right here?" she said, gesturing to her forearm.

Richard squinted, like he was trying to remember. "Maybe. No . . . no, I think he *did* have one now that you mention it! It was in a fancy script."

Diamond took a deep breath. So the shooter had been to their building the day before. He'd been casing the place.

"Do you know who the guy was, Mrs. Grey?" Richard asked.

"No," she whispered, "but I wish I did. Thanks for telling me all of this, Richard. Do you mind if I tell the cops what you said . . . what you told me?"

"No, of course not! If it helps, I can talk to them again. And I'll keep an eye out for any other bad characters from now on, ma'am. Don't worry!" he called to her as she continued to the elevators. "No more thugs will get in here on my watch!"

"Thanks, Richard."

She waved goodbye, pressed the up button, and stepped inside the elevator when the doors opened.

Diamond knew in her heart that the tattooed man Richard had spoken to the day before the shooting had to be the same guy who shot Cyrus. But now she wondered if it was the last she'd seen of him? Would he come back to finish the job? Did he work for Julian, her former pimp and ex? Or maybe he was one of Julian's friends.

He has to be connected to him somehow, she thought.

The whole setup certainly seemed like something Julian would do. Julian had no problem with murder, but he preferred not to get his hands dirty. Hell, she had witnessed him killing someone with her own eyes—and had lied about it when Julian told her to. She knew what her ex was capable of.

Her cell phone ringtone suddenly began to play. She reached into her purse, pulled out her cell, and saw the name on the screen. "Speak of the devil," Diamond muttered.

It wasn't Julian himself. She'd tried his old number yesterday and discovered that it had been disconnected. So Diamond had called a few members of his old crew and some of girls she used to turn tricks with. She'd left messages and sent texts to a few, all asking if they had spoken to Julian, if they had seen him since he'd gotten out of jail. So far, none of them had responded—until now.

"Hey, what's up?" she said after pressing the green button to answer.

"What's up, girl?" Honey yawned, sounding even more tired than Diamond.

Diamond wasn't surprised. Honey, who had gotten her name from the honey-colored weave and wigs she always wore, hadn't stopped doing sex work like Diamond did when Julian went to prison. She kept a few regular clients and found new ones online. It was a job that meant having irregular hours. Diamond remembered what it was like to head out to meet a trick at ten o'clock at night and not get back until dawn. She'd used to sleep until noon or later when her work was done and be awoken by either a hard shove by one of the other girls or Julian loudly clapping his hands next to her ear, startling her.

"I saw you called me last night," Honey now continued over the phone. "I haven't heard from your ass in a hot minute. Where you been at girl?"

The elevator doors opened, and Diamond stepped onto her floor. "Same place I've always been."

Honey had been her only real friend back then, the only person she'd told where she was going when Julian went to jail, just in case her bestie ever needed anything. Diamond had wanted to start a new life and not be weighed down by the baggage and the people of her past. She'd sworn Honey to secrecy. She'd made her not tell anyone that she'd moved to Baltimore, but now she wondered if Honey had kept her secret like she'd promised.

"Uh-huh," Honey murmured. "Well, you sure ain't been around here. Don't even visit a bitch. Can't send me a birthday card or nothin'."

"You didn't send me any cards either," Diamond said, walking down the hall. "You could've come up here to see me, too."

"I'm too busy down here. Gotta make that paper!" Honey popped her gum. "So why you call me? What you want?"

"I heard Julian got out early." Diamond heard the elevator doors close behind her. "Did you know?"

Honey didn't immediately answer her. After a long pause, she yawned again. "Yeah, umm . . . I heard."

"Have you spoken to him? Do you know where he is?"

Again, Honey went silent.

She was Diamond's friend, but she'd always had a sort of reverence for Julian. Diamond had loved him almost like a father figure and wanted to make him happy, but Honey had treated him like he was damn near God himself. Like Diamond, she'd never been willing to rebel against him. Probably even less so now.

Diamond came to a stop in the corridor. "Have you spoken to him, Honey?" she repeated slowly.

"Yeah, he hit me up," Honey finally admitted. "He's at The Men's Village now, I think. You know . . . the halfway house. He gotta stay there until next year."

"Did he ask about me? Did he ask where I went?"

"Why do you think it always gotta be about you? Like we can't talk about anything else."

"Did you tell him where I went, Honey? I need to know. Something . . . something happened here, and they think Julian might have done it."

"*They?* They who?"

"The police!"

"Why the popo think it was him? What happened?"

"Someone was shot. Someone close to me. Just tell me if you told him if I was up here in Baltimore. Please! That's all I need to know."

"Well, when did it happen?"

Honey still hadn't answered her question. She seemed to be outright refusing to do it, so Diamond guessed she already had her answer; Honey had told Julian where she'd gone. Diamond wasn't surprised, just disappointed. She dropped her forehead into her hand.

"It happened yesterday afternoon at around three o'clock."

"It wasn't him," Honey said with certainty. "It wasn't

Julian! It couldn't have been. Those cops don't know what the fuck they're talking about! He was down here in bed with me."

Diamond felt neither anger nor jealousy at Honey's revelation. Again, just disappointment. They had both managed to get out of Julian's clutches, only for Honey to happily climb back into his talons again within a few days of his release. The escaped prisoner had returned to her jailer with her wrists extended, eager to slap on the shackles again.

"I never said he did it himself. He could've—"

"Look, he didn't have anything to do with that shit! He ain't worried about you. *Okay?*" Honey insisted. "He's out of jail and he got other things on his mind. We finna do big things! Don't worry about us, College Girl."

College Girl . . . It was the nickname the other girls had given her, thanks to the two years of college she'd had before she started doing online porn to make fast cash and help pay the bills that her student loans couldn't cover. Eventually, online porn became meeting clients and then full-time sex work when Julian convinced her that she could make even more money the other route. He'd offered to guide and protect her, to take her under his wing. By the second semester of her third year, she had dropped out of college and started turning tricks exclusively.

Since some of the other girls hadn't finished high school, let alone gone to college, she'd taken the nickname they gave her as a compliment—at first. At least it wasn't "Chunky" or "Fat Ass" which is what the kids used to call her at school before she grew up, lost weight, and her chub became voluptuous curves. College Girl sounded like something to denote she was better than the other girls. She certainly didn't talk like them. She had read books and been places. Julian chose her for the clients who requested somebody "classier" and "less ratchet," who they could take to a restaurant or on the town before they took her back to their hotel room. Diamond had foolishly thought she was special, but she figured out they were only ridiculing her when they called her College Girl.

"Yeah, you think you're so fuckin' smart, College Girl! Well, what did all those classes and books get you when you're suckin' dick and fuckin' randoms just like the rest of us?" one of the girls had asked, making the rest burst into laughter. "Not a goddamn thing!"

Now when Diamond heard the nickname, she winced. She took it as the jab it was intended to be. She didn't know why Honey was using it now. She'd thought they were friends.

"Yeah, well, I hope you do big things if that's what you want," Diamond said. "And I hope he treats you right."

"Don't he always?"

Diamond dropped her hand from her forehead, knowing from the sound of Honey's voice that she wouldn't be able to convince her that Julian had been and would always be bad for her. "Look, I'll talk to you later, all right?"

"Yeah, okay. Hit you up later." Honey then abruptly hung up.

Diamond stared down at her phone for a long time before continuing down the hall to her condo.

She still wasn't convinced Julian was innocent, despite Honey's assurances that Julian had nothing to do with what had happened to Cyrus. Just because he didn't shoot the gun himself, didn't mean he didn't send someone up here to do it for him. Honey's blind defense of him actually made Diamond more suspicious, not less.

I gotta figure this out, she thought as she shoved her cell back into her handbag.

Her eyes landed on her front door, on the yellow crime tape crisscrossed over the doorway and the blood still smeared on its wooden surface. It flooded her with angst.

"I'm gonna figure this out," she repeated before reaching up and ripping down the tape. She unlocked her front door and shoved it open.

Chapter 10

Noelle

Noelle gazed up at the towering building in front of her, holding her hands over her eyes like a visor.

It was part of a business complex along a busy highway in Montgomery County, over the border in Maryland. It was tall—fifteen stories—though nothing compared to the skyscrapers she remembered back in Manhattan. But when the sun hit the building's tinted windows at the right angle, it looked almost green against the blue sky, projecting a light that could be seen from more than a mile away, making it look like the tower in the Emerald City from *The Wizard of Oz*.

This was the building where Cyrus and Tariq worked. This is where they housed their consultancy firm, which consisted of Cyrus, Tariq, and one other employee.

Noelle stepped through the revolving doors and strolled inside. She walked across the marble-tiled atrium straight to the bank of elevators, pressing the button to head to the tenth floor.

As the elevator ascended and Noelle watched the numbers tick by on the digital screen overhead, she realized how little she knew about what Cyrus and Tariq did all day.

She'd seen his office, but for all she knew he and Tariq could have a secret enterprise going on that had absolutely nothing to do with their company. Maybe Cy made all his money by some other means, like something illegal.

She had to find out the truth, especially now that Cyrus's secrets were putting her in a precarious situation with the cops. She'd come here in person instead of calling Tariq by phone to not only ask him every question that was on her mind, but to also watch him and pay attention to the details, things she may have ignored or dismissed before.

The elevator doors opened, and Noelle strolled down the hall, stopping by a door with the gold plaque, GREYDON CONSULTANTS, posted beside it. The company's name came from both Cyrus's and Tariq's last names: Grey and Donahue. She pushed the door open and found a young woman sitting at a reception desk in the center of an airy waiting room filled with understated modern furniture. A few pieces of artwork adorned the white walls. A coffee carafe along with a few empty cups sat on tray cart in the corner. Magazines were fanned along the center of a coffee table in front of three armchairs.

The young woman was Kelsey. She served as the company's receptionist and office assistant. Noelle had always been friendly to her, exchanging greetings and even bringing her a small Christmas gift the past two years.

Nothing seemed nefarious or unusual as Noelle looked around her. It was your typical, mundane front office, like every other front office in buildings across America. But Noelle knew that looks could sometimes be deceiving.

Kelsey raised her dark head, looking up from the stack of paperwork she'd been reviewing. She saw Noelle and shot to her feet. She walked around her desk and practically ran toward her.

"Oh, Mrs. Grey! Tariq told me what happened to Cyrus. He said he went to see him at the hospital. I'm so sorry, ma'am!" she said, taking one of Noelle's hands within her own.

Noelle grimaced. "Thank you, Kelsey. I appreciate it."

"Are you okay? I mean . . ." The young woman furiously shook her head and released Noelle's hand. "I know you're not okay. That was a silly question. I bet you're devastated. But . . . do you need anything? Is there anything I can do for you? What . . . what can I do?"

Kelsey was staring at her eagerly with doleful big brown eyes.

Noelle wondered if all this sympathy was real—or was Kelsey pretending like Cyrus had and like Tariq had done as well. Had Kelsey put on a smile and lied to Noelle over the years to cover up Cyrus's sins? Was the young woman conning her now too?

"Did you know?" Noelle asked in a hushed whisper, making Kelsey blink in confusion.

"*Did I know?* Did I know what, Mrs. Grey?"

"Did you know the truth about Cyrus?" she repeated, this time in a louder voice.

Kelsey frowned. "What . . . what truth?"

"Did you know about his other wives? Have you met them? Did you know that he was—"

"Noelle!" Tariq suddenly boomed, making her jump.

She turned to find him standing in the hallway leading to his and Cy's offices. He was wearing a gray single-breasted suit with no tie today that showed off his lean frame. He strode down the hall into the waiting room, giving her a censuring look the whole time, making her instantly go quiet.

"Hey, I didn't know you were coming up here." He leaned forward and gave her a hug. "Have you lost your damn mind?" he quickly whispered into her ear, before stepping back and rubbing her shoulder. "I thought you might be at the hospital. Any updates on Cy?"

Kelsey glanced between them both, still looking distressed and confused.

So, we're playing pretend again, Noelle thought with annoyance. *Fine. I'll play along.*

"No. No updates so far. The doctor says he's pretty much the same," she lied. "I decided to take a break from the hospital though, come here, and take you up on the kind offer you made last night."

"Did you now?" Tariq inclined his head. "Well that's good to hear. So a late lunch it is." He turned to Kelsey. "Kel, Noelle and I are going to grab something to eat. I'll be back in an hour. Okay?"

"Uh, o-okay," Kelsey said, nodding sluggishly, still looking off kilter. "I'll . . . I'll update your schedule, sir."

"Thanks." He headed toward the door leading out of the waiting room and opened it. "Ladies first," he said to Noelle.

She walked in front him, striding into the corridor. He followed her, shutting the door behind them.

"You shouldn't have done that," Tariq said ten minutes later as his silver Porsche Boxster zipped down the four-lane roadway. Noelle sat in the passenger seat beside him, cringing as he abruptly switched lanes.

"I shouldn't have done what?" she asked, digging her nails into the leather armrest as his speed increased another ten miles per hour.

"You shouldn't have said that to Kelsey," he now elaborated, giving her that same censuring look that he'd given ten minutes ago. He returned his attention to the road. "She doesn't know about any of that shit with Cy. She's never met his other wives either."

"Why not?"

"Because neither of them are as nosy as you are," he said, side-eyeing her. "You always asked the most questions. That's probably why you're the only one who's been to the office building. He told the others that he works from home and rents co-working space somewhere in Silver Spring, I think."

"And they believed him?"

"Yeah. Why wouldn't they? He always makes sure they call his cell or his direct line. The only address for our company that's listed online is a P.O. Box. Diamond hasn't been with him long enough to dig deeper than that, I guess, and as long as Vanessa's bills are paid and her credit cards still work, she doesn't give a goddamn either way."

Noelle winced, hearing Tariq casually use their names: Diamond and Vanessa—the two other women in Cyrus's life. She still hadn't gotten used to the concept. But part of her wanted to know more about them, even loudmouthed, obnoxious Vanessa. Who were they? Why had Cyrus chosen to marry them too? What was so damn special about them? But she wasn't sure if she was prepared to get to know these women better quite yet.

Better to focus on the other stuff for now, she thought.

"I don't get it. Why do you guys have offices in Montgomery at all?" she asked Tariq instead.

He chuckled as he drove. "See what I mean? More questions!"

"Is Greydon Consultants even a real business?" she asked, ignoring him. "Or did Cy make that up too?"

"All of it is real, Noelle—just some of it you may call . . . well . . . questionable."

"Questionable? Questionable how?"

"How do you think? Some of it is questionable legally, but the company still has to function. I still have a business to run, and I don't need you fucking it up just because you're pissed off at Cy, which is what you almost did with Kelsey back there."

"Well, pardon me for not considering the state of your half legitimate, half shady company, Tariq, but my goddamn life is in shambles! I thought Kelsey might know more than I did since she's around you guys so much. It's the only reason why I asked her anything. I just want answers!"

"Kelsey knows what we want her to know, and the less she knows, the better off she is."

"Well, if she's better off not knowing, then why the hell are you willing to tell me the truth?"

"*Honestly?*" He glanced at her again. "I'm still not sure if I should tell you. It's risky for you to know everything, but Cy fucked up. He left that door open. You might as well step on through. I'd rather I answer your questions than you ask the wrong person and . . ."

"And what?"

"Get yourself killed."

Noelle swallowed audibly.

Tariq whipped the wheel, making a hard right into a shopping center, making her clutch the armrest again and the car behind them blare its horn. She thought they were going to pull into one of the parking spaces in front of the high-end Italian or seafood restaurant. Instead, he pulled into the queue at a fast-food joint.

Noelle peered out the window, narrowing her eyes at the golden arches and sign. "*McDonald's?*"

"It's fast and we can eat in the car while we talk."

Despite her anxiety and headache, she laughed. "You're

driving a Porsche and wearing what has to be a seven-hundred-dollar suit," she said, fingering his lapel, "and you're about to eat a Big Mac and fries?"

"Food is food," he said, pulling up to the speaker and lowering his car window. "Besides, I may be in an *eight*-hundred-dollar suit and drive a Porsche, but I'm still a regular dude from Southeast D.C., Noelle. That part of me will never change."

I bet it won't, she thought as she watched him look at the menu and give his order. She stared at his handsome face in profile.

Tariq had always come off to her as a complex guy, a study in contrasts. He liked expensive things from the car he drove to the wine he drank and seemed studiously meticulous in his appearance. But Tariq also didn't believe in putting on airs. He could be laid back and funny when he wanted to be.

Cy had told her once that he considered Tariq to be his right-hand man, his counterbalance that kept him and his business level. She wasn't surprised. She always felt reassured and calmed by Tariq's presence, despite how brusque he could be with her sometimes. Even when he was blunt to the point of being almost abrasive, she'd always felt like his honesty came with good intentions, that he only wanted to help her in the end.

But like Cyrus, there were parts of Tariq she still didn't know. Like, for instance, she knew he wasn't married, but did he have a girlfriend? Of the women he sometimes brought with him when he would go on double dates with her and Cy, she couldn't remember ever seeing any girl more than once. She'd tried to ask him about it in the past, to joke with him and ask him why he hadn't found that special someone yet, but he'd brushed her off.

"I see people," he'd say. "I get around. Don't worry about me. Trust."

Was Tariq single like he claimed, or was he hiding a secret wife, like Cyrus?

He now turned from the window to look at her. "Did you want anything?"

She blinked, snapping out of her thoughts. "Huh?"

"Did you want me to order you anything?" he repeated.

"Oh . . . um. No, I'm okay. Thanks."

"Have you eaten anything today?"

"Not really. But I don't want the first thing I eat to be fast food. I'm tired and hungover. I doubt I could keep anything down."

"Fries," he said, turning back to the window. "McDonald's fries are good for a hangover."

"Tariq, I told you, I don't want—"

"And I'll take a medium fry too," he called to the mesh speaker. "And a cup of water."

"Gotcha'," the fuzzy voice answered. "That'll be ten-fifty-three. Pull up to the first window, please?"

She grumbled as he pressed the accelerator and they lurched forward. "Really?"

He laughed. "It'll help. Believe me. I wouldn't steer you wrong."

He was right. The fries did help abate her headache and nausea a little. She came to this conclusion as they sat in the parking lot, gazing out the windshield at the restaurants in front of them and people watching while they ate their food.

"So," she said between chews, "do you know why Cyrus was shot? Did his shady business stuff have anything to do with it?"

Tariq, who had been drinking his soda, lowered the straw from his mouth. "You're gonna hop right into it, huh? You're not even gonna let me finish my Quarter Pounder first?"

"This isn't a joke, Tariq. Cy's in the hospital. Police are questioning me and acting like I was behind it. This shit is serious. I need to know!"

His face when somber. He frowned. "Police questioned you?"

"Two detectives," she slumped back into the passenger seat. "They came by the house today. They were insinuating that I might have done it . . . that I might have been behind the shooting because I found out that Cy was cheating on me. They brought up my depression and . . . and something that happened a few years ago." She dropped her gaze to her lap, too embarrassed to look Tariq in the eye while she told the story. "Cy and I had an . . . an incident where the cops showed up. I wasn't really trying to hurt him. I wanted to hurt myself."

"Hurt yourself?" he repeated. "You mean you wanted to . . ."

His words faded as she nodded.

"Shit, Noelle. I didn't know that."

"And I hoped you never would. It's not something I'm proud of, Tariq. But anyway, I . . . I had a knife that night. It was a deadly weapon and the cops wanted to charge me with assault, but Cy stopped them. I thought this was all behind us." She took a shaky breath. "But now that he's been shot, and they don't know who did it, they're . . . they're trying to use it against me, and I-I don't know . . ."

She stopped when she felt Tariq's comforting hand on her shoulder. "It's okay. You don't have anything to worry about."

"How do you know that?" she cried. "They said they'll stay in touch. What if they come back and—"

"They're just fishin', Noelle. All detectives do that! It's their job. They have to talk to everyone around Cyrus, including you, Vanessa, and Diamond. They wanna see if you'll confess something, but you don't have anything to confess." He squeezed her shoulder. "You're good. I bet they won't even question you again."

Noelle hoped he was right. "What did Cy do, Tariq? Why would anyone want to kill him?"

Tariq dropped his hand from her shoulder and closed his eyes. "I don't know for sure if they did it. Let me say that outright, but . . . Cy stole money from the wrong people. He knew he was dead ass wrong, but he did it anyway. He didn't listen to me."

"What 'wrong people'? Who?"

Tariq opened his eyes again. "I can't give you specifics. But some of the consultancy we do is with clients who want to invest, but their money . . . how they got it . . . well, it isn't always legit. Cy and I find a way to make it look legitimate. We give them good returns and we collect our fee and our percentage. That's all."

"That's all? And these people are . . . what? Criminals?"

"Technically . . . yeah."

"You guys work for criminals?" she repeated, unable to hide how shocked she was.

"They are our *clients*, Noelle. Just like any other client as far as I'm concerned. We're not involved with how they make their money. We just control how they invest it. But these are the type of clients who don't take kindly to having their money stolen, and they ain't gonna file complaints with the S.E.C. when it happens. Cy was skimming off the top for a long time, and it finally got back to them. I guess he might have paid the price for it."

"Why didn't they suspect you did it too? I mean . . . you and Cy work together, right? You're partners."

"Yeah, but they know I'm loyal. I wouldn't do any shit like that. I especially wouldn't do it to who Cy did it to."

"Did you tell them what he did?"

He tilted his head. "You mean did I snitch on him?"

"That's not what I meant. I just meant that . . . that . . ."

She couldn't find the words because it was exactly what she'd meant. She just didn't want Tariq to think she was blaming him in any way for what had happened to Cyrus. But part of her now wondered.

"Look, I ain't a snitch! They figured that shit out on their own. And Cy had to know that a bull's-eye would be on his back if and when they did find out."

"Have you told the cops any of this?"

"Hell no!" he shouted, staring at her like she'd just announced she was the Queen of Sheba reincarnated. "Why the hell would I tell the cops? I told you, I'm not a snitch and I don't want them coming after my ass, too!" He went serious again. "And you better not tell the cops either. You hear me? It would be very, *very* stupid for you to do that. I'm only telling you this so you know what's been happening . . . so you aren't in the dark anymore."

"But what if they come after Cy again? They didn't kill him the first time, but his life could still be in danger!"

Tariq shrugged, bit into his hamburger, and chewed. "Shit, it might. But like I said, I warned him." He wiped a smear of ketchup off the side of his mouth with a paper napkin. "Besides, I don't even know for sure if they're the ones who did it. But *if* Cy survives this, I suggest you stay as far away from your man as possible. Being pissed off at him is probably a good thing right now. Keep your distance."

At those words, a chill went up Noelle's spine. She stared at Tariq in dismay. "I don't get how you can be so glib about this. Someone tried to kill Cyrus. They could try again. And you're acting like . . . like you don't give a damn! I thought he was your friend, Tariq."

He stopped chewing and looked at her for a long time after that, not saying anything.

She'd pissed him off. She could tell, but she didn't care. Cyrus had trusted him. He'd considered him not just a business partner, but damn near a best friend. Now she was starting to wonder if the men's relationship was one-sided, if Cyrus thought he was a lot closer to Tariq than he really was.

"Let's understand something," Tariq began in a measured voice as he tossed what was left of his burger into the container and then the paper bag and wiped his hands. "I've been watching your man's back for almost sixteen years now. Okay? I've helped him out. I've kept his secrets. I've even covered for him when he needed it. I offered him advice. More importantly, I told him when he was dead ass wrong and when he was making a mistake. I gave him the hard truths that only a *real* friend would give. And even when he didn't take my advice, I stuck by him. So don't question whether I was a friend to Cy." He pointed at her. "My ass was loyal! Much more loyal than that dude ever was to me!"

She quieted, shamed into silence.

"Look, Cy is a grown ass man. He does whatever the fuck he wants to do. He always has! And he has a god complex. What else would explain why he thought he could marry three different women and never get caught? What else would explain half of the other shit he did? He made a bad decision, Noelle—a *very* bad decision, and he has to suffer the consequences. Neither of us putting our neck out for him is going to change any of that! Do you understand?"

She glared stubbornly out the windshield, refusing to answer him, but turned to look at him when he placed a finger under her chin, catching her off guard. The stern expression on his face had softened.

"Do you understand?" he said in a voice that was as

gentle as his touch. "I need to know that you aren't gonna go running to the cops with what I told you . . . that you aren't gonna put yourself at risk by doing anything stupid."

Gazing into his dark eyes, her throat went dry. Her heartbeat quickened. She gradually nodded.

"Good." He lowered his finger from her chin and shifted in the driver's seat. She could still feel a tingle on her skin where he'd touched her. "I promised Cy awhile back that if anything ever happened to him, I'd look out for you. I plan to keep my promise. Don't make it hard for me."

"I can take care of myself, Tariq."

She didn't need any rescuer or protector.

He lowered the car window and tossed his fast food bag into a nearby trash can. "I know you can. Just let me help out a little though."

She shook her head in exasperation, secretly relieved that if anyone had her back right now, it was Tariq.

Chapter 11

Vanessa

Vanessa fluffed her curls around her shoulders as she mounted the last brick stair leading to her colonial. She exhaled before inserting her key into the lock on her front door, returning home in a much better mood than when she'd departed that morning.

She had just left Bilal forty minutes earlier after making love not once, but twice in his office. They'd parted ways with kisses and promises to see one another soon. As Bilal casually strolled back into the gym and she to the gym doors to head back home, Vanessa had locked gazes with his client Keisha, who was still climbing on the stair machine. The girl had probably climbed up the equivalent of the Empire State Building by that point.

"Enjoy your workout!" Vanessa had called to her.

Keisha hadn't responded. Instead, she'd shot daggers at Vanessa with her eyes, knowing full well what Bilal and Vanessa had probably been doing while he was gone. Vanessa had to fight the urge to burst into laughter as she'd stepped out the gym onto the sidewalk.

Hey, either you got it, or you don't, honey, Vanessa had

thought before putting on her sunglasses and striding toward her Mercedes.

And Vanessa Grey still had it, despite what Cyrus had done to her. Bilal could vouch for that.

She opened her front door, still floating on a high of sex and love. But when she saw the chaos around her, her endorphin high came crashing to earth with a splat.

Cy Jr. was sailing around the living room on the glowing hoverboard his father had given him for his birthday. He was wearing oversized headphones and was firmly focused on his handheld and not the world around him, which would explain why one of her potted plants was overturned, spilling dirt onto the area rug. She could see that a metal vase had fallen off one of the consoles and lay on the hardwood. She watched as Cy Jr. bumped into one of her end tables, making the lamp on top wobble. Meanwhile, Zoe and Bryson were fighting in the living room, shoving at one another as they tussled over the TV remote. The sound in the room was deafening thanks to the blaring television and her screaming children.

Where the hell was her mother? She was supposed to be watching them.

"Stop it! Stop it, right now!" Vanessa shouted as she charged across the living room.

But the children didn't stop. Cy Jr. glided around their leather sectional, undeterred, bobbing his head to whatever music was playing in his headphones. Zoe and Bryson were now rolling around on the floor like wrestlers in a ring. Zoe bit her brother's hand to release the remote. He squealed in pain and swung at her, hitting her arm and making her scream.

"I said . . . *stop it!*" Vanessa yelled, reaching down and yanking the two apart.

They both blinked and stared up at her in surprise. She

tore the remote out of Bryson's hands and turned off the television. "There! Now neither one of you can watch it!"

Cy Jr. finally skidded to a halt on his hoverboard. "Hey, Mom, I didn't know you were back," he lisped, tugging off his headphones. "When'd you get in?"

"Just a minute ago," she said, dropping her hands to her hips. "And I'm not happy to see y'all fighting and carrying on this way while I was gone. Look at this place!" She threw out her arms. "It's a mess!"

Her children surveyed the room. They looked chagrined.

"If your father was here, he'd take the belt to all of your behinds, and I'm of half a mind to spank you myself!"

Cy Jr. lowered his gaze. "Sorry, Mom."

"Sorry, Mommy," Bryson and Zoe said in unison.

"All of you, clean this place up, then go to your rooms. I don't want to hear any more yelling or fighting. Do you hear me? And since you all seem to have so much energy, I guess I can let you go back to school tomorrow."

They all let out a collective groan.

"No reason to keep you home another day since you don't seem to be that upset about your dad anymore, from what I can tell. Now clean this place up!"

"Yes, Mommy . . . Yes, Mom . . . Okay, Mom," they all answered before gathering their discarded toys and putting the vase back on its console.

"And where is your grandmother? I thought she was watching you three!"

"She went outside to sit on the deck," Cy Jr. explained. "She said she needed a break."

"She's smoking cigarettes," Bryson said with a conspiratorial giggle before slapping his hand over his mouth.

"*Cigarettes?*" Vanessa exclaimed.

The children nodded.

Vanessa grumbled. "Okay, I'll go find Grandma. All of you . . . clean up!"

Vanessa stepped onto the deck a minute later and shut the French doors behind her. The deck, which was two stories and wrapped around the entire rear exterior of the house, overlooked their swimming pool and basketball court. Vanessa found her mother, Carol, reclining back in one of the patio chairs, under an umbrella, smoking and sipping from a perspiring glass of lemonade. When she heard Vanessa walk up behind her, she turned with the cigarette still dangling from her puckered lips.

"So, the kids were right. You *are* smoking," Vanessa said as she pulled out a chair on the opposite side of the patio table, tucked her sundress beneath her, and sat down. "It's a bad habit, Mama. You know it could kill you! You told me you stopped smoking those things years ago!"

Carol loudly groused before tugging the cigarette out of her mouth and stamping it out on a saucer that she was using as a makeshift ashtray. She blew smoke through her nostrils. "I only smoke every blue moon, Nessa. Just when I feel a craving for nicotine—or when I'm stressed out, which I was thanks to you *and* your children."

Vanessa thought back to the chaos she had just witnessed in her living room. "I know the kids can be a handful, Mama. I'm sending them back to school tomorrow. Don't worry."

"I'm not just talking about those little hellions, my dear. I called you and texted you on your cell at least four times to get an update, and you didn't answer me. You were gone for almost two and half hours, Nessa!"

"Oh," Vanessa said. Her cheeks went bright pink. "Sorry. Guess I was driving or . . . or busy."

"I bet you were," her mother replied sarcastically, before reaching for her glass and taking a sip. "You said you were going to talk to that boy to find out information. And here you come back two and half hours later, with no lipstick on and in a wrinkled dress, looking freshly fucked and—"

"Mama!" Vanessa cried before whipping around to look at the French doors then the window.

She hated when her mother got this crude, but the older woman wasn't someone to beat around the bush. Alcohol made her blunt lips even looser. Vanessa was starting to wonder if maybe her mother's glass of lemonade was filled with more than just ice.

She turned back to Carol and dropped her voice to a whisper. "Watch your language! What if the kids heard you?"

"Oh, they aren't listening," her mother said dismissively, fluttering her fingers. "They're watching TV or playing video games or uploading stuff on that Instagram. Whatever children do nowadays!" She leaned forward and narrowed her eyes at Vanessa across the table. "The only child you need to be concerned about is the one you're screwin'."

"He's *not* a child, Mama," she said tightly. "Stop acting like I'm some pedophile. He's twenty-four—a grown man!"

"So you say." Carol leaned back in her chair again. She took another sip from her glass. "Did this grown man have anything to do with what happened to your husband yesterday?"

Vanessa hesitated, remembering Bilal's initial reaction to the news of Cyrus's shooting. He hadn't reacted at all. Not even surprised. It had been so strange, even a little alarming at first, but Bilal swore he didn't do it. And she suspected if he did do it, he wouldn't lie about it. He was so eager for Cyrus to be gone that he'd rub it in her face if he was the one to pull the trigger.

"*Well?*" her mother persisted.

"No, he didn't do it, and he doesn't know who did."

"And you believe him?"

"He wouldn't lie to me."

Carol turned her gaze. She stared at the pool, letting her eyes linger on the blue water that turned darker as a cloud passed overhead. "So, what y'all did today . . . it was the last one for the road? You aren't going to see him again, right?"

Vanessa looked at the water, too, fidgeting anxiously in her chair, unsure how to answer that question.

She knew she shouldn't see Bilal again. Their affair came with too many risks, especially now that Cyrus was in the hospital with a bullet wound. She didn't want anyone to misconstrue that she might have, in any way, set up the shooting so she could run away with her lover. But the sex with Bilal was *so* good. It hadn't been that good with Cyrus in years, maybe even since the beginning when they first started dating. And Bilal loved her like crazy. Yes, she was never going to be with him in the way that he wanted, but why couldn't she enjoy their relationship just a little bit longer? Why did she have to go cold turkey? Especially now when this whole ordeal with Cyrus was making her feel powerless and insecure. With Bilal, *she* was in control. She had him wrapped around her little finger.

"I'll take your silence as a no," her mother said, sucking her teeth in disgust.

"Mama, it just isn't that simple. I want to, but—"

"Yes, it is that simple, Nessa! You think you're the first woman who got some good dick? Well, you're not, honey. I got quite a bit in my day, too, but I wasn't dumb enough to risk everything to get it and keep it! What do I always tell you? What do I always say? If a man doesn't serve a purpose, then why the hell would you keep him around?"

Vanessa clenched her hands in her lap. She wanted to yell back at her mother to mind her own damn business for once, but she knew better. Vanessa may be a tigress, but Carol Walters was a lioness. You did not spar with her.

"When you fell head over heels in love with Cyrus, I didn't tell you that you were being a damn fool because I saw that he was rich. He was handsome. He could take care of you and whatever children you had. Even if you two got divorced, you would be set for life. But what does Bilal offer you besides a stiff dick? What can he give you besides rug burns and a sore cooch?"

Vanessa loudly exhaled. "It's not always about money, Mama, or . . . or sex!" she argued, though she could inwardly admit that it was mostly about sex when it came to Bilal. "It's about having a connection and—"

"Oh, save it for the poor and unwashed, honey," her mother replied dryly. "I don't need a speech. I just need a straight answer, which is why I'm asking you again . . . what can he give you? What will he do for you, Nessa?"

"What . . . what do you mean?"

"I mean how much is he in love with you? How far is he willing to go to please you? If you asked him to do anything, would he do it? Some men don't have the means to buy you a diamond necklace—but they might be willing to steal you one, if you asked. I had men like that, too. They're useful as well—in the right context. But would he consider you worth the risk? How far is he willing to go to please you?"

Vanessa thought for a moment. She remembered their conversation in the gym, back at his office.

"So, you were hoping I had shot him because of what he did to you?"

"No! Of . . . of course not."

"You don't sound convincing. Tell the truth. You hoped I did it, didn't you? You wanted me to take him out."

She could've sworn she saw something in his eyes when he said that last part, like he'd be willing to kill Cyrus if she asked. All she had to do was say the word. But she would never ask for such a thing.

"I think so," she finally answered.

"You think so?" her mothered echoed. "Either it's a yes or a no, Nessa."

"Yes. He loves me and he's not just saying it. He wants me. He wants to please me more than anything, and he'll do whatever he needs to do to accomplish that."

"Good." Her mother raised her glass to her lips once more. "Then keep him around for now. He might be useful later," she said before finishing off the rest of her lemonade.

Chapter 12

Diamond

Diamond gradually rose to her feet, wincing at the cracking in her knees and the pain in her lower back. She dropped her brush into the red-tinted bucket of soapy water, yanked off her rubber gloves, and sighed.

The cops may have been thorough in collecting evidence, but none of the dozen or so people who had traipsed in and out of her condo yesterday were part of any cleanup crew. They'd left her foyer in the same disordered state as they'd found it, leaving Diamond with the honor of cleaning up all the dried blood and tissue by herself. Fortunately for Diamond, this wasn't the first time she'd had to clean up a mess like this. She knew what cleanser to use and to get a scrub brush instead of a sponge to make the work go faster. But she still had been at it for almost two and half hours, trying to remove the mess from her front door, floor, and walls. She'd gotten most of it off, but there were a few pesky smudges she'd have to take a second swipe at later.

"After I take a long, hot bath," she mumbled.

But that meant she probably wouldn't make it to the hospital today. She wanted to see Cyrus again so badly, to hold his hand and sit by his side, but she was too exhausted from the cleaning and the rough night's sleep. She would try to do it tomorrow before her shift started at the restaurant.

Diamond walked into her bathroom and dumped the bloody water into her toilet, watching it as it swirled down the drain when she flushed. She then began to tiredly peel off her clothes, leaving them piled on the tiled floor. She opened one of the counter cabinets and looked at the assortment of bubble baths, bath gels, scented soaps, and bath bombs in her collection, trying to decide how she should soothe her sore limbs and muscles.

Before she'd met Cyrus, she didn't take long, languid baths or wear facial masks or get foot massages. She'd always been a scrub your face at the sink or a ten-minute shower kind of girl. He'd taught her how to lavish attention on herself though.

"Why not be the princess that you are?" he'd asked her once. "Don't you think you deserve it?"

The truth was she didn't think she deserved to be treated like a princess. Not after years of Julian's putdowns and letting him sell her out to the highest bidder every night. Not after a decade before that of being called chunky or "fat ass" or "fat girl." It wasn't easy to erase all that conditioning, to build a sense of self-worth. It was a slow, painful process, but Cyrus had been there to help her part of the way.

Diamond had never met a man as charming or as gallant as he was. In fact, the first time they'd met was because Cy was being a gentleman and defending her.

It was more than a year ago. She'd been the hostess that night at the restaurant where she worked. The Seneca had been a mad house—all the tables were booked, and the waitlist was about two hours long. Even the bar was crowded with patrons waiting to be seated. A guy had come in off the street, insisting that he get a table right away.

"What do you mean you can't squeeze me in?" he'd yelled over the clamor in the restaurant. He was a short, wide man in a polo shirt and khakis with thinning, slicked back hair that showed his liver-spotted scalp. "Do you know who the hell I am?"

"I'm sorry, but I do not, sir," she'd said, pasting on a polite smile despite his shouting and his attitude. "I would be happy though to add your name to the waitlist that we have—"

"I don't want to go on the waitlist! Did I ask to go on the goddamn waitlist? Where the fuck is the manager? I want to speak to the manager! Get him over here! Now!"

"My man," she'd heard a heavy baritone rumble beside her, "is that language really necessary?"

Diamond had turned to her right, surprised to see a tall black man standing there.

He was dark-skinned and handsome with a bald head and a thick beard threaded with a few gray hairs. He'd worn a black pinstriped suit and pale blue shirt. He'd looked sharp and debonair, but not like he was trying too hard. He'd given her a reassuring wink, making her heart flutter and her cheeks warm.

"Are you the manager?" the patron had asked, looking him up and down. "What's your name?"

"My name is Cyrus. Cyrus Grey. And no, I'm not the manager. I'm waiting for a table just like you. We *all* are," he'd said, gesturing to the lobby area where about a dozen people stood along the walls and sat on the padded benches. "It's not this young lady's fault that the restaurant is crowded. Don't take it out on her. Why don't you just—"

"Why don't you just shut up and mind your business, pal?" the patron had said, glowering up at him. "Or I'll—"

"Or you'll what?" Cyrus had challenged, taking a threatening step toward him. His face had hardened. "What are you gonna do? Tell me." He'd beckoned. "I wanna hear it."

The people standing around them who had been watching the exchange, had gone silent. Diamond had seen something in Cyrus's eyes that made her clamp her mouth shut, too. It made her throat go dry. For a few tense seconds, she had been very worried for the balding man in the khakis despite how badly he'd been treating her.

The patron must have been worried too, because his face had gone pale. He'd loudly cleared his throat. "Look, pal, I-I don't w-w-want any trouble."

"Neither do I. So I suggest you add your name to the list, quietly stand somewhere, and wait like the rest of us—*or* you can turn around, head to that door, and leave this establishment right now. In both cases, I'll advise you to leave this young lady alone and let her do her job. Those are your choices as I see it." Cyrus had tilted his head. "Don't you agree?"

Diamond had watched the exchange, absolutely riveted. No one had ever stood up for her like that, definitely not any guy. And Cyrus hadn't shouted, cussed, or used his hands to defend her. He'd done it simply with his words in an even tone in the smoothest, casual sort of way.

What a Zaddy! And he's fine too, she remembered thinking at the time. *Goddamn!*

The restaurant patron had nodded sheepishly before turning back to Diamond. "Uh, my . . . my name is Alexander Mitchell. I'd . . . I'd like a table for four."

"Yes, sir, I'm adding you to the list right now," she'd said, holding back her laughter as she typed his name into the computer screen. "I'll let you know when it's ready."

As it turned out, Alexander left before his table opened

and Cyrus lingered after closing to escort Diamond to her car. Even then, he was a gentleman—he didn't try to grab or kiss her. He didn't stare at her tits or leer at her ass. She didn't know who Cyrus Grey was at the time. She didn't know a damn thing about him, but she was already hooked. When he asked her out after shutting her car door behind her, she felt compelled to say yes.

Diamond thought back to that day while lying in her bathtub.

Cyrus was her knight-in-shining armor and she was his princess, and now she wondered if their fairy tale had come to an end. Would he survive this?

Diamond let her head loll back against the edge of the bathtub and closed her eyes tight, fighting back tears. But they fell anyway, sinking along with her into the hot soapy water. She couldn't lose her husband. She didn't know what her life would be like without him. She began to wipe away her tears with a washcloth, but paused when she heard a series of thumps that sounded like footsteps outside her bathroom door. She quickly sat upright and looked at the crack in the door, showing a sliver of her bedroom.

"Hello?" she called out. Her voice echoed in the high-ceilinged bathroom.

Of course, no one answered, but Diamond squinted when she heard another thump.

What the hell is that noise? she wondered. Was it one of her neighbors? Was it coming through the bathroom wall?

She slowly stood from the tub, feeling her skin light with goosebumps as she went from the hot water of the bath to the cool air of her bathroom. She reached for the towel hanging on a nearby rack and stepped onto a towel on the floor, drying herself as she listened more carefully for sounds in her condo.

Had she locked the front door when she finished scrubbing? She struggled now to remember if she had. She had been so engrossed with getting rid of all the blood that it may have escaped her mind. Could someone have crept into the condo if she'd left the door unlocked?

Maybe it was the tattooed man. Maybe he had come back to take another go at her and finish the job. Richard, the guard at the front desk, had assured her that he wouldn't let any more "thugs" into the building, but maybe he hadn't kept his promise.

She started to shiver a little, and not because she was cold. Diamond wrapped the towel around herself. She wished she had taken her cellphone into the bathroom with her. Maybe then she could call the police and tell them she thought someone had broken into her home. But she knew her cell sat on her coffee table in the living room, connected to its charger.

"Fuck the cellphone," she mumbled. She wished she had a gun. Perhaps she would get one later this week, or even tomorrow.

What's the waiting period to buy a handgun in the state of Maryland, anyway? she mused.

Diamond slowly crept to the bathroom door and eased it open farther, peering into her bedroom through the widened crack. The thumping noise had stopped. The condo was achingly silent, but what she'd heard a minute ago hadn't been her imagination. She knew she'd heard something.

Diamond eased the door open several more inches and stepped into her bedroom. Nothing was out of place. The king-sized bed was still unmade from yesterday when she'd rushed out the door to work. The door to Cyrus's mahogany armoire stood open slightly from the last time he'd been in there more than a week ago, revealing his ties and belts. The shades on the floor-to-ceiling windows were open as well, filling the room with bright light, but the brightness didn't comfort Diamond. The hallway beyond her bedroom was steeped in total darkness. She kicked herself mentally for not turning on more lights around her home, for relying on natural light while she scrubbed. She now tightened the towel around herself even more and crept across the room and around her bed to the opened door. When she drew closer, she took a deep breath, bracing herself for what or who could be waiting for her out there. She leaned her head through the doorway but, once again, saw nothing.

"Hello!" she called. "Is somebody out here? I've got a gun!" she lied, feeling ridiculous even as she said it.

Diamond began to creep down the hallway. When she neared the living room, she heard a thump again, making her come to an abrupt halt.

"Shit," she whispered as her heart began to race.

She felt like one of those fools in horror movies who should have run out the door or locked themselves in a closet, but instead walked right into the murderer's or monster's clutches. But she couldn't hide in her bathroom or bedroom all day; she at least had to get her phone.

She finally put one foot in front of the other and started walking again. She stepped into her living room, expecting to find the tattooed gunman waiting for her, but instead, she found the room just as she'd left it. No one was in here. She nearly ran to the coffee table, grabbing her cellphone just as she heard another thump. She saw a shadow looming on the hardwood in her periphery. Someone was behind her.

Diamond whipped around and screamed when she saw a man staring at her through her living room window.

"Is okay! Is okay!" the window washer shouted.

His voice was muffled by the double-paned glass. The

little Latino man in a gray uniform held up his hand and his squeegee, as if to show her he meant no harm. "I clean! I clean!"

She dropped her hand to her chest and closed her eyes. So that's what she'd been hearing in the bathroom: the window cleaners. Her heartbeat decelerated. She stopped shaking and laughed instead at her paranoia and foolishness. Suddenly, her phone began to chime.

"Hello?" Diamond said after raising the phone to her ear and pressing the green button. She was still laughing. Mentally, she kicked herself for freaking out.

"Hey, College Girl, what's up?" a familiar voice answered, making her eyes flash open.

She gaped. "Ju-*Julian?*"

"Yeah, girl! It's me. I heard you were lookin' for me."

Wednesday

Chapter 13

Noelle

Noelle sat at her desk in the office at the back of Azure, her boutique, with the door closed, staring at her laptop screen. The office was a tight space, but neat and chic like the shop itself and the woman who occupied it. It included a white lacquer desk with gold accents, a matching leather chair, a printer, and a petite file cabinet. Noelle had wanted the space to be calming, to be an ideal setting for getting work done, but that wasn't the case today. Her mind kept drifting. She'd tried to focus on inventory spreadsheets and invoices that needed to be logged into their database, but she kept going back to Google. She'd type in "Diamond Grey" or "Vanessa Grey," only to delete either name or close out the web page entirely. This would be the fifth time she'd done it in the past hour.

The truth was, Noelle couldn't forget about them— Cyrus's other wives—just like she couldn't forget about everything Tariq had told her about Cyrus yesterday. Her husband's dirty business deals and his secrets were now impacting her, possibly putting her freedom and life at risk. Was that also the case for Diamond and Vanessa? Did their proximity to Cyrus mean they ran the risk of getting hurt or even killed as well?

"Why do you even care who they are?" Tariq had asked her yesterday as he drove them back to Greydon Consultants headquarters. During the drive, she had asked him more about the other women and their lives. "Why do you even want to know about them at all? Shit, *especially* Vanessa! Didn't you say she threatened to fight you at the hospital?"

"She rubbed me the wrong way. I rubbed her the wrong way. But looking back on it, we were both shocked, angry, and frankly, hurt, Tariq," she'd conceded as he drove. "Cyrus married all three of us. We're all going through the same fucked up experience right now. We just found out there are big gaps in our husband's life . . . aspects of him that we know nothing about. I just want to close those gaps. Maybe . . . maybe they do, too."

Tariq had turned his attention momentarily away from the road to look at her. "You aren't going to reach out to them, are you?"

"Of course not! I'm not that crazy!"

"Noelle," he'd repeated slowly, "I mean it. I'll tell you more about them only if you promise me you won't talk to them and you damn sure won't tell them all the shit I just told you."

"Yes, Tariq, I promise! You have my word."

But now she was on the verge of breaking that word. Using the basic info Tariq had given her, she typed in "Vanessa Grey, Maryland," and within minutes found the woman's Facebook page.

She knew from Tariq that Vanessa didn't earn an income and hadn't in more than a decade, but she loved spending Cyrus's money on anything and everything. In her photos, that was pretty evident. Vanessa's social media page was filled with pictures of her preening for the camera in tight Versace tops and Dolce and Gabbana dresses, in flashy jewelry and designer shoes, looking like the wannabe diva that Noelle remembered tangoing with in the hospital waiting room. But some of the photos also featured her proudly posing with children. In one photo was a boy with braces who looked to be eleven or twelve in a soccer uniform. In another was a little girl of maybe five blowing out candles on a birthday cake while Vanessa stood beside her. In yet another was a little boy of maybe six or seven, smiling as he sat on a diving board with his feet dangling over a pool.

"She has *kids?*" Noelle whispered, more than just a little surprised.

Noelle's persistent longing to hold an infant in her arms had become a painful journey. She was even considering a round of IVF, though the doctor had told her everything seemed normal on her end and theoretically she should be able to get pregnant. Noelle had assumed the problem was Cyrus, but how could he be if these were all his children? Or maybe he and Vanessa had done some type of medical intervention, like undergoing their own rounds of IVF, or had they adopted?

Noelle's finger itched to press the "friend request" button so that she could reach out and ask Vanessa directly, so that she could finally get some answers or hints as to why she and Cyrus had been struggling so long to get pregnant. Or maybe she could do another search to find Vanessa's phone number so that she could . . .

"No," she whispered.

She had promised Tariq that she wouldn't talk to them. But as she surveyed Vanessa's Facebook page and the pictures of Vanessa's beautiful children laughing and smiling, she had to admit the temptation to talk to Cyrus's other wife was indescribable.

Noelle kept searching, this time for anything related to

Diamond Grey. Tariq had told her that Diamond was the youngest of the wives at twenty-three. She was also a hostess at The Seneca restaurant in Baltimore. Noelle had assumed that because of her age, Diamond would be easy to find on the internet. Twenty-somethings had Twitter accounts and Instagram pages, didn't they? Noelle had thought it was practically a requirement at that age. But Diamond didn't have either, or at least, Noelle couldn't find them. Instead she only found a photo of Diamond on a local news web site. It was an article related to Cyrus's shooting. Noelle hadn't seen it before because it was from a news station in Baltimore.

Noelle hadn't known that the young woman had been there when Cyrus was shot, or that she'd been wounded. Diamond—with her pretty nutmeg-hued face and dimpled apple-cheeks, with her long braids and big doe eyes— could've been killed that day.

Noelle winced. And that could have just as easily been her, if the shooter had decided to come after Cyrus last week instead of this one. Or maybe it could've been Vanessa who was there when he'd gotten shot, or one of her three children. Were their lives still at risk? Should she warn them that their proximity to Cyrus could get them killed like Tariq had warned her?

"Shit," Noelle muttered, gnawing her bottom lip. The promise she had made to Tariq was weighing heavier and heavier on her conscience. How could she keep it?

Noelle turned when she heard a gentle knock on her office door. She found Miranda, her assistant manager, poking her dark head through a crack in the doorway. Music from the main floor suddenly filled the space.

"Hey," Miranda said in almost a whisper, "just . . . uh . . . seeing if you needed anything."

Miranda's dark brows were drawn together. Her thin lips were pursed. She looked worried. She had looked worried since Noelle had arrived at the shop that morning, eager to distract herself with work.

"I'm okay. Really, I am."

"Are you sure?" Miranda asked, opening the door a little more so that she could step inside Noelle's office.

She crossed her freckled arms over her chest. She was almost as tall as Noelle though she'd played basketball in college, not modeled on any runways. She wore a teal cap-sleeved dress today that was belted at the waist—one of the many dresses they sold at the boutique.

"I mean . . . what happened to your husband just happened two days ago, Noelle. If it were me, I couldn't imagine coming back to work this soon. And you've been back here for hours. You seem like you want some time alone." She glanced at Noelle's opened laptop. "You know, it's okay if you want to go home. If you need more time. We've got it all covered here. We'll survive."

"I would go stir crazy with worry if I stayed stuck in that house all day." She lowered the lid of her laptop, closing the screen on Diamond's smiling face. "Besides, I'm done working in here. I was just headed out to the floor. I wanted to see the new swimwear display you guys were setting up."

Miranda still eyed her warily. "Okay. We're ready whenever you are."

A few minutes later, Noelle strolled through Azure. The boutique was decorated in the same color as her office—white with gold accents. Two pendant chandeliers hung from the ceiling along with canned lights. A wall of shelves displaying purses, jewelry, and shoes stood behind the sales counter and along the back wall. The rest of the space was filled with sales racks and glass display tables, all showing stylish, reasonably priced clothing that Noelle would wear herself. Nothing made it onto the racks or show floor without her approval.

After two years, Azure still hadn't made a profit, but the sales had gone up annually. She'd figured by the fourth or fifth year, the business would be in the black, but Noelle wasn't sure if she could do it now without Cy's backing. He was a deceiver and a cheater, but he'd kept her boutique afloat all this time. She couldn't see herself asking him for more money though, not after knowing what she now knew about him.

Noelle fidgeted with her wedding ring as she walked toward the display window where a series of mannequins now sported colorful bikinis and one-piece swimsuits, wraps, and floppy beach hats. Her six-carat diamond seem to weigh heavily on her finger. She wanted to tug it off.

"What do you think, Mrs. Grey?" Janise asked, pointing to one of the mannequins as Noelle approached.

"Janise worked on it all by herself," Miranda said proudly. "I told her she did a great job! She should try pursuing window design if she ever decides not to do that whole doctor thing."

Janise laughed.

Janise was biracial girl with curly hair that fell around her shoulders. The pre-med student went to nearby George Mason University and worked in the boutique three days a week. She depended on the extra money from her sales-clerk job to help pay for her books and unexpected expenses. Noelle now wondered what would happen to Janise . . . what would happen to *all* of them, if Noelle had to close her shop.

How many people would Cyrus affect because of all of his lies? How many lives had he put in jeopardy?

When Noelle didn't immediately respond, Janise's eager smile disappeared. She lowered her hand. "You don't like it, huh? Well, I can take this version down and—"

"No! No!" Noelle insisted. "It's fine. Really. I just . . . I just . . ."

"You just what?" Miranda asked. Her brows were knitted together again.

Noelle looked between them both, at their concerned faces. She couldn't take it anymore.

"Look, I'm sorry that I've been acting strange lately," she began.

Miranda held up her hand. "You aren't acting strange, Noelle. Your behavior is perfectly understandable. Your husband was shot. He's still in the hospital and—"

"It's not just that," Noelle interrupted. "There are other things . . . other stuff that's happened, and I'm . . . I'm facing some questions . . . some dilemmas now, and I'm not really sure what to do."

"What questions, Mrs. Grey?" Janise asked.

Noelle began to tug anxiously at her wedding ring again but forced herself to stop. She loudly exhaled. "Look, I'm gonna ask your opinion. I'm gonna ask the both of you, and I need an honest answer."

They gradually nodded.

"If you knew something . . . if you knew something that could be important, but you made a promise not to share that information, would you keep that promise? Would you not tell anyone?"

"What do you know that you can't tell anyone?" Janise's eyes widened with panic. "Are you about to shut down Azure? Is that what you can't tell us? Are you saying we're *about to be fired?*"

"No! Nothing like that!" Noelle insisted, making the young woman sigh with relief.

"What does important mean though?" Miranda asked. "You're gonna have to be more specific."

"Important as in serious," Noelle explained.

"How serious?" Miranda grimaced. "As in potentially life or death?"

Noelle hesitated then nodded, making Miranda and Janise glance at each other.

"Umm, I can't really say without knowing all the details, but anything that's life threatening, you can't keep to yourself, Noelle," Miranda said. "Morally, it's irresponsible. You at least have to tell the police!"

"You know what they say on the metro, Mrs. Grey: See something, say something," Janise chimed in, sounding every bit of her naïve nineteen years at that moment. "It's dangerous to hide something if lives are at stake."

Noelle gazed at them both. "Thanks, guys. I needed that advice."

It validated what she already suspected.

Noelle wouldn't be calling the cops like Miranda suggested, but she knew who else she had to call, despite Tariq's warning to the contrary. It was the only responsible thing to do. For her own mental health, for the sake of her own conscience, she had to reach out to Vanessa and Diamond. She just hoped they would listen.

Chapter 14

Vanessa

"Oh, yes! Oh, yes! Oh, God, yes!" Vanessa groaned breathlessly. "Keep going, baby!"

She lay naked on her California king with her bed sheets fisted in her hands, her legs akimbo, and Bilal's face firmly nestled between her thighs. He was licking her pleasure spot like it was a Toostie Roll pop, trying his very best to get to the candy in the center. He was making her squirm and moan in the process. Vanessa had almost screamed a few times, but bit one of her decorative pillows instead, forcing herself to keep the noise down.

She didn't want the neighbors to hear, after all.

Since she and Bilal began their affair, she'd never invited Bilal to her house. It seemed too risky. What if someone in the neighborhood grew curious about the unfamiliar car parked out front in her driveway? What if her nosy neighbor across the street spotted Bilal going inside her home?

But now that Cy was in the hospital, still in an induced coma, and Vanessa knew all the things he'd been doing behind her back *for years*, she felt more emboldened to take chances. Besides, she was getting tired of having sex in

Bilal's sad little apartment, his office, and the backseat of his car. She wanted him to make love to her in her own shower, on the kitchen counter, and on her comfortable, spacious bed. And she could do it now. She was alone at home; the children were back at school and her mother had returned to her place in D.C.

Why not invite him over? Vanessa had thought that morning before sending Bilal a sexy text with promises of all the nasty, freaky things she would do to him when he arrived.

He'd shown up a little more than an hour ago, sneaking around the back of the house as she'd instructed and through the deck's French doors that she'd left unlocked. They'd been at it since then, and Vanessa was well on her way to another orgasm when her phone began to ring.

Vanessa stopped groaning. Her eyes fluttered open and she frowned as the ringing continued.

Who the hell was calling her in the middle of the day? She hoped it wasn't the kids' school. Did Bryson get in trouble again?

Vanessa grumbled as she shifted so she could sit up on her elbows. She reached for the cordless on her night table and checked the number on the Caller ID screen. She didn't recognize it.

Must be a sales call, she thought with annoyance before pressing a button to stop the phone from the ringing.

Bilal paused mid tongue-stroke and raised his head. He gazed up at her. "What's up? This ain't workin' for you no more, bae?"

"No, it's wonderful, honey." She reached down and pat his head, like he was her good little puppy. "It was just the damn phone. It was distracting me. Keep going. I was almost there."

He chuckled and lowered his head again. Within minutes, the moaning and groaning resumed. This time, even biting her pillow couldn't contain all her screams. When they were done, Bilal climbed back to the top of the bed, licking his lips.

She grinned. "Ready for another round?" she asked, making his eyes widen.

"Damn, girl, aren't you tired? You trying to give me lock jaw? Shit, I need a break!"

"*A break?* Are you serious? You're more than ten years younger than me!" She laughed, making him laugh too. She nudged his shoulder. "Don't tell me you can't keep up, Mr. Fitness Trainer, or I might have to replace you with another lover. Trade you in for a better model."

His laughter abruptly tapered off. His face went stern. "Oh, you're gonna replace me now?"

She rolled her eyes. "Oh, here we go!"

"*Here we go?*"

"Baby, I was just joking with you!"

"Yeah, well, that shit ain't funny!" He shoved her off him, climbed off the bed, and rose to his feet. He glared down at her.

"Why are you being so goddamn sensitive?" she lamented, sitting up and leaning against the headboard. "It's not that big of a deal!"

"Yes, it is! Yes, it fuckin' is a big deal! I love you, Nessa, and I'm tired of you yanking me around! One minute you want me, the next minute you're yelling at me to stop calling you. A few days later, you call me to tell me to come over, and then you joke about replacing me with some other nigga! I mean . . . what kinda shit is that? *Which is it?* Do you want to be with me or not?"

Vanessa hated when Bilal ruined her sexual afterglow by getting all in his feelings. She wanted to chalk it up to him being twenty-four, but she swore she didn't know a man of any age who was as insecure as he was. Still, the sex was good, and she did like his company—*most* of the time. And she remembered her mother's words encouraging her to keep Bilal around.

"He might be useful later," her mother had warned. Vanessa didn't know how he could be, but in this case, she felt it was best to take her mother's advice.

She had to make it up to Bilal. She had to placate his ego before he went storming out of here.

"Of course I want to be with you, baby," she lied, as she climbed off the bed and stood next to him. She wrapped her arms around him. "I'm sorry I upset you with my bad joke. I didn't mean to."

He didn't respond and instead, continued to glare down at her. He was being stubborn, but she knew how to win him over. Insecure men loved to have their egos stroked as much as their dicks.

That's never changed, she thought.

"You are the handsomest, sexist, best lover I've ever had, baby," she said. "That's what I meant when I said I was joking. I know I could never replace you!"

He stared at her, looking doubtful. "Laying it on a little thick, bae," he murmured dryly.

"No, I'm telling the truth!" She stood on the balls of her feet and gave him a quick peck. "Come on. Let's get in the bubble bath so you can relax, and I can show you just how much I appreciate you. I'll rub your shoulders . . . your back . . . your feet."

"*My feet?*"

"Yep! I'll rub whatever you want," she whispered before giving the corner of his mouth a saucy lick. "Your wish is my command."

His face finally softened. He smirked. "Don't test me. You don't know what I'll ask you to do."

"I'm game to try anything at least once. Start the water," she said, reaching down to give his bare behind a squeeze. "Just let me pin up my hair and I'll meet you in there."

As Bilal strolled into her bathroom, Vanessa walked across her bedroom to her vanity table. She reached for a stack of bobby pins that sat near a picture of her and Cyrus on their wedding day. She examined the photo—him in his tuxedo, her in satin, mermaid gown that she'd had custom made. She then slammed down the sterling silver picture frame on her vanity tabletop, almost shattering the glass.

"You son of a bitch," she muttered.

"Hey! Where's your bubble bath?" Bilal called over the sound of running water.

"On the bathroom counter next to my makeup!" she called back while twisting her long hair into a bun at her crown and securing it with two bobby pins.

"Huh?" he called back. "I can't hear you!"

"On the . . . never mind," she mumbled, deciding it was best to just find it for him. She swore she had to do everything around here.

Vanessa strolled toward the bathroom, but paused when she saw a flashing light on her cordless phone, signifying that someone has left a message. She wondered if it was the call from earlier. She reached for the phone and pressed the code to check the message, planning to quickly erase it if it was the sales call she suspected.

"*H-hello? This is uh . . . this is Noelle Grey. I found your number online. We . . . we met at Johns Hopkins Monday in the hospital waiting room,*" Noelle said, making Vanessa's heart rate kick into overdrive. Her grip around the phone tightened as she listened.

How the hell had this chick gotten her number? What on earth gave her the damn nerve to think it was appropriate to call here?

"*Well, 'met' isn't the right word,*" Noelle continued. "*You wanted to kick my ass. I wanted to kick yours, and it's all understandable, considering the circumstances but . . . God, I'm rambling, aren't I? I have to stop rambling. You see I'm nervous because there's no easy way to say this so I'll just . . . just come out and say it. I'm reaching out to you because I think we should talk. I think we all should talk about Cyrus. I mean, about what happened. I don't know if you know this but . . . he has another wife, a third. Her name is Diamond. He married her earlier this year, and I think she should be in on this, too. She was with him the day that it all happened . . . the day he was shot.*"

There was a pause on the other end after that, giving Vanessa only a few seconds to grapple with what she'd just heard. Cyrus had yet another wife? Could that be true?

You son of a bitch, Vanessa thought, furious all over again. *You son of a bitch!*

"*Look, we don't have to hate each other,*" Noelle said on the voice mail. "*We didn't do this—Cyrus did! I know things about Cy that you should know, and you probably know stuff as well that Diamond and I would want to know about him. We can help each other, Vanessa. And there's some stuff that's important that I don't want to just blurt out on the phone. I'd rather do it in person. If you're willing to meet up, please call me back. My number is 703-555-2837. Hope to hear from you.*"

Vanessa listened to the end of the message until it beeped, startling her. She stared at her phone, thunderstruck.

"You okay?" Bilal asked, glancing over his shoulder at her in the sunken tub. He sat between Vanessa's legs as she massaged his shoulders and back.

"Yeah. Why?" she asked.

"Because you're rubbing me so hard, it's starting to hurt, bae," he said with a wince.

"Oh, damnit!" She dropped her hands into the soap suds. "Sorry!"

Vanessa probably was doing such a horrible massage because her mind wasn't focused on kneading Bilal's muscles. She'd been distracted since she'd listened to Noelle's voice message. She'd replayed it twice and saved it, trying to grasp everything the woman had said. Vanessa still was struggling to grapple with the two new bombshells—that Cyrus had three wives, not two, and that Noelle had important information about Cyrus that she wanted to share with them both.

Just when Vanessa thought she was finally orienting herself to her new existence after discovering her husband was also married to another woman, she was now finding out there were even more secrets she didn't know about him. Where did it end? What else had he hidden from her?

Bilal turned around completely now, frowning. "You sure you're okay, bae? Why the hell are you looking like that? Like you saw a ghost or somethin'."

"It's that damn phone call from earlier."

"Yeah?" he said nodding, encouraging her to continue. "What about it?"

She hesitated. "It was from Cy's other wife."

"For real?" Bilal raised his brows and shifted to the other end of the bathtub. "Why did she call you?"

"She asked me if I wanted to talk . . . if I wanted to meet up. She said she has stuff she has to tell me. Stuff that's important. She's inviting Cy's other wife, too. Some woman named Diamond. Even her name sounds ridiculous!"

"Wait . . . back up! Cy was married to a *third* broad too? Why am I just hearing about this?"

"Because I just heard about it!" she shouted, slapping the water. "That's what she said in the damn message. Diamond was there when he got shot. I didn't know he was juggling three wives. I don't know how he even managed to juggle two without us knowing!"

Bilal slumped back in the tub, looking as dazed as she felt. "Damn. That dude got around! So what are you gonna do? Are you gonna meet them?"

Vanessa scrunched up her face. "Absolutely not!"

"Why not though? I thought you said she had important stuff to tell you."

"Because I don't want to sit down and kiki with the two other bitches my husband was fucking! I don't have anything to say to them and I damn sure don't wanna hear the garbage they would tell me! They probably want to gloat . . . to rub it in my face that Cyrus married them too, and I'm not his only wife. They probably want to know what assets he has. What money they could sue his estate for if he dies. Oh, no! They don't fool me!"

"Bae, you don't know that. They might really have some serious shit to share with you. You still don't know who shot him. If his third wife was there, maybe she could give you some info. Who knows what other shady shit that dude was doin'?"

She shook her head. "No! No, I don't want to talk to them and I'm not going to. It's crazy!"

Bilal narrowed his eyes at her. "You know what I think? I think you don't wanna talk to them cuz you're scared of what else they might tell you . . . what else you'll find out about him."

"Why would I be scared? What else could they tell me at this point that would devastate me any more than I've been devastated already?"

"Admit it, Nessa. You still got that nigga up on a pedestal, don't you? Just because he bought you all this stuff . . . this big ol' house!" He gestured to the bathroom around them, at the marble tile and expensive finishes. "But the truth is, he ain't shit. Just a liar with a lot of fuckin' money!"

Vanessa closed her eyes, shutting out the truth in Bilal's words, but she opened them when Bilal brought his lips to her in a sensuous kiss.

"I think you should talk to them," he urged. "Find out the truth about him—*finally*. Then maybe you'll leave his tired ass and finally be with me. Come on, bae. Just call her back!"

He really wasn't going to let this go, was he? She swore sometimes he was more persistent than her five-year-old. "I'll think about it," she said, hoping that concession would make him drop the topic.

"You promise, bae?" he asked, kissing her again, making her smile.

"Yeah, I'll think about it."

"Okay. Now enough talkin' about that nigga. Get your ass over here, girl," he said, yanking her across the tub as she giggled and water sloshed onto the bathroom floor.

Chapter 15

Diamond

Diamond pulled up to the curb only a few feet away from where Julian stood on concrete stairs leaning against the side of a brick building. He was smoking a cigarette and talking to a guy she didn't recognize. He'd told her to meet him here at The Men's Village, the halfway house where he was staying, but Diamond had been hesitant to make the drive all the way to southeast D.C., especially if it meant she could be walking into an ambush.

"You . . . you want me to come down there?" she'd asked him over the phone yesterday as she stood shivering in her living room with a towel wrapped around her.

"Yeah, they gave me a pass that lets me out for about an hour a day. I ain't got no car yet, and I need to pick up a few things from the store. You can pick me up about two o'clock. I'll be waitin' by the curb."

"But I have to go to work, Julian. I have a job here in Baltimore. I have a life! I can't just drive down to D.C. to—"

"Why the fuck not?" he'd shouted, making her wince.

"I don't give a fuck about your job! I told you to come down here, so your ass better come down here like I said!"

"But I—"

"But you what? What's with all the arguin'? Since when did you start buckin' to me anyway? Has it been that long, baby? You forget who Daddy is? Do I have to come up there and remind you?"

Diamond had instantly gone quiet at that threat, and she'd hated herself for it.

She should have told him that he wasn't her damn daddy—he never had been. She should have told him that he couldn't give her orders because he wasn't her pimp anymore. But old habits die hard. Whenever Julian got loud in the old days, she would clamp her mouth shut, keeping it sealed like a Ziploc bag for fear of getting a smack to the face or some other form of punishment or humiliation. He had trained her well.

"Yeah, I thought so," he'd muttered over the phone, chuckling at her silence. "Be here at two o'clock tomorrow, and don't make my ass wait. You know how I hate that shit."

He'd then hung up on her.

The voice inside her head—the one of caution—told her not to come here, despite his threat. Diamond knew it was foolish. If Julian really had tried to kill her the day Cyrus was shot, why make it easier for him to make a second attempt on her life? Why deliver herself to him like an expedited package? But she had to know the truth. She had to know why her husband was lying in the hospital bed, and if Julian had anything to do with it. She had silently promised Cyrus that day in the hospital that she would find out for sure.

And if Julian did it, I'll make him pay, she thought now

as she watched him laugh and talk to his companion in front of the halfway house.

She didn't know how she would, but she'd make sure he didn't go unpunished.

She tapped the horn and Julian turned to look at her car. When he saw her, his eyes widened. He pushed himself away from the wall and strolled toward her unhurried, irritating her. She was already in a bad mood. She'd gone to the hospital that morning, hoping to see Cyrus again, only to be told that she couldn't go back into his hospital room.

"Why not? I'm his wife!" she'd argued with the same nurse who had grudgingly let her in the last time. "I want to speak to the doctor! No, I want to speak to the hospital administrator. Now!"

"You can if you like, but from what I understand, it wasn't their decision, ma'am. Only hospital personnel are allowed into Mr. Grey's hospital room. The police requested it," the nurse explained.

Diamond had stilled at that. All her arguments had evaporated. Maybe the cops were doing it for Cyrus's own protection since they still weren't sure who had shot him. She couldn't fault them for that. She suspected she knew who was behind it though, and he was currently standing next to her car.

She let her eyes rove over Julian.

He'd lost weight since she'd last seen him. He also looked a lot shabbier. Gone were his signature expensive leather jackets, silk shirts, and gold chains he'd purchased with the proceeds of his girls' hard work. He now just wore a plain white T-shirt and worn, saggy, skinny jeans he kept tugging back up his bony hips. He also sported a patchy beard and dreads that desperately needed some loc butter and a re-twisting.

Diamond watched as Julian tugged open her car door and hopped inside.

"Where am I taking you?" she asked as he slammed the car door shut.

"Damn? I can't get a hello?" he joked.

When she continued to glare at him, he sucked his teeth. "Marlow Heights," he said as he looked around the Aston Martin's interior. "I gotta pick somethin' up from the jewelry store."

She shifted gears, signaled and pulled off.

"This shit is nice!" He looked around him again appreciatively and ran his hand over the dashboard. "You movin' up in the world, College Girl! Is this your ride, or you borrowing it from the dude you live with now?"

"He's not 'the dude I live with'. He's my husband, Julian."

"Yeah, I heard you was married." Julian chuckled as he leaned back in the passenger seat. "So, you finally got a nigga to put a ring on it, huh?" He looked her up and down. His gaze lingered on the shadow of cleavage peaking over her V-neck blouse. "Well, married life suits you, baby. You lookin' good as fuck!" He reached out and trailed a finger along her chin and neck, but stopped when she shrank away him. "*What?* I can't touch you anymore?"

"I told you I was married!"

"I don't give a fuck what you are! You still mine, girl."

"Is that why you had someone shoot him?" she asked, keeping her eyes on the road. She didn't think she'd work up the courage to ask Julian the question if she had to look him in the eyes. "Is that why you tried to kill my husband a couple days ago? Because you think I'm still yours?"

"I don't think—I know!"

"So you *did* do it then? You tried to kill him?"

He didn't answer her; he started to laugh again, instead.

"Julian, stop playin'! *Please!*" she said desperately.

"Just tell me the truth. Do you know who shot my husband?"

This time she did look at Julian, disheartened to see that his smile had widened into a full grin. He looked like a cat who had just swallowed a mouse.

"Keep drivin', baby," he said, gesturing to the windshield. "I only got fifty minutes to make it there and back or they gonna throw my ass in jail again."

When they arrived at the jeweler, he continued to pretend like their conversation in the car hadn't happened. For almost half an hour, he perused the glass cases, trying on gold chains, diamond pinky rings, and expensive watches. He shopped with an unconcerned air, infuriating her even more.

"Yeah, that looks nice," Julian whispered, gazing at himself in one of the jewelry counter's mirrors, admiring his reflection. He'd finally settled on a chunky gold rope chain that cost a little under five thousand dollars. It was flashy and garish; it fit him perfectly.

"And how will you be paying for this, sir?" the jeweler asked, returning the chain to its velvet-padded display. "Cash or credit?"

"I don't know." Julian glanced at Diamond. "You gotta ask her."

Diamond choked out a laugh. "*Are you serious?* I'm not paying for that!"

"What I tell you about buckin' to me," he said in a low menacing voice, making her quake a little on the inside. But she reminded herself that she wasn't his girl anymore, despite his insistence that she was. She was married to Cyrus. She had his love and was under *his* protection, not Julian's.

"I'm not buying you that chain," she repeated, saying it more firmly than before.

He raised his brows, almost in amusement. "Oh, yeah,

you will, College Girl. If you want me to answer that question you asked me in the car, you'll buy it. Or I'm not tellin' you a goddamn thing!"

They stared at one another for a full minute, engaged in a silent standoff. Finally, she broke his gaze and reached into her purse. She opened her wallet and tugged out her American Express, gritting her teeth so hard as she thought one of her fillings might chip. She slapped the card on the counter.

"I'll be right back," the jeweler mumbled, taking her credit card.

Less than ten minutes later, they walked back to her car. Julian whistled as he walked, twirling the small, gilded shopping bag that now contained his new gold chain. He tugged the handle to the passenger side of her sports car and frowned when the door didn't open. He turned to her.

"You gonna unlock this shit or what?"

"No," she answered, shaking her head. "Not until you finally tell me the truth. I did what you asked. You got your damn chain. If you know who shot Cyrus, just *tell* me. I need to know!"

He strolled around the car and got up in her face, bearing down on her. "You know I really ain't likin' this new attitude of yours, College Girl. It's gettin' on my nerves. You keep talkin' your shit and I'm gonna—"

"*What?* Slap me? Punch me? *Shoot me?*" she challenged, glowering right back up at him. "I don't care! I am not opening that door and I am not taking you back to that halfway house until you answer my question. You left at two o'clock. You only have fifteen minutes to get back there or your ass is going to jail! You really wanna chance it?"

His nostrils flared. He looked furious, but she didn't care. She knew she had him. He was squirming in her grasp and she wasn't letting go.

"Answer my question, Julian. Answer, or your ass is going back in lock up!"

"No, I didn't shoot your husband, bitch!" he yelled back, sending spittle flying into her face. "Shit! And I don't know who the fuck did! You happy now?"

"You mean it? Don't lie to me just to—"

"For the second time, no, I didn't shoot him! I don't even know who the fuck your husband is!"

She closed her eyes. She finally had her answer—and it filled her with relief. Her past hadn't come back to haunt her. It hadn't come back to rob her of her present and future. Julian had nothing to do with what had happened to Cyrus, therefore *she* had nothing to do with what had happened to him. She was worried about her husband, but she hadn't realized she'd been carrying guilt all this time as well.

Diamond opened her eyes again and pressed the button to unlock the car door. "Get in."

He angrily strode back to the passenger side and tugged the door open. "Dumb bitch," he mumbled. "I'm tired of your ass!"

Yeah, well, I hope I never see you again either, she thought as she walked to the driver's side.

They drove back to The Men's Village in silence. When she pulled up to the curb, instead of hopping out, Julian turned to her.

"So when we doing this again?" he asked.

She stared at him in amazement. "You're joking, right?"

Had he forgotten what had happened in the last half hour?

"Nah, I got a few more other things I need to get. I need you come back by here tomorrow. You can do it around the same time."

"Julian, I'm not coming back tomorrow. I'm not taking you on another damn shopping spree! You answered my question. We're done!" she said, slicing her hand through the air.

He began to smile again and, instead of making her feel better, the sight of his yellow teeth made her blood run cold. "No, we ain't done, baby. Because I didn't try to kill your man this time around, but I might take a shot at him if you don't keep me happy. You know I'll do it. I've done it before."

Yes, he had done it before; she'd seen it with her own eyes four years ago.

Julian had owed his long-time dealer money—a lot of it—and his dealer had come to their apartment one day to collect after Julian had been evading him for weeks. Diamond had been the one to answer the door when the hulking man came bursting inside their place, shoving her out of the way, ready to kick ass and take names if he didn't finally get his money.

Julian started to argue with him. The guy wouldn't back down. The two men started to tussle in the living room and the entire apartment fell into pandemonium—screams and shouts, punches being thrown. Several of the girls leapt forward to defend Julian while Diamond hung back, not wanting to jump into the fray. She remembered watching in alarm as Julian reached for the handgun he'd left sitting on the end table. She remembered him raising the weapon and firing it into the man's chest and head.

At that moment, time seemed to slow down to a snail's pace. Diamond could remember the dealer crumbling to the floor. She could recall the girls all standing around with dual expressions of shock and horror on their faces.

"Don't just stand around lookin' stupid!" Julian yelled at them all. "Clean this shit up! Move!"

That's when time seemed to speed up again. The girls frantically raced around the living room. One grabbed the gun, wrapped it in a washcloth, and took it away for disposal. The others like Honey, grabbed the dealer's body and wrapped him in several blankets like a mummy being prepared for his sarcophagus. They would remove him from the apartment and dump the body somewhere. Diamond was given the task of scrubbing up the remaining blood stains and brain tissue with Pine-Sol and later, bleach when the traditional cleaner didn't work. She tried her best not to vomit as she did it, but didn't succeed. She had to clean that up, too.

The girls had thought they'd taken care of Julian's mess, that they had protected their man. But the cops found the dealer's body a few days later in a dumpster about a mile away from the apartment building. The police were able to trace it back to Julian through eyewitnesses and text messages that said the last place the drug dealer was seen alive was at Julian's apartment. All the girls had lied for him, insisting they had no idea what had happened. The cops and district attorney had known the girls were all full of it, but the prosecutor hadn't been able to prove it. The most the state could get was an involuntary manslaughter charge against Julian. The judge had sentenced him to a measly eight years for murdering a man in cold blood, and Julian hadn't even served the full eight.

"The only reason why you got away with it the last time is because we helped you. *I* helped you," she clarified, "but I'm not doing that shit again."

"*And?* I don't need a ho like you who ain't loyal, but Honey is . . . and so are all my other girls. They'd do anything to help their man if I asked them to. They'd take a bullet for me. Maybe even shoot one if I asked them."

"You always make them do your dirty work, don't you?"

He laughed. "What the fuck else are they there for?" He then shoved open the passenger side door and hopped onto the sidewalk. "See you tomorrow," he said before slamming the door shut.

Chapter 16

Diamond

"You're late," Alejandra hissed as Diamond strode to the reservation desk, excusing her way past waiting patrons.

Diamond shoved her purse underneath the lacquer counter and adjusted the front of her blouse. She took her position next to Alejandra, the other hostess at The Seneca restaurant. "I had to do something, and it took longer than I expected," Diamond explained.

The pretty Latina tossed her dark hair over her shoulder. "Yeah, well, David was asking where you were. When I told him I didn't know, he walked away and didn't look too happy about it." She then glanced down at the screen in front of her. "Wilson, party of four!" she called out. "Your table is ready."

Diamond had just arrived back from D.C. after dropping off Julian, and she still was a little shaken by the whole ordeal. She'd found out that he hadn't shot her husband, but that didn't mean he wouldn't try to do it if she didn't bribe him with more gifts—maybe another chain or a gold watch or an expensive leather jacket. She could go to the cops and tell them what Julian had said and how he had threatened her, but she didn't want the cops to know she was talking to Julian again, let alone that she went to visit him. She could only imagine what conclusions they would jump to.

"Diamond," David, the restaurant's floor manager, said a few minutes later as he strode toward the reservation desk. He was tall and wiry and walked around the restaurant, in Diamond's opinion, like he had a broom shoved up his ass. "I need to speak with you *now*!"

He didn't wait for her to respond. Instead, he turned around and headed to the back office, expecting for her to follow him.

She exchanged a look with Alejandra. "I'll be right back."

A minute later, Diamond stepped into David's office. It was one of the least glamorous spots in the restaurant, a short second to the broom closet. Unlike the hardwood floors, leather upholstery, and crystal chandeliers at the front of the house, David's office had linoleum tiled floors, particle board furniture, and a water-stained paneled ceiling. The only adornment in the entire room was his wall calendar and a picture of his dopey cocker spaniel he kept on his desk.

"Where the hell were you?" David asked as soon as she stepped into his office.

"Uh, I went to go see my husband at the hospital," Diamond began, "and I—"

"You were supposed to be here an hour ago, before we even open," he interrupted. "And you didn't come in at all yesterday even though I had you on the lunch and evening shift. *And* you left early Monday. This isn't acceptable, Diamond!"

She forced herself not to grumble, though she was getting annoyed. "My husband was shot, David! I'm sorry if I had to—"

"And now this woman is calling here, asking if she can speak to you," David continued, ignoring her. "I told you about getting personal calls on our reservation line. It's for diners only."

Diamond frowned. "What woman?"

"I don't know, but she's called here twice asking for you. She keeps saying that its important, which is the *only* reason why I'm letting you talk to her at all." He pointed down at his desk phone that was flashing red. "Five minutes. That's it. Then I want you back out there. And no more personal calls to the main line. Do you understand me?"

"Y-yes."

She watched as David strode out of his office with his imaginary broom still firmly in place. She then looked down at the phone again. Was it Honey or one of the other girls calling her? She doubted it, since none of them knew she worked at The Seneca and they could just call her on her cell. So who the hell could it be?

Diamond raised the phone receiver to her ear and pressed the red button for line two.

"H-hello?" she answered hesitantly.

"Hello?" a woman replied. Her voice was warm and deep, almost smoky, but it didn't sound familiar. "Hi, is this Diamond? Diamond Grey?"

"Yes," Diamond said, her frown deepening. "Who is this?"

"Umm, well . . . my name is Noelle Grey. I'm . . . I'm Cyrus's wife. Well, his *other* wife. I don't know if you . . . if you've heard about me."

Diamond's heart skidded to a halt and then started up again.

The cops had said Cyrus was married to another woman,

but she had pushed the thought to the back of her mind because she hadn't believed the detectives. She didn't want to believe it was true. But it was hard to deny the truth now that the woman was speaking to her on the phone.

"How did you . . . why? I mean, I don't . . ." she sputtered helplessly.

"Look, I know this is a shock. It was for me, too," Noelle rushed out. "Believe me! I found out about you through a . . . a friend. He told me you worked at The Seneca so I decided to call there to see if I could reach you. I'm sorry for just dropping this bomb on you, but I wanted to talk to you. I felt like we needed to talk."

"About what? What do you gotta say to me?" she asked, her voice tightening and going up an octave. Her shock had now switched to anger.

So she was going to have to fight for her position all over again.

So be it, she thought. She wasn't giving up Cyrus to some other woman. She didn't care if that other woman also happened to be his wife. He was her man, her protector, and her provider. She wasn't going to hand him over easily.

"Look, I didn't call to pick a fight, if that's what you're wondering," Noelle replied. "That's the last thing I wanted to do. Trust me! I heard that you were with Cy when it happened . . . when he was shot. Are you hurt?" Noelle asked. "Are you okay?"

Diamond blinked in surprise. Her anger abruptly disappeared. She hadn't expected the woman to show concern for her, let alone ask after her.

"Yes, I'm . . . I'm okay." She anxiously began rub her forearm. "I just have a bandage on my arm and a few bruises on my legs, but besides that I'm fine. Nothing compared to what Cy went through."

"Well, I'm happy to hear that. I'm happy to hear it wasn't

more serious, but I worry that it could have been, Diamond. I worry that something could still happen to any one of us because of what our husband has done . . . because of who he associates with."

"*What?*" Diamond frowned. "What has he done? What do you mean?" She stopped rubbing her arm. "Wait. Do *you* know who shot Cy?"

"No, not for sure. But I figure if we all put our heads together and share information, we might be able to figure this out. We might be able to help each other. I don't know about you, but I don't want anyone else getting hurt, if I can avoid it. I wanted all of us to meet in person, if that's possible. I'd like to do it soon."

"What do you mean 'all of us'? Who else would be there?"

"Brace yourself for another shock. Cyrus has a third wife named Vanessa. She married him over a decade ago."

Diamond's mouth fell open. "*What?*"

"Yeah, I know. Cy definitely got around. I have no idea how he juggled it all. Since I found all this out, I stop and think about the sheer logistics of it all. How did he keep us from running into each other? How did he keep all his stories straight? How did he even remember which wedding ring to wear? But that's Cy. He's too charming and convincing for you to ever question him."

Diamond didn't know how she felt about another woman talking about her husband with such familiarity. Even worse, Noelle's description of Cyrus was totally accurate. He did exude a charm that made him seem beyond reproach, so she had never questioned him like Noelle said. But then again, she never thought it was possible that he would lie to her on such a grand scale.

"So, will you do it?" Noelle asked. "If I can set something up with Vanessa, will you come?"

Diamond hesitated.

This was a lot to take in and she wasn't sure if she was ready mentally or emotionally to sit in the same room with these two women, but she was interested in finding out who had shot her husband. She wouldn't forget that vow. If Noelle and this third wife, Vanessa, could offer some hints or give her an outright answer, she couldn't pass this up.

"Y-y-yeah," she heard herself say. "Yes, I'll do it."

"Good," Noelle said, sounding relieved. "If Vanessa says yes, I'll follow up with you to schedule a time and place that works for all of us. Is this the best place to reach you?"

Diamond gave Noelle her cell phone number to call instead, then hung up. She stood in the aching silence of the office for several minutes, wondering if what had just happened had *really* happened, or if she had hallucinated the whole thing.

She'd just gotten a phone call from Cy's other wife, and she was probably going to meet her later this week.

"This is crazy," she murmured before turning and walking out of David's office. "This is completely nuts."

Chapter 17

Vanessa

Vanessa stretched and stood from her bed, tightening her robe belt around her waist as she watched Bilal tug his T-shirt over his head and shove his arms into the sleeves.

This was his second attempt to put back on his clothes. He'd only managed to get his shirt and boxer briefs on before she dragged him back to bed an hour ago so they could make love again. Vanessa honestly wouldn't mind one more round, but she had to pick up the kids from school and he had to head back to the gym. He had a training session with a client a half hour from now.

"Thanks for coming over," she purred as he raised his jeans zipper and turned to her. She draped her arms around his neck, gave him a lip-smacking kiss, and grinned. "It was just what I needed."

Sex with Bilal was better than any juice cleanse, mud bath, or bikram yoga session combined. She always felt relaxed and refreshed after a few rounds with him.

He chuckled. "I bet it was. Maybe I could stop by tomorrow, too. I don't have any sessions all afternoon. We'd have plenty of time together."

She loosened her arms from around him. "I don't know, baby. It might not be a good idea to hook up again so soon." She glanced at the drawn curtains on her bedroom window. "What if someone sees you come in and wonders why you were here two days in a row?"

He cocked an eyebrow. "No one saw me today. No one will see me tomorrow! Just leave the deck door open again. Don't make it complicated."

Vanessa was still hesitant. Two days straight of mindblowing sex was tempting, but doing it at the house might be too risky. But honestly, she wasn't relishing the idea of going back to having sex in the backseat of Bilal's hatchback or worse, getting down and dirty in his sad little bedroom on a bare mattress.

"Fine! Text me when you're on your way. I'll make sure I'm ready for you."

"No need for anything fancy. You just being butt-ass naked is good enough for me," he said before reaching down, squeezing her behind, and giving her one last heated kiss.

"Do you remember the way out?" she asked a minute later as he headed to her bedroom door.

"Yeah, I'm good," he said with a wave before disappearing into the hall.

She grinned again, remembering all the carnal pleasures that they'd enjoyed today and what awaited her tomorrow. She shivered all over and moaned before walking into the bathroom to take a shower and then dress before she headed to the school campus to pick up her children.

Vanessa hummed along with the music as she drove to Winston Preparatory Academy, zipping through traffic as she went. She felt lighter. All memories of her cheating bastard of a husband, who was still in a coma, the discovery of his third wife, and the phone call from his other wife Noelle earlier that day and the woman's odd request to meet in person floated on the periphery of Vanessa's mind. *Nothing* was going to destroy her natural high. She refused to let it. She stopped humming, turned up the volume of the music on the radio so that the speakers nearly vibrated, and began to sing along with the Mary J. Blige tune, snapping her fingers to the up-tempo beat.

The academy's campus soon came into view: the rolling Kelly green lawn that resembled a golf course, and the stately brick buildings with white ionic columns that housed the classrooms, gym, and auditorium. Vanessa fell in line with the rest of the luxury cars that slithered in snake formation along the curb to the school's entrance. Most of the drivers were mothers like herself or, in some cases, nannies or housekeepers who were there to pick up their charges.

Vanessa watched as a crossing guard—a pimply faced kid of no more than twelve, wearing the academy's burgundy and gray uniform and a neon orange belt—stood several feet away. Beside him was the Academy's smiling principal. The older woman seemed to wear sweaters no matter what the season and her gray hair was always in a severe bun, today being no exception.

The crossing guard waved forward cars with a military-like precision, making them come to a halt a foot in front of him before children raced to car doors and hopped inside. Vanessa finally pulled up to where the crossing guard stood and spotted her sons and daughter. Bryson and Zoe were shoving each other, per usual, while Cy Jr. was staring down at his cell phone.

"Guys!" Vanessa shouted over the music after lowering the passenger side window. "Come on! Let's go!"

"Ah, Mrs. Grey!" the principal said, stepping toward one of the car windows as the kids raced to the rear door. "How are you?"

"Uh, fine," Vanessa answered distractedly as she frowned

over her shoulder, watching the children as they climbed onto the SUV's leather seats and slammed the door shut. "Zoe, stop hitting your brother! Junior, did you remember to pack all the books you need for homework? I want you to finish it all this time. No excuses!"

"I was so sorry to hear about Mr. Grey," the older white woman continued.

"Huh?" Vanessa said, finally turning to look at her.

"I said I was sorry to hear about Mr. Grey . . . your husband!" the principal shouted over Vanessa's music. "The children told their teachers that he's been at the hospital for several days!"

Vanessa finally lowered the volume on her stereo, remembering that she was supposed to be playing the concerned, distraught wife and mother. She fixed her face, trying to look solemn. "Yes. Yes, that is correct. My husband is still in an induced coma, unfortunately. But we're praying he'll wake up soon."

"Oh, dear!" The older woman pursed her wrinkled lips. Her gray brows knitted together. "He didn't fall ill from something contagious, did he?" She glanced at the Grey children who were still arguing in the back seat. A worried expression was on her face. "Not meningitis, I hope."

"No, he had a car accident," Cy Jr. said just as Vanessa answered, "No, he was shot."

When she said that, the principal, Cy Jr., Bryson, and Zoe did a double take. Vanessa inwardly kicked herself. She forgot the lie she and her mother had told the kids.

Damnit, she thought. *I messed that up.*

"Daddy was *shot?*" Bryson whispered in awe. "But you said he had a car accident, Mommy!"

Vanessa rolled her eyes. "I know what I said!"

"Aww, Mommy lied!" Zoe exclaimed. "Bad Mommy! Bad Mommy!"

"Why didn't you tell us Dad was shot?" Cy Jr. asked.

The principal looked anxiously at Vanessa and the kids. She eased back from the car like it was a bomb that could go off at any moment. "Well, I'll . . . I'll let you be on your way. It . . . it looks like I'm holding up the line. See you tomorrow, children!" She waved and fled.

Vanessa pulled off. She couldn't believe she had let it slip that Cyrus had been shot, but she couldn't very well take it back. The truth was out now.

"I didn't tell you guys that Daddy was shot," she began during their drive home, "because I didn't want to upset or scare you. You don't have to worry. Daddy is at the hospital asleep right now. He's giving his body a chance to heal. He should be okay."

"*Should* be okay? What do you mean, 'should'? You don't know if he's gonna be okay, Mom?" Cy Jr. asked.

"Well, we'll have to wait and see, honey," Vanessa tried to sound reassuring and keep the irritation out of her voice.

And the truth was that she was starting to wonder if maybe she would be better off if her husband did die. The house was in her name. Being his first and only legal wife (unless *another* one came out of the woodwork), she'd argue that she and her children rightfully should inherit Cy's estate upon his death. If Cyrus didn't make it out of this alive, Vanessa would become a very rich widow and the kids would be taken care of for life.

You're already making plans for when he dies? a voice in her head questioned.

Maybe she was. She was finally coming to terms with everything that had happened. The rage and sadness were giving way slowly to acceptance, and she could look at things more clearly now.

Cy had lied and cheated on her. He'd humiliated her, but a divorce from him could get messy. Maybe he'd challenge it. Or the case could get tied up in court for years. Vanessa hated to admit it, but it would be much better and easier if Cy just . . . died.

"Will *we* be okay?" Bryson asked, snapping her out of her thoughts. "No one is going to shoot at us, are they?"

"Of course not, honey!"

"You don't know that," Cy Jr. mumbled.

"I don't know what, baby?"

"You don't know that we're not gonna get shot, too!" He gnawed his bottom lip. "I almost did."

Vanessa looked in her rearview mirror and stared at her eldest son's reflection. "*What?* Why on earth would you say that? When did that happen?"

"This weekend. When Bryson and me were with Dad. This guy walked up, and I thought he had a gun, Mom, but . . . but then I thought I was wrong. I thought I was wrong! But maybe he really did have one!"

"You saw a gun?" Bryson asked in a hushed whisper. His dark eyes went as wide as saucers. "Why didn't I see it too?"

"No, your brother did not see a gun!" Vanessa insisted.

"Yes, I did, Mom!" Cy Jr. yelled back. "Now I know I saw it when he—"

"Stop! Enough! We're not going to talk about this right now, Junior! Do you understand me?"

The car went silent again. The radio DJ's banter was the only voice in the car as she pulled into their neighborhood.

Vanessa could see the fury on Cy Jr.'s face—along with the fear and anxiety. She didn't doubt that her son had seen what he'd claimed he'd seen, but she didn't want to talk about it in front of her younger kids. They were all freaked out enough as it was. She had to talk to Cy Jr. privately about this.

Vanessa pulled into their garage a few minutes later and

came to a stop. The back doors to the SUV flew open and Bryson and Zoe went rushing out, thundering up the wooden stairs to the door leading inside the house. Cy Jr. climbed out too—though much slower than his siblings—with his head bowed. He slammed the door closed behind him and stomped toward the house just as Bryson and Zoe ran inside, squealing as they did it.

"Junior!" Vanessa shouted after him, hopping out of the driver's seat. "Junior!" she said as she raced after him. "Wait!"

He paused and turned to look at his mother.

"When did you see the man with a gun, baby? Where?"

Cy Jr. seemed to hesitate. "B-but I thought you didn't believe me."

"I believe you," she whispered. She drew close to him and placed her hands on his shoulders. "Now tell me when you saw the man with the gun. Tell me everything."

Cy Jr. gnawed his lower lip again. She worried with his braces, he was going to make his lip bleed. "It happened on Saturday while Dad, Bryson, and I were at the shoe store."

Because she was taking Zoe to ballet practice, Cyrus had agreed to take the boys to get sneakers. Cy Jr. had been growing like a weed lately. He'd gone up two whole shoe sizes since winter. She also thought the shopping excursion would offer the chance for Cyrus to bond with the boys since he'd been away on so many "business trips" lately.

"I was trying on a couple of Air Jordans and Dad got a phone call," Cy Jr. began. "He said he had to step outside and take it. Bryson was still trying on a pair too, and I really liked my shoes and I wanted to show them to Dad, you know?"

She nodded, silently encouraging him to continue.

"I wanted him to see how they looked, so I walked

across the store and knocked on the window to get Dad's attention, but he didn't hear me. He kept talking on the phone. And then I saw this guy walk up. He had cornrows and all these tattoos. Dad didn't see him though. I could tell. His back was facing him." Cy Jr. grimaced. "And the guy started to pull up the front of his shirt. It looked like . . . it looked like he had a gun tucked in his jeans, Mom! I thought he was reaching for it so I . . . I banged on the window again, really hard. I started shouting to get Dad's attention. I opened up the shop door and ran out. That time Dad saw me—and the guy saw me, too. He dropped his shirt and kept walking down the sidewalk."

He paused to clear his throat, making his Adam's apple bob over the collar of his school uniform.

"The guy in the shop thought I was trying to steal the tennis shoes and started yelling at me to come back. Dad asked me what was wrong. He told me I was interrupting a business call. Dad started yelling back at the shop guy, telling him that I wasn't stealing anything. They started arguing and . . . and with all that happening around me, I guess I got confused. I . . . I didn't know what to say. They were all saying stuff at the same time . . . Dad and the guy in the shop. And then I started to wonder if I really saw what I thought I saw. I thought maybe I was wrong! I didn't want to look stupid." Cy Jr. lowered his eyes again. They flooded with tears. "I should've told Dad though, shouldn't I? If I had told him Saturday, maybe he wouldn't have gotten shot. It's all my fault, Mom!"

Vanessa wrapped her arms around her son. At ten years old, he was already a few inches taller than her, but he still rested his head on her shoulder as he cried, and she rubbed his back like back when he was a baby.

"Shush! Shush, sweetheart," she whispered. "Don't cry. You weren't the reason your dad got shot. It wasn't your fault."

Cy Jr. raised his head, sniffing and wiping his tears on the sleeve on his blazer. "B-but if I w-w-would've t-told him—"

She placed a finger to his lips and shook her head. "It wouldn't have made a difference either way. You don't even know if the person who shot your dad is the man you saw. It could've been anybody, Junior!"

Cy Jr. frowned. "You think so? Really, Mom?"

"Absolutely," she said, lying through her teeth. "Now don't you worry about this anymore. Go inside, have a snack, and get started on that homework. Mommy's orders. I'll be inside in a sec. Okay?"

Cy Jr. nodded before adjusting his backpack on his shoulder and climbing up the stairs.

Meanwhile, Vanessa stood in the garage, cursing under her breath.

So someone besides herself thought Cyrus would be better off dead, and they had been following him around for days to do it, including following him while he was with their kids.

This won't do, Vanessa thought. *This shit won't do at all!*

Had her children been in danger this whole time? Who the hell were these people?

Noelle had said she knew information about Cyrus that Vanessa should know. She hadn't really considered calling the woman back, even though she'd told Bilal that she would, but now she knew she had to do it, in order to protect her own. She could be a lioness like her mother when she needed to be. She was going to protect her children— even if it meant reaching out to her enemy, which is what she considered any other woman in Cyrus's life to be.

Vanessa stalked up the stairs to head straight to her kitchen, grab her phone, and finally return Noelle Grey's message.

Chapter 18

Noelle

Noelle turned the corner and peered out her sedan's windshield at her mostly deserted neighborhood. It was evening. Many of her neighbors were starting to settle around their family dinner tables and in front of their televisions for the night. She tiredly rubbed her neck as she drove and yawned. Noelle planned to do something similar when she got home—kick off her shoes, drink a glass of wine, have a quiet meal alone, and maybe some television or reading before falling to sleep.

She'd stayed at Azure later than she'd intended, but it had felt good to keep busy, to do something besides worrying and agonizing. She'd gotten a lot accomplished today, including reaching out to Cyrus's other wives. To her surprise, Diamond had said right away that she'd be willing to meet them all in person. Vanessa had also called Noelle back later that afternoon and left a message on her cell, saying that she was willing to meet too.

"Something is going on here and I want to know what the hell it is," Vanessa had said on the voice mail. "If someone is trying to kill my husband, I want to know who. My son said he might have seen him. That asshole could have hurt one of my babies, and I don't play that shit!"

Noelle had nodded as she listened. She was relieved that Vanessa understood why they had to meet, why it was so important. Of course, Tariq wouldn't understand the sense of urgency. He wouldn't approve of her decision to contact Vanessa and Diamond either, but Noelle already felt better now that she'd done it—like a weight had been lifted off her shoulders. She was trying her best to regain some control of the situation. She was, in the words of all the spiritual gurus, taking back her power.

Noelle would set it all up tomorrow if that worked for the other ladies since time seemed of the essence. She knew the perfect restaurant in D.C. for them to meet each other in person—a central location for all three women.

Noelle drew closer to her house and slowed to a stop a few feet away from her driveway, surprised to see that another car was already parked there. She recognized the silver Porsche Boxster instantly and the driver who was throwing open the car door.

"Shit," she murmured as she watched him step onto the asphalt.

Was Tariq psychic? Why had he chosen today of all days to visit her, only hours after she had done exactly what he'd asked her not to do? Though he had lied to her to cover up for Cyrus, she knew that she would find it hard to lie to him.

Noelle watched as he closed his car door behind him and strolled toward the end of the driveway to wait for her.

Tariq was an attractive man, even from a distance, with the physique to match. The muscles in his arms strained slightly against the cotton fabric of his shirt. The slim fit of his black suit pant showed off the contours of his thighs. Tariq also had a great walk—and as a former model, Noelle knew walks. He had the gait of a tiger or better yet, a jaguar. It was beautiful to watch, all sinewy muscle rolling in unison with each stride. But like a tiger or a jaguar, he looked almost predatory, like if she weren't careful, he could pounce on her and gobble her up if the inclination came over him.

Noelle swallowed audibly as she pressed the accelerator and pulled into her driveway beside his Porsche.

She couldn't tell him the truth—that she was setting up a meeting with Vanessa and Diamond. He'd warned her that both their lives could be in danger if it got back to the wrong people that she was sniffing around, trying to find information on her husband. She didn't want Tariq to get angry or worry, or more importantly, stop telling her things.

"Hey," he said as she climbed out of her car.

"Hey! What . . . what are you doing here?"

"I just stopped by to check up on you . . . to see how you were doing. You seemed freaked out yesterday about the cops questioning you. They came to the office to question me today, too."

"They did?"

"Yeah, but it was quick and painless. I wondered if they came back again since we last spoke, or if they called you for a follow up."

She threw the strap of her purse over her shoulder. "Uh, no. No, they didn't come back or call."

He beamed. "See! I told you that you had nothing to worry about. It was just routine questioning. All cops do it. They're talking to all of us . . . covering all their bases."

"Y-yeah! You were right." She laughed nervously.

Tariq eyed her. "Are you okay?"

"Yeah, why?"

"I don't know. You just seem . . . off." He took a step toward her, his dark eyes scrutinizing her more closely now. "Did something happen today?"

"No! Why-why do you th-think something h-happened?"

"Because your stuttering and acting weird as hell, Noelle."

Shit, she thought again.

"I'm not acting weird! I don't know what you're talking about," she said, making herself not stutter. She glanced at her front door, feeling her façade faltering, wanting to escape before it fell off completely. She wasn't as good a liar as Cyrus and Tariq. That was obvious.

He followed her gaze to the front door then looked at her again. "Can I come inside?"

"Why do you want to come inside?" she asked suspiciously, now eyeing him too.

Had he really come here to check on her—or to spy on her? Maybe he knew she'd reached out to Vanessa and Diamond, and was waiting for her to confess. Had one of the women called him?

"Because I wanna rob the place," he deadpanned then chuckled. "I'm just kidding. I wanna come inside because it's a forty-five-minute drive from here back to my house and I'd like to use the bathroom before I make the trip." He inclined his head. "If you don't mind."

She breathed an inward sigh of relief. So he didn't suspect anything and he wasn't spying on her. He just had to pee.

God, I'm getting paranoid, she thought. And she was turning that paranoia on Tariq—of all people, the one person who told her the truth about Cyrus and assured her that he had her back. This whole ordeal was bringing out the worst in her in some ways. Noelle hoped she wouldn't have to ask her doctor to up the dose on her meds when it was all over—*if* it would ever end.

"Sure, you can come in. That's not a problem."

A minute later, they walked through the front door and she turned on all the overhead lights, revealing her tidy living room and kitchen. Nothing was out of place, except for all the framed photos of her and Cyrus that had once dotted the space. They all now sat at the bottom of her garbage bin. Tariq scanned the two rooms when he entered and closed the front door behind him.

She bet he noticed the difference, even if he didn't comment.

"You know where the bathroom is," she said, pointing towards her left.

"Yeah, I know." He then walked in the direction she pointed.

She sat her purse on the kitchen island and then opened the fridge to take out a bottle of Moscato.

"I should probably buy stock in the company," she muttered, considering how much she'd been drinking the stuff in the past few days.

Noelle opened one of the overhead cabinets and pulled out a wineglass. As she started to pour herself some wine, she heard the toilet flush down the hall. Tariq appeared a few seconds later. He stared at the glass she raised to her lips. He smirked. "Getting the party started right away, huh?"

"It's been a long day," she grumbled after taking a sip. "I've been drinking a lot more lately though. I need it to calm my nerves. All this stuff with Cy has been a lot to take in."

Tariq's smirk disappeared. "This isn't . . . this isn't messing with you, is it? You aren't feeling . . . well . . . you know—"

"*Suicidal again?*" she finished for him, cocking an eyebrow and licking the wine off her lips. "No, not yet. But I have a feeling I should say thanks to Mother Zoloft for that one. It helps smooth me out—for the time being, anyway."

He lowered his eyes and grimaced. "Look, Noelle, I'm sorry about all this shit. You were right. I should have warned you and told you about what Cy was doing way back in the beginning. I should have told you that he was already married. I should have looked out for you, but I didn't say a damn thing!"

She sat her glass back on the island and exhaled. "Don't be so hard on yourself. He's your business partner. Telling me the truth would have put you in a very awkward position, shall we say. It could have affected your relationship with Cy and ruined the company."

"But none of that shit matters though! By me staying silent, I hurt you. I didn't want to, but I did and . . . and I just hope you can . . . that you can forgive me."

Her face softened. He looked so earnest—and vulnerable. She was used to him being wry and confident; she had never seen him this way. "I could never stay mad at you, Tariq. Besides, you've made up for it ten times over since then. You were the only damn friend I had down here for months when I was at my worst. Of course, I can forgive you!"

"*Really?*" he asked, still eyeing her like he didn't quite believe her. "You aren't just saying that to make me feel better?"

"No!" Noelle laughed as she walked toward her refrigerator again. "I'll prove it. Do you have to go home right away? Are you in a rush?"

"Not really. Why?"

"Stay and have dinner with me. I was just about to heat up some tortellini soup."

He relaxed again. The tension in his shoulders, in his entire body, seemed to visibly loosen. "Did you make it yourself?"

"No, I bought it from Balducci's," she said, removing the container from the refrigerator shelf and sitting it on the counter. "Why?"

"'Cuz you can't cook!" he said, leaning against the island, making her burst into laughter again. She gave him the middle finger, making him laugh as well. "Shit, girl, I wanna eat, but I don't wanna die! Mess with your cooking and I might end up with food poisoning. But since you didn't cook it, I'd be happy to stay. I appreciate the invite."

An hour and a half later, she was laughing all over again as they sat at the dinner table. They had finished devouring their bowls of soup along with French bread and were now finishing off her Moscato. Tariq was regaling her with a story about his childhood, a dare that had gone awry and had landed Tariq in his Superman underwear in front of the whole playground at school.

"I knew I never should've listened to that dude," he said, leaning back in his chair. "After that day, I never did that shit again."

"But you could've established a long career as a stripper," she said between giggles.

"Yeah and got tipped in Now and Laters and Hot Fries," he muttered sarcastically before taking a sip from his glass. "No thanks."

Noelle grabbed her belly and leaned forward. He'd had her laughing so hard that her stomach hurt, and she was near tears. It felt good to laugh, to finally have some form of emotional release that wasn't crying or a screaming fit born of hurt or anger.

"All right," he said, lowering his wineglass back to the dinner table. "I told about four funny stories from my younger days. I'm done embarrassin' myself." He beckoned her with his hand. "Come on. It's your turn."

She gradually stopped laughing. "I don't really have any funny stories."

"Oh, come on, girl! You gotta have one. Everybody does!"

"No, actually everyone doesn't, Tariq." She went somber and stared into her glass. "My childhood didn't have a lot of funny times. When you're being raised by an undependable junkie, you don't really have a lot of good moments on the highlight reel. If you know what I mean."

"You're talkin' about your mom?"

She nodded. "The only good moments I remember were the calm ones when the chaos stopped. When she wasn't locking me in my room for twenty-four hours at a time because she had one of her crackhead friends over to party and get high, and she wanted to 'protect me' from them. But she'd always pass out and forget she left me in there. I can remember screaming and banging on my bedroom door, begging for her to let me out. I was so terrified that no one would ever come to get me . . . that I *die* in there. Then there was the time I called nine-one-one. It was the first time she OD'd. I was ten years old and I dragged her all the way from her bed into the shower. I turned the water on and kept slapping her face to wake her up."

Noelle went quiet as she was overwhelmed with memories of her mother. She'd inherited the woman's build, height, and cheekbones, but not much else. Her mother had seemed so weak to her even back then, so easily won over but men, drugs, and whatever else could offer her a fleeting escape from the drudgery that was their daily lives.

"The calm moments were either at my great aunt's house in the South Bronx when my mom was in rehab, trying to get clean," she continued, "or just after she'd get out of rehab. Mom would make me all these promises that she would try to do better . . . *be* better, but she'd always go back to those same old ways. She'd always start using again. I was seventeen the last time she OD'd. That time she . . . she didn't wake up."

Noelle finally looked up from her wineglass when she felt Tariq reach out and briefly squeeze the hand she'd rested on the table. She saw him gazing at her with neither pity nor shock, but true empathy.

"I promised myself that I would be better than her, that I would do better with my own kids. That's why I wanted so badly for Cy and me to have a baby. He thought it was because I thought we weren't whole enough as a couple without a child, but the truth was *I* didn't feel whole without one. I was starting to worry that we weren't compatible, that he didn't want kids because he was fighting me so hard about it—but now I find out that he had kids with Vanessa and—"

"Wait. How did you know they had kids?"

She halted. She now remembered that Tariq hadn't mentioned Cy's children. She'd discovered that on her own during her internet search.

Damn, she thought, now realizing that she had let that one slip.

"Uh, you . . . you told me," she lied.

Tariq squinted and slowly shook his head. "I didn't tell you that."

"Yes, you did! Anyway, that's not the point. The point is Cy had kids with someone else and not with me and now . . . now I'm . . . I'm so confused!"

"Don't try to figure out Cy's reasoning for things, Noelle. You'll go in circles."

"I know. I just wonder if . . . if maybe—"

"Stop," he said, holding up his hand. "Stop yourself right there. You're never gonna understand him. You know it and I know it. Besides, why waste your time trying to figure him out? You know damn well he's not worth it. Especially with how he treated you . . . with how he treated *all* of you."

Noelle gnawed the inside of her cheek.

"What?" he asked, inclining his head again. "You're thinking somethin'. Just go ahead and say it."

She loudly exhaled. "Look, I know you're right. What Cyrus did was fucked up—to say the least. He was wrong and selfish and manipulative, but I still can't help but wonder about things."

"What things?"

"Like why did he keep putting off going to the fertility doctor even when I begged him to go? Why did he act like he wasn't interested in having a baby at all? Maybe he just . . . maybe he just didn't want to have a baby with me, Tariq. Maybe he thought I was too unstable or too fragile to be a good mother. Maybe something really is wrong with me!"

Tariq went quiet again. He then leaned forward in his chair.

"I'm gonna tell you another story. This time about the first time I met you."

"Oh, this should be good," she muttered wryly, wondering what smartass thing he would say, or joke he would crack to liven the mood and make her laugh.

"When Cy introduced me to you that day five years ago at that little hole-in-the-wall Cuban restaurant in Midtown, I saw you walking toward me, and you looked like this . . ." He paused as if to find the words. "This goddess in stilettos and a red dress."

"*Goddess?*" Noelle took another sip of wine and

snorted. She rested her elbow on the dining room table and her chin in her hand. "Okay, now I know you're full of it."

"Nah, I'm serious! And every man in that room was thinking what I was thinking that night, too. I could see it on their faces. My next thought was, 'There is no way in hell a girl who looks *this* good . . . *this* fire ain't a cold bitch or dumb as dirt or both. I don't care what Cy says!' And I know how Vanessa is. I knew Cy's taste, so I figured I had you pegged the moment I saw you. I thought, 'Oh, here we go! She might look good, but I bet I'm gonna be bored out of my mind. This is gonna be a long ass night.' "

"Well, that was mighty cynical of you."

"I'm a cynical dude, if you haven't noticed. And are you gonna keep interrupting my story, or are you gonna let me finish?"

She laughed and made a sweeping gesture with her free hand. "By all means, please proceed, Mr. Donahue."

"Anyway, we had dinner and after about an hour of talking to you, I had to admit I was wrong. You weren't cold. You were warm and smart. You were deep and sexy, and I thought, 'Cy is one lucky motherfucka' to get this girl. I wonder if he even realizes it.' "

She stilled, taken aback by his words.

"He lucked out marrying you, Noelle. He would've been even luckier having a kid with you. Fuck what Cy thought! You'd make a great mother. You still might one day."

She then watched as Tariq abruptly rose to his feet and stretched. "Well, thanks for the wine and the meal, but I better head home now. It's a long drive."

"Thanks for stopping by," she said, rising from her chair too.

She had been wary when he'd first arrived, but now she felt markedly better after being with Tariq a couple of hours. *Like I always do*, she thought.

"No problem," he assured. "Like I said . . . I wanted to check on you. See how you're doing."

She walked him to the front door and watched as he unlocked it.

"Let me know if you need anything, okay?" Tariq said. "Nothing too big or too small. I got time."

"You aren't my personal butler service, Tariq."

"No, I'm not, but it's okay to do things for people. I know you've had . . . uh . . . bad experiences with your mom . . . with Cy, but not everybody is out to hurt you, Noelle. Some of us really want to help. Let me do it. You deserve it."

She wanted to cry happy tears. His kindness had no limits. She didn't know what she had done to deserve it. Without even thinking, Noelle stepped forward and gave him a warm hug that was long overdue. He hugged her back, and they stood there lost in each other's embrace. Noelle liked it—the feel of Tariq's strong arms around her, the comfort that came with resting her head on his broad shoulder. Noelle closed her eyes and inhaled. She loved the sandalwood undertones and the spicy hint of mint in his cologne. She even liked the faint smell of the laundry detergent in his shirt.

After a few seconds, the comforting feeling started to turn into something else though. It made her tingle all over. It made Noelle throb in places that she hadn't felt throb in quite some time. At the overwhelming sensation, her eyes flashed open. She did a sharp intake of breath and stepped back, trying to find a way to break the connection and to dissipate the sensations she was feeling. But it didn't work. They locked gazes for a few charged seconds. Noelle didn't know who made the first move, but their mouths collided.

She relinquished herself to the feel of Tariq's full, strong lips pressed against hers, of his warm wet tongue sliding into her mouth, of the tickle of his goatee against her cheeks and chin. It was intoxicating, getting swept under by a surge of passion, of having someone desire her so badly. When he shifted her so that she was flat against her front door, the kisses became even more amorous. The couple barely came up for air; they were almost panting. She only fell back to earth when she felt Tariq opening the buttons of her blouse. She lurched back and wrenched her mouth away from his.

"What?" he asked, searching her face. "What's wrong?"

"I'm sorry." She took his hands within her own and slowly pulled them away from her shirt. "But I can't."

"*Why?*" His eyes drifted to her open blouse. "I went too fast?"

"No. No! It's just . . ." She struggled to find the right words. "I'm a married woman, Tariq."

"But you aren't married! Not legally anyway. You never were!"

"I know! I know, but I feel like I am. Our vows may not have meant anything to Cy, but they meant something to me, and I can't . . . I can't just turn it off now that I know he's a liar and a cheater." She cleared her throat. "He hurt me. He broke my heart. But I . . . I still think of him as my husband."

Tariq stiffened at her words. He took a step back from her, then another. He didn't look angry; he just looked mystified.

To be honest, she didn't understand it herself. Cyrus didn't deserve her loyalty or fidelity, but she couldn't convince herself to do to him what he done to her. She may have put his pictures in the garbage, but she still wore his ring and it weighed heavily on her. She desired Tariq and she suspected she had for quite some time—unwittingly. Maybe Tariq had desired her, too. But they had both held back out of faithfulness, fear, friendship, or any number of reasons. And she would hold back again tonight. She couldn't cheat on Cyrus—even if she desperately wanted to right now. She just couldn't work up the will or the courage, even after what he'd done to her.

"I'm sorry," she whispered again.

"Don't be," Tariq said.

Less than a minute later, Tariq walked out her front door and she closed it behind him. She pressed her fingers to her lips, feeling the phantom sensation of his kiss even as she heard the rev of his car engine as he pulled out of her driveway. She swore she still felt his kiss even when she climbed into bed alone that night.

Thursday

Chapter 19

Vanessa

Bilal cried out and shuddered all over, like his body was zapped by an electric current before he collapsed onto Vanessa's chest. A minute later, he rolled from on top of her and onto his back, sinking into her crumpled bed-sheets in a sweaty heap. She gazed up at the ceiling and sighed contentedly.

"And you were worried about me being here," Bilal chided. "Aren't you happy I came?"

"I'm happy whenever you come, honestly," she joked, making them both crack up in laughter. He leaned over and kissed her again.

Today had played out the same as yesterday. Vanessa had left one of the French doors leading to the deck un-locked and Bilal had walked around the back of the house, strolled inside a little after two o'clock, and climbed up the stairs to find her waiting for him in her bedroom exactly as he'd requested: buck naked with her legs spread wide open in willing invitation. They'd been at it for the past hour.

He now glanced at the clock on her night table. "Shit," Bilal muttered.

"What?" she asked as he pulled his mouth away from hers.

"I gotta go! I gotta get back to the gym."

"Already?" she almost whimpered. "You said you'd be free all afternoon and we wouldn't have to rush! Mama's even picking up the kids today. I thought we'd have more time together."

"Yeah, sorry, bae. One of my clients scheduled a last-minute session. I got to be there in thirty minutes." He tossed off the sheets and rolled across the bed. She watched as he hopped onto his feet and stretched.

This was new. Since when did his clients start booking him at the last minute? It wasn't like Bilal was a doctor on-call twenty-four, seven. Vanessa suddenly thought back to his last training session she'd witnessed.

"Last-minute session, huh? Got another appointment with Miss Keisha?" Vanessa asked suspiciously, pushing herself up to her elbows. She watched as he removed his condom, knotted it, and tossed it into the bathroom trash can. "I'm sure another trainer could fill in for you. They can help guide her through all that moaning and groaning she does."

Bilal snickered as he walked back into her bedroom and stepped into his boxer briefs. "Are you jealous of Keisha, Nessa?"

"Hardly!" she lied. "Why would I be jealous of a woman who's made of more plastic than my daughter's Barbie dolls?"

He tugged his T-shirt over his head and grinned. "Well, even if you were jealous, you got nothin' to worry about. Keisha's not even my type. I like my women more mature . . . more ripe. She's too young for me!"

"Ripe?" Vanessa curled her lip in disgust. "What am I? A damn grapefruit?"

He cracked up with laughter again as he stepped into his gym shorts. He tightened and tied the drawstring of his shorts over his washboard abs. "You know what I mean! Besides, you're the chick that's already taken. I ain't got nobody on the side! *You're* the one with the whole ass husband, but hopefully not for too much longer, thanks to that little meeting you've got going on tonight. Maybe you'll finally dump his ass and move on when you find out the full truth—like him having a fourth wife or a prison record or some shit."

Bilal was referring to the dinner she was having at eight o'clock tonight with Cyrus's other wives at a restaurant in D.C. Noelle had called that morning to schedule it, and Vanessa had agreed. Bilal thought she was doing it so that she could find out all of Cyrus's secrets and finally close the book on her sham of a marriage, but Bilal didn't know she was well past that point. Instead, she was going to the meeting to find out who else her husband had crossed, who was trying to kill him, and why. She wanted to know whether that person or persons posed a real threat to her family. That's all she wanted out of those heffas. Once she got her answers, she wanted nothing else to do with Cyrus's other wives.

"I'll be waiting when you finally make up your mind," Bilal continued. He strolled back to her side of the bed. "I told you already that I'm the right dude for you, but I don't know if you'll ever believe me."

She slowly rose from the bed and wrapped her arms around him. "I'm warming up to the idea," she answered honestly.

Vanessa knew without a doubt that Bilal believed he was the right man for her; she just wasn't equally convinced. Not yet anyway. There were a lot of areas he had to improve to show he was worthy of her making a long-term investment in him. But maybe he was up to the challenge.

A minute later, Vanessa walked down the stairs to the first floor, holding Bilal close, trailing her fingers along his broad shoulder. When they descended the last riser, the doorbell rang, making them both pause in their steps.

"Who the hell is that?" he asked, eyeing the front door warily.

They could both see two distorted figures in the door's stained-glass window.

Most of her neighbors were at work at this time of day. Many of the children were just getting out of school, like her own. "Probably just a salesman or a Jehovah's Witness." She waved him toward her kitchen's entrance. "Go stay in there until I can get rid of them. Okay? I'll be quick."

Bilal nodded before backing into the kitchen while she continued to the front door. Vanessa unlocked it and slowly cracked it open, only to find two men standing on her welcome mat, waiting for her. She recognized them instantly as the two detectives she had spoken to when she arrived at Johns Hopkins on Monday.

What are they doing here?

"Yes?" she asked.

One of the detectives—the shorter black one—stepped forward. "Hi, Mrs. Grey. Nice to see you again. It's Detective Turner and Detective Macy with the Baltimore City P.D.," he said, gesturing to his partner. "We spoke with you after your husband's shooting and—"

"Yes," she said impatiently, cutting him off, "I know who you are. Why are you here? Did something else happen?"

Vanessa tried not to make a panicked glance over her shoulder to check to see if her lover was still hiding. She hoped he could hear their conversation, that he knew to stay unseen in her kitchen.

"That darling husband of yours might be a bigamist," her mother had warned, *"but you're still supposed to be the dutiful wife no matter what, Nessa."*

"Uh, no. Nothing else happened," Detective Macy said. "At least, nothing that we're aware of. We just wanted to follow up with you. You know . . . update you on our investigation into your husband's attempted murder."

"We thought as his wife you might be concerned about our progress," Detective Turner elaborated.

Detective Turner was looking at her in a way she didn't like. Like he could see something strange on her face. She wanted to reach up and wipe it away.

"Of course, I'm concerned! I want to know who shot my husband and for that person to be brought to justice. Of course!" she cried, almost sounding shrill.

"Can we come in then?" Detective Macy asked.

"Why?"

"Well, because something like this we really don't want to discuss on the sidewalk, ma'am," Detective Turner explained, still eyeing her.

This time she did glance over her shoulder. "Oh! Well, actually this isn't a good time, detectives. I-I have to pick up my children from school in less than an hour," she lied.

"It'll only take a few minutes. I promise. We won't keep you long," Detective Turner assured.

Vanessa loudly exhaled, making her shoulders sink. She didn't want them in her house, especially while Bilal was hiding in her kitchen. But they claimed it wouldn't take long, and if she insisted they not come inside, that might only raise their suspicions.

Reluctantly, Vanessa opened the door by several more inches and stood back. "If it'll only be a few minutes," she muttered.

The two men stepped inside, and she shut the door behind them. "You've got a nice place here, Mrs. Grey!" Detective Macy exclaimed, looking around the room. "Quite a lot of square footage!"

"Thank you. Please have a seat," she said, pointing to her living room sectional. She took the seat opposite them and sat down, forgetting that she was naked underneath her robe. The front panel almost flew open, giving the cops a full peep show, but she caught it before it did. They must have seen a little something though. Their eyes widened in unison.

At their expressions, she blushed. Vanessa loudly cleared her throat. "You said you had an update on your investigation to give me."

The two men glanced at one another. "Uh, yeah," Detective Turner said, "we do, but we wanted to ask you a couple of things first."

Vanessa looked at him warily. "What did you want to ask me?"

"Well, we understand that you were made aware that your husband was married to someone else . . . that he had relationships with other women during your marriage."

Vanessa clenched her hands in her lap. "Yes, I've been made aware of this."

"Have you had any interactions with these women? Outside of the altercation at the hospital, that is," Detective Macy said.

"No," Vanessa answered hesitantly, now feeling more than wary of their questions.

She had received a voice mail and text messages from Noelle and was supposed to have the meeting with her and Cyrus's third wife this evening, but she didn't know why something like that would be relevant to their investigation.

"Well, we've discovered a few things about those past

relationships and, uh . . . there's no easy way to put this, but we have reason to believe that one of these women might have been involved in Mr. Grey's shooting on Monday," Macy said. "We wanted to know if prior to that or even recently, if anyone has threatened you or—"

"Wait! Wait, you think one of them shot my husband?" she shouted, now gaping. Her gaze shifted between the two men. "Which one?"

"We can't divulge that information quite yet because we're still gathering evidence. But we're developing a pretty strong case, ma'am," Macy continued before pursing his thin lips. "When we make our arrest, we'll let you know. We just wanted to make you aware of what's going on. It's best just to keep your distance from *all* of these ladies for now—to be safe. We don't want you to be at risk."

Vanessa's heart began to pound rapidly. She was clenching her hands so tightly in her lap, she swore she was digging her nails into her flesh. Had the reason Noelle invited her to this evening's little get-together not been so that all three wives could share info? Had Vanessa been about to walk into a trap?

That conniving bitch, Vanessa thought.

The detectives left a few minutes later. As she closed the door behind them, she slumped back against it, feeling her knees go weak. Bilal peeked his head around the kitchen entryway. He stared at her expectantly. "Are they gone?" he asked.

She couldn't respond. She was still fighting to catch her breath and calm her racing heart. One of Cyrus's other wives wanted to kill her, and she bet it was Big Bird Bitch Noelle. She had caught bad vibes the instant she'd met the other woman. Of course, Noelle wanted to get rid of her. It made sense for her to remove both Cyrus and Vanessa out of the picture. With Cyrus and his first wife gone, maybe then Noelle could have his money and estate all to herself. And Vanessa had been willing to blindly walk into Noelle's trap, leaving her poor babies defenseless.

"What's wrong, bae?" Bilal asked, walking toward her. "They didn't figure out you weren't alone in here, did they?"

"No!" she cried, making him jump back. "Did you hear what they said? That bitch Noelle tried to kill Cyrus and she's trying to kill me too!"

"Uh, I caught a few bits and pieces, but I didn't hear nothin' about her trying to kill you. Did they even say her name?"

"They didn't have to! I know it's her!"

"How? I thought they were still collecting evidence and stuff."

"It was her! It has to be! That's why she invited me to that dinner tonight. She's probably going to have some guy come up and shoot me in the parking lot or . . . or the restaurant or—"

Bilal groaned. "Nessa, you don't know that! That dude could've been fuckin' around with any number of broads. Maybe it was one of *them* who set him up!"

"The cops told me to stay away from her, Bilal . . . from all of them! It's too risky. I can't go to that dinner!"

"But I thought the whole point of you going there was to find out the truth about Cyrus. To find out the shit the cops may be talking about! That nigga could die, and you may never get answers!"

She crossed her arms over her chest. "Are you really so obsessed with me finding out more dirt about my husband that you think I should risk *taking a bullet to the head* for it?" She sucked her teeth in disgust. "And you swear you love me. You are so full of shit!"

He grabbed her shoulders, catching her off guard and shaking her hard. "I am *not* full of shit and I do love your selfish, ungrateful ass, though sometimes I wonder why, to be honest! If you're so worried about tonight, then . . . shit . . . I'll go with you! I'll protect you."

She barked out a caustic laugh. "How? By bench pressing her to death?" she taunted.

"No and fuck you." He finally let go of her. "I'll bring my Glock with me. I hope I don't have to use it, but I will if I got to."

She cocked an eyebrow. "Since when do you have a gun?"

"It really ain't mine. It's my uncle's. But he owns about six of them. I know where he keeps them. I can take one for one night and he won't know the difference. He won't care."

Vanessa tried to imagine Bilal holding a gun, aiming it, and firing on her command—and the prospect turned her on. She started to get wet all over again just thinking about it. She gazed up at him and licked her lips. "Would you really do that? Just for me?"

"Sure, bae. I can't let anything happen to you."

She wrapped her arms around him and beamed. "Oh, baby, you always say *exactly* what I wanna hear."

A little after eight p.m., Bilal pulled to a stop at the valet station and cut the engine. For a split second, Vanessa almost regretted inviting him to come along. Or at the very least, she wished they had driven her Mercedes to D.C. and not his Versa hatchback. Her cheeks reddened with embarrassment as the valet held the door open for her and she climbed out. Bilal handed him the keys and she threw her purse over her shoulder and strode ahead of him to the restaurant's entrance, leaving Bilal to catch up.

"Wait!" he shouted as he came up behind her at a near run. "I'm supposed to be here protecting your ass! Remember?"

She didn't respond. Instead, she strolled up to the reservation desk where another couple already stood speaking with the maître d'. She gazed around her.

The venue was low lit and filled with candlelight. It was mostly decorated in wood and leather. The back walls were covered with wine racks where hundreds of wine bottles of different vintages were on display. All the tables and banquettes were filled with patrons, but Vanessa was searching for one patron in particular.

"You see them?" Bilal whispered into her ear, making her jump and look over her shoulder at him.

He had worn a tracksuit jacket to cover the Glock 17 tucked into the back of jeans. The gun was secured in the waistband of his boxer briefs. Bilal had shown it to her back at the car and the full magazine. She'd trusted his word that he knew how to use it if it came to that. Vanessa was now questioning that trust though, watching as he nervously adjusted his jacket.

"No, not yet," she muttered, still scanning the room. "Damn it, where is that bitch?"

"Can I help you?" the young man standing at the reservation desk asked.

"Yes, I'm looking for Noelle Grey," Vanessa replied. "I'm supposed to be meeting her here at eight o'clock."

"Indeed! You are her first guests. I'll show you to your table." He then picked up two leather-bound menus and turned toward the seating area.

They followed the maître d', zigzagging through tables until Vanessa finally spotted Noelle. She was sitting alone toward the back of the restaurant.

Cyrus's other wife had traded her silk wrap dress for a silk, one-shouldered multi-print top. Her short hair was upswept into gold hairclips tonight, making her high cheekbones look even sharper. When she saw Vanessa approach, she smiled then immediately frowned when she noticed Bilal trailing behind Vanessa. Her dark brows crinkled together.

"*That's* her?" Bilal whispered in shock as they drew near the table.

"Yeah, why?" she whispered back.

"You said she was big, dark, and ugly, Nessa!"

"*And?*"

"So I was expecting some big ass Shrek lookalike. That's not what she looks like at all! I'll say one thing . . . your husband's got good taste. She is a fuckin' gorgeous," he murmured in awe, making Vanessa halt in her steps and turn to stare up at him.

"*Is she?* Would you say she's ripe, too?" she asked sarcastically, raising her brows.

Bilal chuckled. "Yeah, kinda!"

She sucked her teeth and continued following the maître d'. They finally arrived at the table and Noelle sat upright in her chair. Her eyes shifted between them in confusion.

"I didn't know you were bringing a guest," Noelle said.

Vanessa crossed her arms over her chest as the maître d' pulled out a chair for her. She didn't take a seat. "Did you think I was crazy enough to just come in here by myself?"

The maître d' sat down their menus and slinked away, probably wanting to get out of the line of fire.

"Uh, yeah. I did. *I* came by myself." Noelle held out her hand to Bilal. "Hi, I'm Noelle Grey and you are . . ."

"Bilal Cullen," he said, shaking her hand and grinning like a jackass. "Pleased to meet you, Lovely."

"*Really?*" Vanessa asked, glowering at him again.

She couldn't believe it. The son of a bitch was actually flirting with Noelle—the same woman who was probably on a mission to kill her.

"What?" He pulled his hand back. "Hell, I'm just being

polite! Besides, she seems okay. I don't think you got anything to worry about."

"What do you mean, 'I seem okay'?" Noelle asked, her frown deepening. "What's going on?"

Vanessa loudly exhaled. This was starting to feel ridiculous. She had envisioned Bilal as some slick bodyguard, ready to defend her with his life, if necessary. But instead he was acting like the twenty-four-year-old guy she knew him to be—immature, cocky, and undependable. She should have known he'd come in here thinking not with his head, but with his dick.

"Just go wait for me at the bar," Vanessa mumbled. "But stay in my sight, okay? Don't disappear."

He looked a little dejected that he wouldn't be eating dinner with them, but he nodded anyway.

"It was nice meeting you, Noelle," he said, actually having the audacity to give her a wink.

"Nice meeting you, too," she said with a wave as he walked off, though she still looked bemused. Vanessa sat down in the open chair and pulled up to the table.

"Do you mind telling me what that was about?" Noelle asked, pointing to Bilal's receding back. "Why did you bring your friend with you?"

"For protection," Vanessa answered succinctly, dropping her purse onto her lap.

"*Protection?* Protection from who?"

"I don't know. You tell me."

Noelle shook her head again. "I'm sorry, but I have no idea what you're talking about."

"Of course, you don't!" Vanessa let out a bitter laugh then abruptly stopped. "You think you're fooling me, but you're not, sweetheart." She jabbed her finger at her. "One of you bitches tried to kill my husband and you could've hurt my child. And I told you, I don't play that shit!"

Chapter 20

Diamond

Diamond rushed to the restaurant doors, relieved that she was only ten minutes late. To make it up to David, the floor manager at The Seneca, for skipping out on previous shifts, she had served as hostess during the lunch shift today. But that had meant leaving the restaurant at a little before six p.m. and sitting in slow evening traffic in downtown Baltimore *and* D.C. so that she could meet Cyrus's other wives for dinner.

Of course, the entire time she'd been working, her phone had buzzed with phone calls and texts from Julian. She'd gotten more than a half dozen irate messages from him, all asking her why she hadn't picked him up today for yet another shopping trip, like he'd ordered.

"Where the fuck are you, bitch?" he'd barked into one of his voicemail messages. "I told you come here at two o'clock. I only get one of these passes a day and I'm wasting it on you! You better be here in the next five minutes or, I swear to God, I'mma—"

She'd deleted his message at that point, no longer interested in listening to his tirades. Diamond just assumed it would include more threats to her or to Cyrus or them both. But she had a chance to think about what Julian had said the last time she'd seen him, and she'd decided that his threat to harm Cyrus had been an idle one. Cyrus was in the hospital under police protection. Even *she* couldn't get access to him anymore. Julian really thought that one of his girls could just roll up in there to do her man harm? He was delusional.

Instead of focusing on Julian, she needed to focus on finding out the truth of what had happened to Cyrus. That was why she was here today. Nothing else mattered.

"Hello," she said to the skinny gentleman who stood at the wooden reception desk.

He slowly looked up from a computer screen. He painted on a smile. His eyes brightened. She knew she did something similar whenever a customer walked up to her at The Seneca. "Yes, how may I help you, ma'am?"

"I'm meeting Noelle Grey. Is she here?" Diamond glanced at her cellphone screen to check the time again. "She should be. I'm running a little late, but I wonder if she is, too."

An expression flickered across his pale face, one that she couldn't decipher. "Uh, yes. Yes, she is here indeed. I will . . . uh . . . show you to your table."

Diamond narrowed her eyes as she followed him across the dining room. Why had he acted so strangely when she mentioned Noelle's name?

As she drew closer to their table, she figured out why he'd reacted the way he had when she said she was here to see Noelle. She caught sight of two women, and it looked like they were arguing. She assumed they were Cyrus's other wives.

Diamond was surprised to see neither one resembled her in the slightest. One was light-skinned, pretty, and petite with long curly hair that hung down her back. She looked to be in her mid-to-late-thirties, but was trying to look younger in her skin-tight, low cut dress and heavy makeup. The other one seemed taller with skin the color of hot cocoa, short hair, and pillowy lips that women paid good money to plastic surgeons to get. She vaguely resembled the model Naomi Campbell in her younger days. In fact, the only thing the three Mrs. Greys all seemed to have in common was that they were attractive black women.

"You think *I* tried to kill him?" the dark-skinned one asked, pointing at her chest.

"It would make sense! You got pissed at him for being married to someone else and you thought you could take your revenge out on him!" The light-skinned one inclined her head. "Did you plan to come for me too? That's what this whole restaurant meet-up was about, I bet!"

"You're not serious, are you? Am I supposed to have some assassin on standby *at a restaurant?* Is he supposed to be hiding in the bathroom or the kitchen?"

Diamond came to a stop at their table and both women turned and looked up at her in surprise.

"I guess the fun's started without me," she said dryly, as the maître d' held out a chair for her. "I'm Diamond." She took her seat, glanced up at him, and gave him a silent nod in thanks before he walked back across the dining room. "Let me guess. You're Noelle," she said, pointing at the dark-skinned woman.

Noelle nodded. "So, we finally meet in person."

"Yeah, and it's as strange as I thought it would be." She then turned to the other woman. "And you must be—"

"Vanessa," the light-skinned woman answered, cutting her off. Vanessa slowly looked her up and down, like she was sizing her up. "And I guess you're the woman claiming to be Cy's third wife."

"It's not a claim," Diamond said tightly, not liking her tone. "I brought a copy of my marriage license like you guys asked so that I can prove we're married."

She reached into her purse and removed the folded sheet of paper. She sat it at the center of the table. Noelle hesitated before flipping open the lid of her clutch and doing the same, sitting her marriage certificate next to Diamond's. Vanessa rummaged around in her snake-skin handbag before tugging out a sheet and slapping it on the table as well. They all read them silently.

February 3, 2020 in the State of Nevada signed by Diamond Moby and Cyrus Grey . . .

April 22, 2016 in the State of New York signed by Noelle Simmons and Cyrus Grey . . .

June 18, 2009 in the State of Maryland signed by Vanessa Walters and Cyrus Grey . . .

All different wedding dates. All different states. Three different women and the same groom. His signature was almost identical on all the marriage certificates.

Diamond took a shaky breath as stared at the sheets of paper, feeling the blood drain from her head. She couldn't ignore the truth now that it was plain as day and sitting right in front of her face.

"Well, this proves it for a fact!" Vanessa pronounced. "I knew it all along, but this shows it for sure. He and I were married first. *I'm* Cyrus's true wife!"

"That's what you get from all of this? This isn't a competition!" Noelle said, looking like she was trying to hold onto her patience, but losing the battle.

Frankly, Diamond was getting irritated as well. The situation was challenging enough without this woman trying to pick a fight with them. But if Vanessa wanted a fight, Diamond would give her one.

"No, it's not a competition, because if it was, both of you would have already lost." Vanessa tossed her hair over her shoulder and raised her button nose into the air. "Cyrus Grey is my husband according to the eyes of the law. I don't care who he married after that. I—"

"Look, we all know you're legally his wife," Noelle countered. "You've marked your territory. He's yours. We get it! That's not—"

"No, we *don't* get it!" Diamond snapped. "Just because she married him first, doesn't mean he's hers. It doesn't mean she's the one he wanted to be with. If their marriage was so goddamn great, then why did he move onto other women? Why the hell did he marry me?"

"He didn't move on," Vanessa said icily. "He just decided to put a ring on his side pieces for whatever reason. I guess you'd have to ask Cy. But that man is still mine, sweetheart." She chuckled. "He was sleeping in bed with me the very morning he was shot."

Diamond leaned forward, meeting Vanessa stare for stare. "And he was just about to climb on top of me in our bed that same afternoon," she hissed back. "So what's your point?"

Vanessa's mouth twisted with outrage. "You little tacky heffa! I should reach across this table and slap the shit outta you!"

Diamond slowly rose from her chair. "I'd like to see you try, bitch!"

"Stop! Stop! Look, this is *not* what we came here for!" Noelle shouted over them both, laying her hands on the tablecloth. "I am not here to bicker. I'm especially not here to have a death match over a man who cheated on all of us . . . who played all of us! Because that's exactly what Cy did!"

Diamond fell silent. So did Vanessa—to her surprise. That was a good thing because several diners at the surrounding tables was starting to look at their trio anxiously. If they got anymore boisterous, Diamond assumed they would get kicked out of the restaurant. She reluctantly lowered herself back into her chair as she and Vanessa continued to glower at one another.

"We're here to share what we know," Noelle argued. "We're here to find out who shot Cyrus and if that person still poses a threat to either one of us."

"Oh, please! Stop pretending like you don't already know the answer to that question," Vanessa said. "You know who shot Cy!"

"Why do you keep saying that?" Noelle asked.

"Yeah, why do you?" Diamond chimed, turning to Vanessa. "Why are you so damn sure she knows who did it?"

Vanessa stubbornly raised her chin again. "I don't have to tell you who told me, but I have it on a good source that one of Cyrus's wives was likely behind his attempted murder."

"One of Cyrus's wives?" Noelle tilted her head. "Well, if that's the case, couldn't it just as easily be Diamond or you?"

"It certainly wasn't me!" Vanessa laughed. "And I highly doubt it was her, either." She gave a scant glance at Diamond. "This little girl doesn't look like she could think her way out of paper bag, let alone conspire to commit murder."

Diamond pulled her lips back, ready to spew venom at Vanessa, but Noelle spoke before she could.

"I didn't try to kill Cy and I doubt Diamond did either, considering she got hurt too, and could've died that day! Neither one of us had anything to do with this! It was more than likely someone else that Cy crossed, someone that he stole money from. That's the person who's behind this."

"*What?* Who did Cy steal money from?" Diamond asked, now genuinely shocked.

Say what you will about Cyrus Grey's personal life, but

Diamond had always assumed that he was a good business-
man and a well-respected one. She didn't know a lot about
his line of work, but it had seemed far from suspect.

"I think Cy may have stolen from one of his clients."
Noelle glanced around the restaurant and lowered her
voice to a whisper. "And they may have put a hit out on
him."

"What the hell are you talking about?" Vanessa cried.
"Cy is a financial planner. He gives investment advice to
rich retirees! Little old ladies who live in mansions. Who
would put a hit out on him?"

"Those aren't his only customers," Noelle said. "Someone told me—"

"*Someone?*" Vanessa repeated, sounding doubtful.
"Someone who?"

"If you can't divulge your sources, I can't either," Noelle
insisted. "Just know that this person is credible, and they
told me that not all the clients for Greydon Consultants
are who we think they are. Some of them are . . . well,
they're criminals looking to move money around, to hide
or invest it in other places. Greydon Consultants helps
them do that, but Cy has been skimming money off the
top and . . . and they found out."

"Shit," Diamond said in one exhalation. "Shit! Is this
for real?"

"I wouldn't have said it if it wasn't," Noelle insisted.
"That's why I wanted to tell you two. I thought it was important to know."

"Criminals? What kind of criminals?" Vanessa yelled
hysterically.

Noelle raised a finger to her lips, motioning for her to
quiet down.

"Like the mafia? *Drug dealers?*" Vanessa said in a
lower voice.

"I don't know. The person didn't go into detail," Noelle

whispered. "They just said they were bad people who you don't want to cross."

"Well, that would explain why that son of a bitch was following Cy and my son! He sounded like some damn gang member," Vanessa said. "I can't believe Cy did this! How could he be so stupid?"

"So maybe the guy your son saw was working for the people who Cy stole money from," Noelle argued. "Did he say anything that day? Did your son recognize him?"

"No, he didn't say a damn thing! Cy Jr. said he just walked off, but he saw that he had a gun. Damnit, this is a lot! Do the police know any of this? Should we—"

"No, and they can't know! All of what I just told you has to stay at this table," Noelle said. "If we tell the police, it could make things worse."

"*How*?" Diamond asked. "How could it possibly make things worse? Cy was shot! He could have died!"

"Because the people who tried to kill Cy, if they knew that *we* knew they did it, they would come after us, too," Noelle explained. "There wouldn't be a question if our lives were in danger at that point. We'd be walking dead women."

"Oh, God! I need a drink. Where the hell is the waiter? Waiter! Over here!" Vanessa raised her arm to flag down someone.

Diamond opened her mouth to speak. She was just about to tell them about the mysterious man who had shot Cy, about how he had stopped by their building the day before, and had a nine tattooed on his forearm that both she and the building's guard had noticed—but she closed her mouth before the words came out. Something held her back.

She wasn't sure what it was. Maybe it was Vanessa's attitude. It didn't exactly endear her to the woman or make her want to share information with her. Or maybe it was because she still wasn't sure if she could trust Vanessa, Noelle, or what they were telling her now. Maybe one of them or both were lying to her, trying to fool her into believing they had nothing to do with the shooting. For those reasons, she would keep that tidbit to herself. Perhaps she would tell them later tonight or another day, but she wasn't ready to do it yet.

A waiter finally arrived to serve them drinks and to take their dinner orders. Diamond had the shrimp scampi and after an hour, barely finished one glass of Chardonnay. Noelle had the lamb and pureed potatoes and had downed two glasses of wine, but only picked at her food. Vanessa had the lobster risotto, finished her entire dish, and seemed to make it her mission to finish the rest of their wine bottle as well. The entire time, the women talked more about their lives and Cy.

Diamond found out that Noelle had a dress shop in Ballston, Virginia, and had once been a model. She'd traveled the world—walking runways in Paris, Milan, Madrid, and New York, only to settle down with Cyrus in the suburbs of Northern Virginia.

"I did it because he asked me to," Noelle confessed. "I thought it would be a way to keep him close, but it didn't turn out that way. I felt more alone and without him when I got here. Now . . . looking back and seeing all this drama, I wish I would've never left. I should've stayed in New York."

Diamond discovered that Vanessa was a stay-at-home mom with three kids who lived in Anne Arundel County, Maryland. Diamond was amused to see Vanessa's abrasive façade disappear when she spoke about her children. Her face softened and her eyes went bright as she showed pictures of her sons and daughter, flipping through them in her cellphone.

"This is Bryson, and this is Cy Jr.," she said, proudly

tapping the screen. "Doesn't he look just like his daddy? I tell him that all the time!"

Diamond also shared a little about herself. She told them she'd gone to school in D.C. but that she didn't finish college. She said she'd moved to the Baltimore area four years ago and had met Cyrus a few years later. For obvious reasons, she didn't tell him about her sex work or Julian's murder trial and release. She planned to never tell them about that part of her life.

"I should've known he would cheat," Vanessa drawled two hours into their dinner. Her words were slightly slurred. She sounded drunk. "Cy seemed too good to be true. Men that fine can never keep their dick in their pants."

"That's a cop out," Noelle said. "There are plenty of attractive men and women who don't cheat. I didn't cheat on Cy!"

"I didn't either," Diamond insisted.

Diamond noticed that Vanessa stayed conspicuously silent on that one. Instead, she raised her glass to her lips and took a sip. "Well, Cy is fine *and* rich, which makes it even less likely that he wouldn't sleep around. I wonder what other women he had over the years."

"It wasn't just the other women that I wonder about. What other stuff has he kept secret? It's like Cy had all these other lives he was living . . . all these other parts to himself and I only know a sliver of it. I barely know my own damn husband!" Noelle lamented, lowering her fork to her plate and dabbing at her mouth with her dinner napkin.

She did it in such a ladylike fashion that Diamond wondered if Noelle had taken etiquette classes to learn how to do it. She seemed so classy, so refined—and so unlike Diamond or Vanessa. Why had he decided to marry them all? The three women seemed so different physically and their personalities were disparate, too. Did he seek something unique in each of them, or were they all facets of the perfect woman he'd wanted, but was unable to achieve in one single package?

"I'm still not sure if I want to know everything," Diamond confessed. "Maybe Cy kept some secrets for a good reason, like . . . I don't know . . . he wanted to protect us."

"You mean protect himself from getting his ass whupped," Vanessa said.

"No, I mean protect us! Maybe he just didn't want to hurt us. That's why he kept things from us. It is possible that he loves us . . . all three of us in his . . . well, in his *own* way. I mean, he took care of us, didn't he? He gave me a condo and a car. No man has ever done that for me! And you said he gave you that money to help start that store, Noelle. And what about that private school your kids go to, Vanessa? He showed us how much he cares. He did it all the damn time!"

"But those are just things," Noelle said. "*Nice* things but that doesn't make up for all the lies. He should have been honest with us. If Cy wanted to keep three women in his life, he should have given us the option of whether we wanted to stay or move onto someone else. He should've given us the option of whether we wanted to be part of his . . . his harem!"

"And no woman in her right mind would say yes to that shit," Vanessa grumbled, downing the rest of her glass.

This time, Diamond didn't respond. She wouldn't tell them that she had actually said yes in the past, and may have been willing to do it again if Cyrus had asked, if he had been upfront about it. She knew even if she were one of many women in his life, Cyrus still would treat her ten times better than Julian had.

"And there were so many other things I wanted that Cy couldn't . . . wouldn't give me," Noelle continued. "That you couldn't buy."

"Like what?" Diamond asked.

"Like him being there with me. I was alone sixty to seventy percent of the time. He was always traveling and away on business," Noelle argued.

Vanessa snorted. "Yeah, well, now we know that was a crock of shit. He was probably with one of us."

"And I wanted a baby," Noelle continued, lowering her eyes to her half-eaten dinner. "I wanted a baby and it just wasn't working. We had been trying for a while and I begged Cy to go to the doctor with me, but he wouldn't go! He knew how badly I wanted it, but he wouldn't get checked out."

"When were you trying to get pregnant?" Vanessa asked.

Noelle gradually raised her eyes, blinking back tears. "We . . . we started about a year and half ago. We still might have been able to conceive naturally, but I wasn't sure if—"

"No, you wouldn't have," Vanessa said, reaching for the bottle at her elbow to pour herself another glass, finishing off the rest of the white wine. "It wouldn't have worked."

Diamond gritted her teeth in annoyance. She was getting so tired of this bitter bitch. "How the hell do you know she wouldn't have gotten pregnant? Why don't you just shut—"

"Because Cy can't have any more kids!" Vanessa said before taking another drink from her glass. "Not unless he reversed his vasectomy."

Noelle and Diamond gazed at her in stunned silence.

"When did Cy get a vasectomy?" Diamond asked.

"Right after Zoe was born. She was our 'surprise baby,'" Vanessa said, using air quotes. "I got pregnant with her only five months after I had Bryson. I wanted to get my tubes tied so it would never happen again, but Cy said he'd get a vasectomy instead because it was an in-and-out procedure and he didn't want to have any more kids anyway."

"He . . . he didn't tell me," Noelle whispered. This time the tears in her eyes spilled over onto her cheeks. "I *begged* him to go to the doctor with me! He . . . he knew how much it meant to me, and he didn't say a damn thing! He knew he couldn't have kids and he just . . ." Her words faded. She abruptly pushed back from the table and rose to her feet. She sniffed. "I'm sorry, but I have to go."

"*What?* Why?" Vanessa cried, lowering her wineglass. "Hey, I understand you're upset, but you're not the only one he lied to. We all have to—"

"This should cover our dinner," Noelle mumbled after reaching into her purse and slapping three hundred-dollar bills on the table. She then walked across the dining room and out of the restaurant, leaving Diamond and Vanessa gaping in her wake.

Chapter 21

Noelle

Noelle bit down hard on her bottom lip as she drove, try-ing to bite back the sobs that threatened to erupt like a volcano from her throat. Cyrus had lied. He had lied like he'd lied all the other times, but for some reason this be-trayal felt worse than the rest. It wasn't like discovering he had two other wives or that his business was a front for dirty dealings that may have landed him on the wrong side of a gun and in the hospital. This was a kill wound that left her writhing in pain. This shook Noelle to her very core. She wished she'd brought her bottle of Zoloft with her. She could use one of her pills right now.

As she traversed city streets, she thought about all those pregnancy tests she had taken, month after month, hoping for a positive sign or a smiley face only to toss them into the trash in disappointment. She had even put a calendar in the kitchen on their refrigerator to track her menstrual cycle, circling the dates and showing Cy the optimum time for them to try to get pregnant. She'd made him promise to be in town on those nights.

Noelle thought about the hundreds of hours she had

spent researching intrauterine insemination, in vitro fertilization, diets that could boost sperm count, and any other health supplements or sexual positions that could help them make a baby. And it all had been a waste. That entire time Cyrus had seen her wanting a baby and struggling to cling to hope, and he hadn't said a damn thing . . . not one single word that he'd had a vasectomy. He could have told her the truth and put her out of her misery. Instead, he made her look like a fool. He'd made her doubt that she was even mentally fit to become a mother, like *she* was the problem.

"How could you, Cy?" she whispered as warm tears spilled onto her cheeks again as she drove. How could he be so cruel?

Diamond had insisted that Cyrus had kept the truth from them to protect them. Even as she'd said those words, Noelle had raged on the inside, wanting to tell her that was complete and utter bullshit, but she'd held back because Diamond obviously was young and naïve, and Cyrus had taken advantage of that. Even though he had shown himself to be a user and a liar, Diamond still clung to the hope that he had her best intentions at heart. But Noelle knew the truth. She couldn't believe it, but she was siding with Vanessa on this one. Cyrus had lied to protect himself—and himself only. He'd done it with no care for the pain he'd inflict as a result. She couldn't think of any other reason why he would not tell her that he'd had a vasectomy and could never give her the baby she'd been trying so hard to have.

Noelle finally pulled to a stop on a side street, found a space, and parallel parked, hoping that she wouldn't get towed. Her left hand felt lighter as she rested it on the steering wheel now that her wedding ring was gone. She'd furiously ripped it off and tossed it to the car floor when she climbed inside and drove away from the restaurant.

She had no desire to search for the missing ring now. Instead, she looked around the residential neighborhood not far from Logan Circle, surprised that she'd made it here this quickly.

She had only been here twice before and Cyrus had been the one driving both times, but she remembered the address and directions from memory. She climbed out of her car and up the wrought iron steps leading to the D.C. townhouse.

She didn't know if Tariq was home. She probably should have called ahead of time, but the moment she'd left the restaurant, her thoughts went straight to him and her steering wheel had followed.

Noelle stared up at the house's red brick exterior and the pale wooden door. Lights shined bright on the inside behind the window curtains so perhaps he was home after all, but she couldn't be sure that he was alone.

What if he has a date in there? she wondered. Either way, she wanted to talk to him. Only he seemed capable of calming her mind, of talking her off this emotional ledge.

Noelle hesitated, took a deep breath, and rang the doorbell. A few seconds later, the front door opened. Tariq stood in the doorway in a white shirt and black slacks, like he'd just arrived home from work. He gazed at her quizzically.

"Hey, Noelle. What . . . what are you doing here?" he asked, frowning.

She sniffed. "Did I come at a bad time?"

He shook his head, still looking puzzled. "No, I just wasn't expecting you," he said, gesturing her inside. "Come in."

She stepped through the doorway and looked around her as he closed the front door behind her. His first floor was decorated in hues of gray and dark blues with African and modern art along the walls. It was understated yet sophisticated. It was an aesthetic she respected and appreciated—just like him.

"Uh, can I get you a drink or somethin'?" he asked, gesturing across the open floor plan to his stainless-steel kitchen.

She blinked back tears. "N-no, no thank you. I'm . . . I'm fine."

"If you're fine then why are your eyes so red? What happened?" he asked, and the sobs that she'd been holding back came out in one burst.

She fell into his arms and he wrapped them around her and held her close while she shook and cried with her head on his shoulder, feeling herself slowly become undone.

"What happened, Noelle?" he repeated with more urgency. "Shit! Just tell me what happened!"

She stepped back and looked at him. "I know now why I . . . why I couldn't get pregnant. Why it wasn't working. Cy knew he couldn't have kids, Tariq. He had a vasectomy and he didn't tell me! He had it *years* ago!"

"What?" His frown deepened. "How the hell did you find that out?"

She wiped her nose on the back of her hand. "Vanessa told me. We had dinner tonight. Me, her, and Diamond."

He dropped his arms from around her. "Wait. Wait! You had *dinner* with them?"

She nodded, deciding to confess everything. "I reached out to them. I set it up. I thought we could all talk to each other. That we could . . . we could share information about Cy."

She watched as Tariq closed his eyes, as the muscles along his jaw rippled. He stepped back from her and clenched his fists at his sides. "Damn it, Noelle, I told you not to tell anybody," he said slowly in an eerie whisper that almost scared her. "I told you how important it was to keep it between you and me."

"I know." She placed her hands on his chest. "I know . . . and . . . a-a-and I'm sorry but—"

"So why the fuck," he exploded, opening his eyes again and making her jump back in alarm, "would you go running to them? Do you understand what you just did? Do you get the situation you've put me in?"

"Yes! Yes, but I did it because I thought their lives might be at stake, too! Diamond was there when Cy was shot, Tariq. Vanessa has three little kids! I didn't want anything to happen to them! They won't tell the police what I told them. I said it had to stay between us!"

"Yeah, and I bet they'll keep their promise just like you kept yours," he said sullenly, making her flinch.

"If they tell the police, I'm the one at risk. Not you."

He closed his eyes again and loudly grumbled.

"It's true! I didn't tell them that you told me. I didn't say how I knew. I would never betray you like that. I just . . . I just didn't want anyone else to get hurt. I didn't want that on my conscience. I'm sorry." She took one hesitant step toward him then another. "Please forgive me, Tariq."

He didn't respond for a long time. Finally, he muttered, "I should've known better. I know how you are. It was my mistake, but what's done is done. We can't change anything now."

He knew how she was. He knew that she couldn't keep a secret to save her own life, that she couldn't be trusted with something this big. No wonder he hadn't told her the truth about Cy for so long. As soon as he did, she went running to his other wives to blab everything he had told her. But she had done it for a good reason. She swore she had.

"I disappointed you. I know I did." Noelle dropped her eyes to the floor and wrapped her arms around herself. "You have the right to be pissed at me. I deserve it."

"Let it go, Noelle," he muttered, turning away from her and walking across his living room.

"I let you down. You can say it! I can take it," she insisted. "I've already been beaten up pretty good tonight. You getting a few licks in isn't gonna make much of a—"

"Is that what you want?" he asked, whipping around to face her. His expression had gone hard again. "For me to be pissed at you? For me to hurt you and talk down to you like Cy does? Is that what you get off on?"

She blinked in astonishment. "N-n-no. That's not what I—"

"You want a man who dogs you out and cheats on you? Who makes you feel worthless and stupid? Is that why you stay with Cy?"

"No! No, that's not . . ." She fought to gain her footing, to find her words. "You know I didn't know the truth about Cy until just a few days ago! I never would have stood for it if I knew!"

"Oh, come on, Noelle!" He rolled his eyes. "You didn't know about the other women, but you knew he wasn't treating you right. You knew your marriage was falling apart. He never treated you like he respected you—and you still stayed. You never left!"

Noelle inhaled sharply, sucking in the nasty truth like it was medicine. Tariq was right. Even before she had met Vanessa in that Johns Hopkins waiting room, she had known her marriage was teetering on the brink. She and Cyrus had been fighting constantly and she could feel the distance growing between them. So why hadn't she challenged Cy or confronted him? Why had she kept stalking off or walking away instead of saying what she wanted, what she needed from him? Why hadn't she given him an ultimatum?

Because I knew it would be the end of my marriage, she admitted to herself.

She knew she'd probably have to walk away from Cyrus, and she didn't think she had to strength to do it. Life with Cy wasn't perfect, but life without him was a scary prospect.

Noelle had transitioned from abandoned daughter of a junkie to runway model and then Cyrus's wife. It was the new persona she had assumed, and it was easy to do it with him financing her shop, Azure, and her life. Noelle had gotten comfortable with being Mrs. Cyrus Grey, so comfortable that she was loath to leave that role behind.

She wasn't as delusional as Diamond or as jaded as Vanessa, but she wasn't as far from either woman's mind-set as she'd thought. All this time, she had been lying to herself.

"Even last night, you pushed me away," Tariq continued. "For what? Vows to a man you're not even really married to? For someone who has two other wives on the side?" He strolled back toward her, staring unflinchingly into her eyes. "You deserve *so* much better, Noelle. I wish you could see that. I wish you would let him go and take a chance with someone who could treat you the way you should be treated."

Noelle considered his words and his offer. She drew up her courage and slowly unwrapped her arms from around herself. Her heart was pounding so hard she swore she could hear it reverberating in her ears. She stepped forward, wrapped her arms around Tariq, and raised her lips to his. He didn't hesitate before kissing her back.

She couldn't believe it, but the kiss had more fervor than the one they had shared last night. Their tongues still dove into one another's mouths. They were still panting and clinging to one another, but Noelle felt like some imaginary flood gates had opened this time. A tide of emotions mixed with longing and desire came rushing out, and, instead of fighting it, she allowed herself to be swept under.

She began to unbutton his shirt and let him tug off the

sleeve of her one-shouldered top, revealing the strapless bra underneath. She reached for his belt and pants zipper and she could feel him pulling her skirt up her thighs and hips. He eased her toward the stairs like he was trying to guide her to his bedroom. They climbed halfway up the staircase, but she could tell they weren't going to make it. They soon became a mass of tangled limbs and uneven steps. The passion was too overwhelming and too strong. They fell back onto the stairs, landing with an audible *oomph*. But even the abrasive feel of the wood grain and floor rug against their backs, shoulders, and bottoms didn't stop them.

Their lips never parted, not even when Tariq unclasped her bra and fondled her breasts, making her moan into his mouth. He kept kissing her, even as he slipped his hand between her legs and rubbed her at her center, making her moans even louder. He only pulled his mouth away when he yanked her thong down her hips and past her thighs, leaving them crumpled on the bottom stair.

What Tariq had previously toyed with through the lace of her underwear, he now touched freely, rubbing her there and making her quiver all over. Her moans quickly switched to whimpers. Noelle spread her legs and started to move against his hand. He slid two fingers inside her, and she began to rock her hips against him, sucking his tongue as she did it. Tariq pulled his hand away and hiked up one of her legs, hooking it around his waist. He tugged down his pants and boxer briefs and centered himself between her thighs again.

She wanted to tell him they should pause to put on a condom. She wasn't on the pill. She hadn't been on anything in more than a year, but she didn't get the chance to tell him anything. He plunged forward and inside her, making her cry out. He did it again and again, increasing the tempo, bracing himself by gripping onto the stairs. She bucked her hips as he drove inside her. Stopping was no longer an option in her mind. Noelle wanted to enjoy the moment for all its worth.

Noelle stared into his eyes, hearing the blood whistle in her ears and her heart thunder in her chest. He gazed right back at her. It was like he was daring her to look away and break the connection, but she didn't. She held on tight until the orgasm hit. That's when she finally allowed herself to close her eyes. She gripped his back as the spasms rocked her body, making her muscles contract and unfurl, making her cry out in agony and bliss. When she opened her eyes again, she could see he was still staring down at her, except this time he was smiling.

"Oww, that hurts," Noelle whispered with a wince an hour later. She shifted on Tariq's bed, changing positions on his chest to get more comfortable.

"Yeah, you got a little bruise sprouting there," Tariq said, lightly touching the tender spot on her shoulder before leaning down and giving it a quick peck. "I was wondering if it was a good idea to get down and dirty on the stairs. I figured we'd pay the price later."

"It was worth it though," she said with a laugh before raising her mouth back to his for another kiss. He happily obliged her.

After they made love on the stairs, they shifted the festivities to his bedroom. Noelle didn't know where all their fervor had come from, but she was more than happy to enjoy herself. She felt almost drunk or high, basking in all the attention and affection that Tariq had to offer. And unlike what she'd gotten from Cyrus, it wasn't some pretense used to win her over. Tariq cared enough to be honest with her. He made her feel wanted and worthy, which she hadn't felt for quite some time. When she'd arrived at his home tonight, she had been terrified of becoming undone, of no longer being the woman she thought she was. Now she relished it.

Noelle trailed her fingers along his skin, pleasantly surprised to find tattoos that started along his arms and snaked their way across his shoulders, chest, and back. So, this was what had been hidden under his dress shirts and suits all this time. It was a tapestry of colors and designs, an elaborate map she longed to decipher.

"How many tattoos do you have anyway?" she asked, squinting down at a Jamaican flag just above his left pec.

"I don't know." He reclined back against a stack of pillows. "I lost count years ago. Somewhere between a dozen and maybe twenty."

"*Twenty?*" she repeated with widened eyes. She trailed her finger over the name, Tanisha, stenciled in cursive on his left arm. "Who was she?" she asked, cocking an eyebrow.

"Tanisha Stanton. The first girl I ever fell hard for. I loved her like crazy, but she left me for some dude who went to North Carolina State. She was my girl for less than a year, but this damn tattoo will be on my arm forever," he said wryly.

"Why not just get it removed?"

He laughed, making his chest shake underneath her and vibrate against her rib cage. "I keep it as a reminder not to do stupid shit ever again, especially stupid shit for a woman."

"Did the reminder work? Have you kept that promise?"

He let his eyes travel over her face. "No, unfortunately."

She trailed her finger over another tattoo. This time of a growling panther, then a buxom woman posing in the semi-nude. Her finger then landed on a number. A black number nine in gothic lettering, no bigger than her thumb, that was tattooed right over his heart. "What's this one? Is it for a team you were on?"

Tariq seemed to hesitate before he answered. "Nah, that's not any team. That's one of my oldest tattoos though. One of my firsts. I got it in my old neighborhood. Everyone in my crew had one."

"*Your crew?*" She traced the number with the tip of her nail. "You mean like your boys in your neighborhood?"

"Yeah, somethin' like that," he said, tugging her hand away and raising it to his lips so he could kiss the knuckles. He then kissed the inside of her wrist, forearm, and shoulder, making her giggle and then moan at the sensation of his lips against her bare skin. "Now if you're finished your examination, Dr. Noelle, I'd like to get back to what we were doin' a little while ago. If you don't mind?"

"Would you now?"

"Yeah, I would," he murmured before easing her onto her back and lowering his mouth to hers.

Noelle couldn't help but oblige.

Friday

Chapter 22

Vanessa

Vanessa awoke to the screeching of her alarm clock. She reached blindly for her night table, feeling her way through the dark before slapping the button on top of her clock, over and over again until the alarm finally went silent. She raised her head from her pillow and winced at the pounding along her temples.

"Damn! How much did I have to drink last night?" she croaked, pushing herself up to her elbows.

Obviously, she'd had too much. That would explain why she was now experiencing a hangover, something she hadn't had in *years*.

She struggled to remember how she had gotten home and into her bed at all.

Oh, yeah, she thought, flashing back to last night. *I remember now.*

Bilal had driven her home after they'd left the restaurant not too long after Noelle had walked out on her and Diamond in a huff. Vanessa wasn't fond of Noelle, but she disliked Diamond even more, and having to sit alone with her across a dining table in a crowded restaurant was the very last thing she'd wanted to do. Once Noelle made her exit, it made no sense for her stay. She'd arrived back at house draped on Bilal's shoulder.

"Are you drunk?" her mother, Carol, had asked with an unmasked hint of revulsion and dismay.

"No!" Vanessa had insisted while shaking her head. She tried to stand upright to prove she was sober but didn't succeed. Bilal had to hold her around the waist to keep her from stumbling forward and landing face first on her foyer's hardwood floor.

Carol had loudly groused. "Thank you for bringing her home, young man. I'll take it from here. Come inside, Vanessa," her mother had ordered before reaching out and yanking her through the doorway.

She'd then guided her upstairs, carrying her and shoving her along the way.

"Are you out of your damn mind? You're lucky that your children and most of your neighbors are asleep and can't see you like this! A married mother of three standing at the door with her shoulder straps coming off, hanging all over that boy like some . . . some *broke down hooker!*" she'd hissed into Vanessa's ear, before opening Vanessa's bedroom door and letting her stagger across the room and collapse onto her bed.

"Get it together, Nessa!" she'd bellowed, pointing her finger at her. "Stop being so careless and goddamn stupid! Do you hear me? You've got a lot a stake and you have no time whatsoever for this foolishness!"

Of course, Vanessa knew there was a lot at stake. Her mother didn't have to tell her that. That's why she had gone to the restaurant in the first place though she still wasn't sure if it had been worth it. Thanks to what Noelle had told them, she had yet another theory on who could have been behind Cyrus's shooting and it conflicted entirely with what the cops had told her. It seemed that she was farther away, not closer, to figuring out who had done it.

Vanessa had mumbled those very words to her mother, but the reply was slurred and unintelligible thanks to her face being buried in her pillow.

"I'm going home," her mother had called to her. "I've had enough of your bullshit for one night, little girl," she'd said before slamming the bedroom door shut.

Vanessa had closed her eyes and fallen asleep soon after.

She now staggered to her feet again toward her master bath. She had about thirty minutes to pull herself together—to take a few aspirin, a quick shower, and change her clothes—before she had to wake up Cy Jr., Bryson, and Zoe, and make them breakfast. Hungover or not, she still had to get her children dressed, fed, out the door, and to school today.

An hour later, Vanessa stood bleary-eyed at her kitchen counter, drinking a cup of French roast coffee and listening to the SpongeBob SquarePants soundtrack on television as Bryson and Zoe argued over who got to keep the prize they found in the cereal box.

"Guys, *please* stop fighting," she said, closing her eyes.

The pounding along her temples hadn't eased yet, even with aspirin. Instead, it now seemed to match the annoying, nursery-rhyme-like syncopation of the music filling her kitchen.

"Can we not start the day like this for once?" she begged.

"But I found it first!" Bryson shouted back, ignoring her request. "She took it, Mommy!"

"No, *I* found it first!" Zoe countered, grabbing for his hand. Her voice was high-pitched and pleading; it made Vanessa's headache ten times worse. "And it's a unicorn. You don't even like unicorns! You just want it because I want it! It's mine!"

"*No, it's mine!*" Vanessa yelled, striding around the kitchen table and yanking it out of both their outstretched hands, making them groan. "Since you two can't figure out how to share it, Mommy will keep it!" She then shoved the toy into the pocket of her jeans.

"Mom, are you okay?" Cy Jr. asked, lowering his tablet.

"No, honey, Mommy is *not* okay. I'm not feeling well today so I would appreciate if you guys would give me a break. No yelling and *no fighting.*"

Just then, the kitchen phone rang, making her wince at the sound and reach for her temples again. She walked back to granite counter, grabbed the cordless phone, and raised it to her ear.

"Hello?" she said.

Someone answered on the other end, but she couldn't hear what the person was saying over SpongeBob and Squidward's dialogue.

"Junior, turn the TV down please," she called to her eldest. When he did, she returned her attention to the phone.

"Yes, hello? I'm sorry I didn't hear you. Who is this?" she asked again before taking another sip of coffee.

"This is Dr. Lewis Chang at Johns Hopkins Hospital. Is this Mrs. Grey . . . Mrs. Vanessa Grey?"

Vanessa halted. She lowered her coffee cup from her mouth to the counter. "Y-yes, this is sh-she," she stuttered.

She hadn't expected to hear from Cyrus's doctor, especially after what had happened in the hospital waiting room Monday. If he was calling her now . . . if he'd tracked her down, it had to be for an important reason.

Had Cyrus finally succumbed to his wounds and died? Was that it?

Oh, my God! Cy is dead. I'm a widow, she thought, letting the realization sink in.

This is what she'd secretly wanted all along, but it was one thing to play with the idea, and another to face the reality of it.

I'm a widow, she thought again.

And she was likely a very rich widow, but her children would be devastated by their father's passing. There would be lots of crying and lots of consoling. But she would help them through it. She would be a rock for her family and rebuild their lives and, ultimately, they would be happier without all the chaos that came with Cyrus Grey.

"Uh, we've met before, I believe," Dr. Chang continued. "You came in the hospital when your husband was shot to check on his condition. I'm sorry I turned you away at the time, but the situation was quite—"

"Yes, I remember. You told me you couldn't let me see my husband. But what's happened now? Is he still alive?" she asked, holding her breath in bated anticipation of his answer.

The children were listening to her conversation now. Cy Jr. rose from his chair.

"Is Dad okay?" he asked. "Can we go and see him, Mom? Is he—"

"Shhh!" she said, holding her finger over her lips. "I'm trying to hear, Junior!"

"Yes, Mrs. Grey," Dr. Chang replied. "Your husband is very much alive. He's also awake now."

Vanessa gaped. She almost dropped the phone.

"He . . . he's awake?"

"Yes, Mr. Grey emerged from his coma last night," Dr. Chang continued. "He's talking now, and he's asked to see you."

"Just . . . just *me?*"

"Yes. Will you be coming down?"

She cleared her throat. "Yes. Yes, I'll be there."

* * *

Vanessa walked down the hospital corridor, blinking rapidly and trying to calm her racing heart. She'd dropped off the children at school before she'd driven straight to the hospital. The kids were full of questions—none of which she could answer. She just knew that their father was alive, talking, and, more importantly, had asked for her to come to the hospital out of all three of his wives. The latter had surprised her. Why had he asked her to come rather than Noelle or Diamond?

I guess I should be honored, she thought dryly as she now continued to his hospital room.

But she wasn't. Instead, she was a giant ball of anxiety, a simmering pot of anger, confusion, and frustration.

What would she say when she finally saw her husband? Would she break down into tears and sobs? Would she start yelling at him, hurling accusations and asking for answers? She honestly didn't know. Her brain couldn't process anything right now.

Vanessa reached the end of the hall and checked the number plaque along the door. She took a deep breath and stepped inside.

She found Cyrus sitting upright slightly in his hospital bed. A nurse stood at his side, adjusting the pillows behind him. The tall, strong John Henry-type she knew as her husband now looked wan and weary. He must have lost at least ten to fifteen pounds even in this short time. Cy's normally rich dark skin looked ashen against the stark white of his hospital gown. Bags were under his eyes. His beard was gone, and the first stubbles of hair had started to appear on his bald head. When she entered the room, Cyrus turned slightly to look at her.

This was her husband of more than a decade. The father of her children. The last time she had seen him, he was joking with Cy Jr. at their kitchen table over a plate of eggs and bacon. She'd never imagined when he'd walked out their front door Monday morning all that would happen after, but here they were, seemingly lightyears from that moment.

When Vanessa had heard he was shot, she'd braced herself for the possibility that her husband would die and had even started eagerly looking forward to it, but here he sat, very much alive. A wave of emotions overwhelmed her, making her eyes flood with tears.

"Hey, baby," he called hoarsely to her.

She took one hesitant step to his hospital bed, then another, crying as she did it.

"It's all right, Nessa. It's okay." He raised his hand, holding it out to her like he wanted to comfort her. "I'm okay now."

She stared at his outstretched hand for several seconds like it was an alien object. She then looked up at his face. Instead of taking his hand into her own, she batted it away, catching him and the nurse by surprise.

"Don't you touch me. Don't you ever fuckin' touch me again, you son of a bitch! *Three wives?* You have three fuckin' wives, you cheatin', lyin' motherfucka!" She then started swinging, slapping and punching his face, back, and shoulder, making him shout out and hold up his arms to protect himself. "You've been lying to me all this goddamn time!"

"Nessa, calm down!" he said, grabbing one of her wrists.

"Don't you tell me to calm down! Don't you tell me to fuckin' calm down, you son of a bitch!"

"Ma'am! Ma'am! You cannot assault the patient!" the nurse yelled, racing around the bed to pull her back. "Security! Help!"

Chapter 23

Noelle

Noelle opened her eyes, rolled onto her back, and grinned. She'd dozed blissfully last night, tumbling into a heavy sleep that wasn't filled with tossing and turning for once. In fact, she'd barely moved at all. She could chalk up such a serene slumber to Tariq's comfortable mattress. But she knew all that sexual healing she'd had before she'd closed her eyes and nestled in his arms for most of the night, had certainly helped her along.

She sat up and stretched, hoping to get a morning cuddle from Tariq before she climbed into the shower, only to find him sitting on his leather foot stool at the end of his bed, putting on his shoes.

She frowned. "You're already dressed?"

He stood and adjusted his necktie. "Yeah, it's almost nine. We slept in late, but I figured I had to head into work at some point."

"*What?* How is it nine o'clock?" she cried, adjusting the bedsheets over her breasts and turning to stare at his alarm clock.

Tariq was right. The black digital numbers said it was 8:52. She had no idea she'd slept that long.

"Why didn't you wake me?"

He laughed. "Because you looked so peaceful. Hell, you were snoring! I didn't want to bother you." He grabbed his suit jacket that he'd tossed across the end of the bed. He now shrugged into it. "Don't worry! You can stay as long as you like. There's no rush."

Noelle's frown deepened. She wished he had bothered her and woken her up. She hadn't wanted their morning after to be like this—him walking out the door while she was just rising out of bed, then her doing the walk of shame *alone* to her parked car. She'd thought they'd have more time together to talk and explore all the things they'd started to discuss last night. Tariq had told her that he cared for her, that he could be a better man for her than Cyrus could. But maybe in the light of day, he'd had second thoughts about those proclamations. Maybe he hadn't meant any of it at all.

Tariq noticed her expression. "What? What's wrong?"

"Nothing," she whispered, lowering her eyes and shaking her head. She tucked a lock of hair behind her ear.

He sat on the edge of the bed, scanning her face. "Noelle, come on. We are well past the guessing games. Just tell me what's up. What's wrong?"

"Last night wasn't . . . it wasn't a casual thing for you, was it?"

"*A casual thing?* You mean like a smash and dash?"

She grimaced. Noelle usually appreciated his bluntness and humor, but not today. "Look, if it was, that's fine! I just . . . I just want you to be honest with me. We're adults so if this is just—"

"No, it wasn't a casual thing. Everything I said to you, I meant. I wasn't just trying to get a piece of ass, if that's what you're worried about," he assured before cupping her face and giving her a kiss. His pressed his forehead against hers and gazed into her eyes and within seconds she got lost in them—two chocolate pools that she wanted to dog paddle in all day. "I just have to go to work. That's all. But as far as I'm concerned, we're resuming where we left off, ASAP. We can get back together this evening, if you want."

She beamed. "I'd like that."

"Good," he said before giving her another peck and rising from the bed. "So tonight it is. I'll meet you at your place at eight."

She watched as he walked to his bedroom door. "Make yourself comfortable. There's food in the fridge and the kitchen cabinets. The remote is on the dresser. Just lock the door behind you when you leave." He stepped into the hall, then leaned his head back through the doorway a few seconds later. "Oh, and don't steal nothin'. I'll be able to tell if any of my stuff is missing," he deadpanned.

Noelle gaped then laughed. She picked up one of his pillows and threw it at him. It landed at his feet. "Go!" she shouted before he disappeared back into the hall.

She heard his footfalls on the stairs and then the front door slam shut behind him less than a minute later.

Noelle emerged from Tariq's bathroom, refreshed from a steaming hot shower. She tightened one of his towels around her and gazed around his bedroom, searching for her clothes. He had been nice enough to leave them in a neat pile on his footstool with her shoes underneath it. She sifted through the pile and noticed that the only thing missing was her underwear. Noelle searched the bedroom, stairs, and his living room floor for the misplaced thong. She scanned his bedroom a second time, accepting defeat.

She could go commando, if necessary, but she preferred not to. Finally, she texted Tariq.

NOELLE: Umm, this is awkward but can't find my undies. Do you remember where I left them?

About a minute later, he replied.

TARIQ: You left them at the bottom of the stairs, but they're in my pocket now

NOELLE: Funny. Seriously, do you know where I left them?

TARIQ: I'm serious!

NOELLE: Sure you are

He then sent her a picture of her crumpled lace thong lying on what looked like his office desk next to a pile of file folders.

TARIQ: Holding onto them for ransom. I'll give them back to you tonight

Seeing his words and the picture, she burst into laughter.

NOELLE: You really stole my underwear! You play too much. You know that?

Within seconds, Tariq sent her a winking emoji in reply.

Noelle lowered her phone, still laughing. She could be annoyed that he had stolen her thong and was carrying it around like some horny fourteen-year-old boy, but the truth was it was fun to be flirtatious and silly with Tariq. She hadn't indulged in this type of playfulness in quite some time. He brought out that side in her.

She dressed and strolled downstairs a few minutes later and bee-lined to his kitchen.

It was neat to the point of being almost immaculate. All the stainless-steel appliances gleamed. Not even a fingerprint marred their reflective surfaces. No food stains or crumbs were on his black granite countertops, even the dark wooden cabinets looked perfect, like they had just come off a furniture show floor. She wondered if Tariq had a house cleaner or if he was really this fastidious about keeping his place neat. She hesitated, loath to touch anything and mess it up, but then she remembered this was the same man who'd made love to her on his stairs, who had told her to make herself at home. Maybe he wouldn't mind her leaving behind a few smudges.

Noelle dialed Azure as she opened his fridge and scanned the shelves for something quick she could eat. Miranda picked up right away.

"Hello, this is Azure boutique. How may we help you?" she answered.

"Miranda, it's me, Noelle."

"Noelle! Hey, how are you? Running late?"

"Yeah," Noelle said, frowning down at the label of a container of cream cheese Tariq had in his refrigerator door. "I just wanted to update you in case you're wondering why I'm MIA. I should get there by eleven o'clock at the latest."

"Oh, no worries! Like I said before, take all the time you need. I know this must be a hard time for you. I think it's amazing that you keep coming into the shop every day. I don't know if I would be able to if I was going through what you are!"

"Actually, I'm doing okay today," she said, as she closed the fridge and shifted her attention to the kitchen cabinets. She opened one and quickly found a box of Cheerios on one of the shelves.

"*Really?*"

"Yeah, really." Noelle thought back to last night and lying in bed with Tariq. "I'm feeling better today than I have all week."

"You *do* sound better! A lot lighter. Did you get good news about Cyrus from the hospital? Is that why you feel better?" Miranda asked.

Noelle blinked as she removed the box of cereal and sat it on the counter. She hadn't thought once about her husband all morning. "Oh, uh . . . no. No word so far. I guess I'm just . . . well . . . coming to terms with everything. Maybe that's why I feel better."

"That's good either way! I'm sure Cy wouldn't want you sick with worry."

Noelle wasn't convinced that Cyrus cared one way or the other about her, but she'd resolved that he wasn't her concern anymore. Vanessa insisted she was his first and only wife and Diamond still seemed solidly in his corner. They could fight over him if they wanted. She wanted no part of a war over a man who obviously didn't love her.

Or at least Cy didn't love her the way she should be loved, Tariq would argue. But maybe she had finally found someone who could do that.

"Look, I have a few things I have to do before I head over there so—"

"Say no more!" Miranda practically sang. "I'll hold down the fort until you get here."

"Thanks, Miranda. See you soon!" Noelle then hung up and opened another cabinet, in search of a bowl.

She was sitting on a stool at Tariq's kitchen island ten minutes later, eating a bowl of Cheerios and watching *Good Morning America*, which was playing on the flat screen television in the living room, when she heard Tariq's doorbell ring. Noelle paused mid-chew and lowered her spoon from her mouth. The doorbell rang a second time and then she heard a loud pounding. The person was knocking now.

"Yo, Tariq? You in?" she heard a muffled voice call out. "I can hear the TV on. I know you home, nigga! Open up!"

Now the person started knocking and ringing simultaneously.

All this noise wasn't doing much for her tranquil morning. *Maybe if I answer and tell them he's not here, they'll just go away*, she thought.

Noelle rose from her stool, adjusted her pencil skirt, and walked across the kitchen and into Tariq's living room. She stared through the front door's peephole and saw a man standing on Tariq's stoop. The visitor was wiry thin, light-skinned, and wore cornrows. Tattoos were on his right cheek and a woman's red lips were tattooed along his neck. He wore a white tank top, revealing tattoos along his arms too. The man raised his fist to pound on the door again.

She hesitated only a few seconds before opening the front door.

"Answer the door, ni—" His words trailed off and he stepped back and stared at her in surprise.

"Hi," she said, leaning against the door frame. "Can I help you?"

"Nah, umm . . . where's Tariq?" he said, staring over her shoulder like he was trying to get a glimpse into the house to see if Tariq was hiding in there.

"Sorry, he isn't home. He left for work about forty minutes ago. I can tell him that you stopped by though, Mr. . . . uh . . ."

"No mister. The names Big El," he volunteered. "Tell 'em Big El came by. He'll know who I am."

She nodded, though she wondered how Tariq knew this guy. He certainly didn't seem like he'd be a friend of Tariq's, but maybe he was. Maybe Big El was an acquaintance from his old neighborhood back in the day.

"I'll definitely tell him." Noelle began to close the front door but stopped when Big El raised his hand and held the door open, catching her off guard.

"And tell him he still gotta pay me in full. All right?" He pointed at her and bore his dark eyes into her as he said it. "Just because he didn't get all that he asked for, doesn't mean he can't pay me what he owe me! I still put time in for that shit. I deserve my money."

Noelle gradually nodded again though she had no idea what this guy was talking about. She thought he was an old friend, but perhaps he was a contractor that Tariq had hired. She knew from experience that they weren't always easy to work with. This one in particular didn't seem to be the professional type.

"Sure, I'll . . . I'll let him know. Does he have a way to contact you? Did you want to leave a card or . . . something?"

"*A card?*" Big El laughed. "Nah, I ain't got no card, baby. But he knows how to reach me."

Big El finally lowered his hand from the door. As he did, she saw that he had a gothic-style nine tattooed on the inside of his forearm—the same tattoo that was on Tariq's chest. It caught her by surprise.

"Just tell him to call me so I ain't gotta come lookin' for him again," he said before turning around and jogging down the stairs, his footfalls ringing off the metal like horse hooves.

She watched as he strolled along the sidewalk then disappeared around the corner at the end of the block. It wasn't until then that Noelle closed Tariq's door, now plagued with a pesky sense of unease.

Chapter 24

Diamond

Diamond was putting away the last of the dishes from her dishwasher into her overhead cabinets when her cell phone began to buzz. She reached for where it sat on the kitchen counter and raised it to her ear.

"Hello?" she said after pressing the green button to answer.

"Uh, hi, Mrs. Grey. It's . . . it's . . . uh . . . Richard down at the front desk."

She tiredly closed the dishwasher door. "Hey, Richard," she said distractedly. "What's up?"

"Well, ma'am, you have some people down here who say they know you. They're asking to come upstairs." He dropped is voice to a whisper. "I remember the incident that happened earlier this week, so I'm not letting anyone up there that you don't okay."

Diamond's brows furrowed as she wondered who could possibly be visiting her at ten o'clock in the morning. No one she had been expecting—that was for sure.

She'd decided to spend the few coveted hours before

she had to leave for work today at home alone. She was recovering from last night's dinner. It had only been two and half hours, but the ordeal had left her emotionally exhausted, especially having to endure the company of Cyrus's other wife, Vanessa—a woman she would be perfectly happy to never see again. Diamond was in no mood to deal with any surprises today.

"Did they say who they are? Did they give you their names?" she asked Richard.

"Uh, the woman's name is Honey, I believe, but the gentleman refuses to give me his name."

Diamond winced. Richard didn't have to get the gentleman's name. She knew instantly that the guy with Honey had to be Julian. Honey must have driven him here, though Diamond wasn't sure why. If he was only allowed a pass out of The Men's Village for an hour a day, there was no way he would make it back from Baltimore to D.C. in enough time.

"Do you want me to send them up, Mrs. Grey?" Richard asked.

Diamond could only imagine Julian gazing around her condominium's luxurious lobby and calculating in his head how many new gold chains or watches she could afford to buy him. Nope. She didn't want to deal with his bullshit today.

"No, Richard. I don't want any visitors and I don't know who they are."

"Okay, Mrs. Grey. No problem. I'll tell them that."

Richard hung up soon after and Diamond loudly exhaled. Honey and Julian would just have to make the drive back to D.C. If they drove fast enough, maybe he could get back in enough time to meet his curfew.

I'm doing him a favor, she thought.

She'd just set down her phone and turned away from

the counter to start another housekeeping task when her phone started to buzz again. She glanced at the screen and saw it was Richard calling back.

"Yes?" she asked irritably after picking up.

"I told him they can't come up, but this guy insists that he speak with you, ma'am. He said it's important," Richard said.

Diamond loudly sighed. "Put him on."

She heard muffled voices in the background then Julian's laugh. "Hey, girl, what's up?"

"You're not coming upstairs, Julian."

"Don't be like that! We came all this way to visit you. You know, to see how you're doin'. You can't let us up to have tea and crackers or some shit? Whatever you rich people do!"

"Why are you here?" she asked tightly as she started to pace, making her bare feet slap against the kitchen tile. "You didn't come here to check on me or for tea and crackers. And I'm not buying you anything else! I told you that already."

"I can't stay at that halfway house no more," Julian explained. "Don't like all those damn rules. And they trying to make me get a full-time job and shit. Talkin' about how I should apply to Walmart or Burger King. I don't have time for that! So I bounced outta there. Honey and I are going away to start up the business again, but we need a place to stay for a hot minute. Maybe a day or two. We thought we could stay with you."

"Hell no! This isn't a hotel, Julian. And besides, you're violating parole. I don't want anything to do with that shit! Tell Honey I said good luck to her wherever you two decide to go, but you can't stay here. It's not an option. I'm sorry."

She was about to hang up when she heard him say. "Oh, it better be an option! Because I'll tell this dude right here and every one of your neighbors who walks through that door, how I know you. I'll tell them how you used to make your money, College Girl."

Diamond stopped pacing.

"I still got a couple pictures too from the old days in my phone. I bet this dude would love to see a couple of 'em. Show him all the stuff you used to be famous for."

Diamond closed her eyes and fought back the scream that threatened to rise out of her throat. She thought she'd hated Julian before, but she hated him even more now.

"So can we come up or what?" Julian persisted. "Or should I show him the pics? You tell me."

"Yeah," she said reluctantly, not knowing what other choice she had, "you can come up."

Diamond heard the knock at her front door less than five minutes later. She took several calming breaths before opening it, trying to get her rage under control but only moderately succeeding. When she opened it, she found Julian and Honey standing in her hallway.

Honey's blond head was bowed. She looked contrite. She also looked tired thanks to the twenty-pound bags under her eyes. The T-shirt and purple gym shorts she wore were so wrinkled, she looked like she might have slept in them. In contrast, Julian was grinning like a Jack-o-Lantern. He seemed wide awake and buoyant. He strode past Diamond and looked around him, spinning in a circle as he took in the spacious condo and her expensive furniture.

"Movin' on up to the Eastside!" he sang with a laugh and a little dance worthy of George Jefferson before returning his gaze to Diamond. "Goddamn, girl! Never thought you'd be here when you were sleeping on a mattress on the floor back at our place four years ago, did you? But you ballin' now! How much this joint set your man back?"

Diamond didn't answer him. Instead, she motioned for Honey to step inside too so that she could close the front door behind her.

"Sorry, Diamond. He ain't tell me we were coming here when I picked him up," Honey whispered.

Diamond turned to find Julian on the other side of her living room, standing in front of the floor-to-ceiling windows, gazing at the panoramic views of the Inner Harbor and the Chesapeake Bay.

"He's gonna get in serious trouble for not going back to that halfway house. You know that don't you?" Diamond asked, turning back to her. "You could get in trouble too. We *both* could. Aiding and abetting is a crime, Honey."

"But we're not gonna get caught. We ain't stayin' long," Honey argued. "I told him we can't. We gotta get out of town . . . outta this state. We were talking about heading to Jersey or New York. Just let us stay here for today, Diamond, and then we're gone. The cops won't even know we were here."

"You don't know that! I can't go to jail for him. I almost did the last time. I lied for him before. I'm not doin' that shit again!"

"Just give us one day. One day, Diamond! Please," Honey begged.

"Hey! What y'all whisperin' about?" Julian called to them.

"Nothin', baby," Honey lied. "I was just tellin' Diamond how pretty her place is. Looks like one of those furniture magazines."

"Well, bring your ass over here and look at this shit," he said, waving her toward him and pointing into the distance. "You can see the cruise ships and yachts and everything, baby!"

Diamond watched the couple as they stood at her window, set against the backdrop of the blue sky, gazing at the view. She'd meant what she said when she told Honey that she wasn't going to lie for Julian again. He wasn't her man anymore. And she'd be damned if she went down for him.

"What you got to eat around here?" Julian asked, stepping away from the window. "I'm hungry!"

An hour later, Honey and Julian sat at her dining room table, enjoying a smorgasbord of food. They had raided her fridge and cabinets and assembled it all between themselves as they sat on opposite sides of the table. The food included opened boxes of cereal that they ate with their hands, leftover Thai takeout, slices of cheese and deli meat, croissants, a bag of tortilla chips, and a container of cookies and fudge ice cream. Julian and Honey both ate like they had not only skipped breakfast, but maybe yesterday's dinner and lunch as well—making her wonder just how good they both were doing before they even got here. Maybe Honey wasn't making as much paper as she claimed. As they chowed down, Diamond began to back out of the room.

"I have to use the bathroom," she said. "I'll be back, guys."

When she entered her master bath, she closed the door behind her and pulled out her cell phone that she'd hidden in her pocket. She quickly looked up the number to Julian's halfway house and began to dial it.

Julian would be furious at her for doing this and Honey would probably hate her for it as well, but she wasn't going to jail for Julian. Maybe Honey would thank her later when he had disappeared yet again behind prison walls and could no longer exert his influence over her. Maybe she wouldn't. It didn't matter either way. Diamond had to do this for her own sake.

"Hello, Men's Village," a woman's voice answered between pops of gum.

"Uh, hey . . . hello," Diamond whispered anxiously into

her phone, all the while staring at her closed bathroom door, "umm, you have a parolee missing right. A Julian Mason. He hasn't been there since yesterday, correct? He didn't check in for curfew?"

"Who is this?" the woman asked suspiciously.

"It doesn't matter who I am. You don't need to know that, but I can tell you where Julian is now if you're looking for him . . . if you guys want to come and get him."

There was a pause on the other end of the line before the woman answered, "Let me get my supervisor on the phone. I ain't the person you should be talking to."

As Diamond waited on hold, she could hear through the door Julian and Honey laughing and talking.

Good, she thought. She didn't want them to wonder why she hadn't come back yet.

"Hello," a man's gruff voice suddenly erupted over her cell, "I'm Executive Director Eric Keating. My assistant tells me you think you know where our client Julian Mason is."

"I don't *think* I know where he is. He's at my dining room table right now, stuffing his face. We're in Baltimore. He'll be here all day so you can send someone to pick him up."

She gave the executive director her address.

"We'll alert police of Mr. Mason's whereabouts. Who do I tell them to make contact with when they arrive though?"

Diamond groused. She really didn't want to use her name, but she guessed she had to at this point. "Diamond . . . Diamond Grey."

"Gotcha', Miss Grey. In the meantime, act normal. Don't alert Julian to our conversation."

"Trust me. I won't," she mumbled.

"Hey, Diamond, you in here?" she heard Honey call out.

"Shit," Diamond cursed under her breath.

"Is anything wrong, Miss Grey? Do you feel unsafe? Do you need to get out of there?"

She didn't answer him. Instead, she hung up, shoved her phone back into her pocket, and leaned over to flush the toilet. She pretended to wash her hands and opened the bathroom door, only to find Honey standing at her dresser, putting on a pair of Diamond's gold hoop earrings as she stared into the mirror. She turned her head back and forth, admiring her reflection.

"Find anything you like?" Diamond asked.

"Oh, shit! I ain't know you were standing there, girl! Just seeing how they looked," Honey said, quickly taking off Diamond's earrings and putting them back into her jewelry box. "We were wonderin' what was up with you. We can't figure out how to turn on your cable box and was calling for you. You didn't answer us. Guess you were on the toilet with a case of the bubble guts, huh?"

"Yeah, I feel better now though."

"You sure?"

"Yeah, I'm sure. Why?"

"Because you still look kinda funny," Honey said, eyeing her.

"Yo! I figured it out! We in business, baby!" Julian shouted from the living room as explosions from what Diamond presumed to be an action film ricocheted down the hall.

"I guess he figured out how to turn on the cable. I better go tell him to turn it down though before my neighbors complain."

She then walked around Honey and out the bedroom, grateful for the means of escape.

Chapter 25

Vanessa

"Now listen to me, and listen very carefully, Mrs. Grey," Dr. Chang began in a slow, grave voice.

They were standing in the hospital corridor. Vanessa was leaning defiantly against the wall with her arms crossed over her chest. Dr. Chang stood in front of her flanked on one side by the head nurse of the unit—a sour-faced, no-nonsense looking white woman—and on the other side by a towering security guard with a buzz cut and big arms. All three were looking at her like she was an escaped mental patient from a psych ward who they were prepared to put in a strait jacket if she so much as sneezed, but Vanessa didn't care.

She had tried to beat the hell out of her husband about an hour ago while he sat in a hospital bed, while he was hooked up to an IV. Left with a choice, she'd probably do it all over again. She hadn't expected her reaction to seeing him after everything had happened would be so volatile, but what had he thought she would do? Give him a hug?

"We will allow you back into your husband's room because Mr. Grey insists he wants you there, though I have

greatly cautioned him to the contrary. But you cannot . . .
I repeat . . . you *cannot* hit, slap, or throw things at your
husband, Mrs. Grey," Dr. Chang continued, speaking to
her like she would one of her children, and annoying her
in the process. "He has suffered a serious injury and just
emerged from a coma. His health is very delicate, and I
will not allow it to be compromised by anyone, including
you. Now do I have your promise that you will not assault
your husband if you are allowed back into that room?" he
asked, pointing down the corridor.

"Yeah," she murmured.

Dr. Chang inclined his head. "Mrs. Grey, I am very serious. You cannot assault the patient again, or you will be
removed from the hospital. You will also be arrested."

"I heard you the first time and I said yes!" She then
pushed herself away from the wall and strolled down the
corridor back to Cyrus's room.

She found him where she'd left him, still sitting up in
his hospital bed. Cy wasn't gazing at her with fear or ap-
prehension. He looked at her head-on, like what had happened an hour ago hadn't happened. She sat down in the
chair nearest to his bed. The security guard stood next to
the door with his thumbs tucked in his belt, mere inches
away from his holstered-pepper spray.

"Can I speak to my wife alone?" Cyrus asked.

The guard glanced at Dr. Chang and the nurse who
were lingering in the doorway as well.

"I'd prefer to have someone nearby just in case the situation gets out of hand again, Mr. Grey," Dr. Chang said,
taking a step forward.

"I can handle my own wife. Besides, she already got her
licks in," Cyrus explained, looking at her. He actually had
the audacity to look like he wanted to break into laughter.
"She got it out her system. Trust me. I know her. We're
okay now."

Dr. Chang seemed to hesitate for several seconds before reluctantly nodding his head. "The security officer will be waiting in the hall on standby," he said.

They all filed out of the room, leaving the couple alone. Vanessa and Cyrus seemed to gaze at one another for an agonizingly long time before he finally spoke first.

"Why you sitting all the way over there?" he asked, gesturing to her chair. "I ain't gonna bite, Nessa." This time, he did laugh.

"You think this is fuckin' funny?"

"Yeah, kind of. Especially with how extra and self-righteous you're bein'," he muttered dryly.

"What?"

What the hell was that supposed to mean? And why was Cyrus acting so unfazed by everything? Why wasn't he making excuses or begging for her forgiveness? All that certainly seemed called for right now. He should be offering to kiss her feet.

"Look," he began, "I'm sorry you found out about Noelle and Diamond the way you did. This isn't the way I wanted this to go down."

"So how exactly were you planning to introduce me to your other wives? Huh, Cy? Were you gonna do it on my damn birthday?"

He chuckled. "No, to be honest, if it were left up to me, it never would've happened at all."

"Well, it *did* happen!" she said, leaning forward in her chair. She wanted to hit him again, but she didn't want to go to jail for it, so she held back. "It did fuckin' happen! I know you married two other women behind my back. Have you called and summoned them, too? Or was I the only one who got that honor?"

"No, I haven't called them yet. I'm still figuring out what to say . . . how to explain this whole . . . well . . . situation."

"*Explain this whole situation*?" she repeated, before blowing a gust of air through her flared nostrils. "You mean you're trying to figure out how to lie! Is that it, Cy? You gotta think up another goddamn lie! Well, good luck to you, because you've been so good at it so far." She clapped mockingly. "But I'm afraid your lucky streak is over. All your lies have caught up with you and now you'll likely go to jail for that shit!"

At those words, his casual façade disappeared. He flinched.

"That's right!" Now she was the one grinning. "You're going to prison for bigamy, but before they put your ass behind bars, I'm getting a divorce and I'm taking you for every fucking cent you have! You hear me?" She rose to her feet and threw the strap of her purse over her shoulder. "So goodbye, Cy. I hope that you—"

"Sit down," he said firmly, making her go still and cock an eyebrow at him.

"*Excuse me*?"

"I said sit down. You're not leaving here and you're not leaving me."

"Yes, I damn well am!"

"No, you're not, Nessa. You're not getting a divorce either, and I damn well ain't giving you a dime of my money! Because I may have done my dirt. I will own up to that. But you aren't innocent either, my love."

She slowly sat back in her chair. "What are talking about?"

"I'm talking about the late-night phone calls. The texts. The little errands that you claim to run that always bring you to Lakewood Apartments in Crofton. I'm talking about the affair you've been having with Coach Bilal."

Her face drained of all color. Her mouth fell open in shock. "I . . . I'm not . . . not having an aff- . . . an affair. I don't know what you're talking about!" she lied feebly making him loudly exhale. It almost sounded like a groan.

"Oh, come on, girl! Don't lie, baby. I've got plenty of evidence of what's been going on between you two for the past few months. I'm not stupid! And if you choose to divorce me, I'd be more than happy to let everyone know what you did . . . to release pictures. Some of those pictures that investigator took were pretty interestin'. You might wanna tell your friend to invest in tinted windows if you're gonna let him fuck you in that weak ass car of his."

She audibly swallowed. Vanessa suddenly felt very sick to her stomach. "You . . . you knew this *whole time?* You had an investigator follow me? Someone was taking pictures?" she squeaked.

She could just imagine how tawdry she looked in those photos, giving a blowjob or doing it doggy style with Bilal in the back seat of his Versa. How had she not realized someone had been trailing her?

"I'll put you on blast," he continued. "I'll send them to the email accounts of all the mothers in your little soccer crew to the principal at the Winston Preparatory Academy to the PTA online message board. I don't give a goddamn! *Everyone* will know who you really are, baby. Everyone will know you aren't the perfect mother and wife you claim to be." He smiled. "So you can be dutiful and stay by my side through all of this. We can unite as a family despite this setback."

"Setback?" she yelled. "Setback!"

"Or you can divorce me. You may still get a settlement and the house, but you won't be able to show your face anywhere in public by the time I'm done. You won't be able to look our children in the eyes—not when they come home and tell you what all their little friends are saying about their Mama."

"You bastard," she whispered. Her eyes flooded with

tears again. This time, tears of rage. He was willing to hurt her like this and humiliate their children just to keep her under his thumb?

"You thought I was gonna let you ride off into the sunset with my kids and that motherfucka? You thought I was just gonna let you take everything from me? *Me?*" He shook his head again. "That ain't the case, baby. Cyrus Grey doesn't go down like that! You're gonna learn that shit today—and *he* will too." She watched as his jaw tightened. "He's gonna rue the day he came for me and mine."

She crossed her arms over her chest. "If you're thinking about beating Bilal's ass, you can try, but you won't get far. You may have been able to do some damage a week ago, but not with all those bandages and the state you're in," she said, gesturing to his hospital gown.

"I'm not talkin' about that nigga Bilal! I'm talking about the ungrateful piece of shit who set me up! He was just a little gutta nigga when I met him and I helped him out of the shithole. I showed him the ropes and made him respectable, and this is how he thanks me? This is how he repays me? He thought he could take me out! He thought he could take what's mine! Well, he's got another thing comin'!"

"What the hell are you talking about?"

Cyrus was ranting. She couldn't follow his train of thought.

He leaned over to look into her eyes. His gaze was so cold and deadly, she wanted to scoot back her chair, but didn't. "He tried to have me killed. I know that motherfucka' did it! But I'm gonna get his ass. He's gonna wish I died after what I'm gonna do to him!"

"*Who?*" She paused. "Wait. Is this the guy who Diamond or Noelle was working with? He was in on it too?"

"What?" This time Cyrus was the one who looked confused.

"That's what the cops said ... that maybe Noelle or Diamond did it. They say evidence points to—"

"The cops don't know what the hell they're talking about! Noelle and Diamond didn't have a damn thing to do with this!" A manic gleam came to her husband's eyes. This time she did scoot back her chair. "It was him! I *know* it was. It couldn't have been anybody else."

"Then why not tell the cops that? If you're so convinced you know who did it, then tell the police! Whoever it is should be in jail, Cy!"

The manic gleam disappeared. Cyrus slumped back against the stacked pillows on his hospital bed, almost in defeat. He gave a hollow laugh. "Because he knows I won't tell anybody he did it. I can't."

This confused her even more. "*What?* Why the hell not?"

"That ain't your concern," he murmured sullenly, turning away from her and reaching for the hospital phone beside his bed. "I'll just have to take care of this shit myself. Look, I got some phone calls to make. Can you bring the kids by this evening after school or tomorrow, since it's the weekend? I want to see them. Give them a hug. Let them know I'm okay."

He then began to press buttons on the dial pad. Vanessa looked at her husband, bewildered. Had she imagined their conversation? Had all of this just happened?

She rose from the chair again and walked toward his hospital doorway. She glanced over her shoulder and found Cyrus talking on the phone.

"Hello, Ralph ... Yes, it's me, Cy," he said casually. "Yes, I've been out of commission for a bit. I'll explain why later, but can you give me an update on the Parker portfolio. How's the stock doing?"

Vanessa staggered dazedly into the hall as her husband continued to talk business. She made her way toward the elevators, only pausing to glance up at the security guard who was now leaning against the wall and reading a magazine. She guessed he'd gotten bored as he waited for sparks to fly in Cyrus's hospital room. Had he heard any of their conversation? It didn't seem like it.

She clutched her purse against her chest as she came to terms yet again with a new reality.

Her husband knew she had cheated on him and had documentation to prove it, and he was holding that over her head now, blackmailing her. But she couldn't stay locked in a marriage to Cyrus. She just couldn't. It would be too humiliating.

"What the hell am I gonna do?" she whispered desperately to herself as she reached the elevators and pressed the down button.

"Mama, I need your help!" Vanessa cried into her cell phone a few minutes later, wiping her nose with the back of her hand.

She was sitting in the hospital parking lot not far from the hospital's entrance, unsure of where to go or what to do. She was no longer a snarling tigress, but a frightened rabbit, trembling all over.

"Oh, Lord," her mother lamented on the other end of the line. "What happened now?"

"Remember I told you earlier today that Cyrus woke up. Well, I went to see him and . . ." She closed her eyes. "He said he knows everything. He knows about my affair with Bilal!"

Her mother didn't respond. Vanessa only heard background noise. She wondered if the reception was bad and the phone call was about to drop.

"Mama, did you hear me? I said I—"

"I heard you!" her mother snapped. "I'm stepping outside so the Vietnamese manicurist can't here our damn conversation! Here I am at the spa trying to get a long overdue mani-pedi and facial and you come to me with this nonsense. What do you mean Cy found out about your affair? How? *When?*"

"I don't know! But he says he has pictures of us together in the back of Bilal's car. He had an investigator following us around. He said if I ever ask for a divorce, he's going to show those pictures to everybody!"

"Goddamnit! I told you it was foolish to start carrying on with that boy. I said it a million times!"

"Yes, you did, but I can't change what's happened, Mama." She started crying again. She lowered her head to the steering wheel. "I can't change the past. I don't know what to do! I don't want to stay stuck in this marriage. Cy lied and embarrassed the shit out of me! And I don't want to be married to a man in prison! But I don't want Cy to send my pictures to the school principal and the PTA. I just—"

"He won't," her mother said firmly. "We'll make sure of that."

"How can we?" She raised her head to gaze out the windshield at the hospital parking lot and the two women in scrubs who walked by her car. "I know what people will think when they see those photos . . . when they hear I've been cheating for three months! All the whispers and—"

"*No one* is going to see those pictures, Vanessa. We won't let that happen. Remember when I asked you days ago if Bilal would be willing to do anything for you? I asked you how far he was willing to go to please you."

Vanessa wiped her nose again. "Yes, I-I remember."

"Well, now it's time to put your claims to the test. Cyrus may be on the mend, but he's weakened now. Anything could happen to him. The world is a dangerous place and he's *so* frail, sweetheart. Who knows if he would survive if something else were to happen to him."

Vanessa narrowed her bloodshot eyes and leaned back in the driver seat, wondering if she heard her mother correctly. "What . . . what are you saying? That I should ask Bilal to . . . to kill Cyrus?"

"No, because I would ever ask you something so stupid over a phone line," her mother answered flatly.

Vanessa cringed. Her mother was right. Phone calls could be monitored. Admitting something like that out loud was very foolish.

"I'm just saying, I think it's time for you to call Bilal . . . and have a little talk," her mother said slowly.

Vanessa wondered what the conversation would even be like. Yes, Bilal hated Cyrus and he wanted her to end it with her husband, but did he hate him enough to kill him?

"I don't know, Mama. It's such a . . . a . . . big thing to ask of somebody and—"

"Give him an incentive. Make up something if you have to, Nessa. Be creative! I've done it. It's easier than you think."

"What? When did you do it?"

"Do you remember your stepfather Eddie?"

Of course, Vanessa remembered him. He was her mother's second husband. She had married him back when Vanessa was ten . . . maybe, eleven years old. She remembered Eddie being a loud, friendly man with a booming laugh. He was several decades older than Vanessa's mother at the time, but he kept himself slimmer and more fit than most men younger than his age by playing golf and tennis regularly. But he died within six years of their marriage.

"The man exercised four days a week and hadn't had a drink in twenty years, and yet he had a heart attack. Poor thing," Carol said with a snort. "I had my own special friend who would do anything for me. Make sure Bilal does the same for you."

"Y-yes, Mama," Vanessa said before her mother hung up.

She sat silently in her car for several minutes, trying to orient herself again. In less than a week she'd had to come to terms with her husband being shot, then with finding out he had two other wives, and then that he had hired a private investigator to follow her and Bilal around to document their affair. Now she had to come to terms with the fact that she had to plot her husband's murder.

"I need a drink," she murmured. "A big one."

She then shifted her Mercedes into drive and pulled out of the hospital parking lot.

Chapter 26

Diamond

"Change the channel," Julian drawled as he slumped back against the sofa cushion and raised his beer bottle to his lips. "This shit is borin'."

Honey, who was snuggled against Julian's chest, raised the remote and flipped from the *Love & Hip Hop Atlanta* rerun on the TV screen to a daytime court show. Diamond could read in the caption that one woman was suing the other for unpaid rent. As Julian and Honey lounged on the sofa, laughing at the judge's one-liners, Diamond shifted anxiously in her armchair. She glanced at the clock on her bookshelf to check the time and stifled a groan. Four hours had passed since her phone call to the halfway house and her conversation with the executive director. She thought the police would be here by now to pick up Julian.

What the hell is taking them so long, she wondered.

She had to head to work at four o'clock, unless she wanted to piss off the floor manager David yet again. She couldn't afford to be late. But she didn't want to leave Julian and Honey alone in her home.

Who knows what they would steal, she thought derisively.

She'd already caught Honey trying on her jewelry. She wondered if Honey and Julian would just raid the place when she wasn't here and disappear. Besides, she had to make sure they stayed in her condo at least until the police arrived. Until the cops made their appearance, she guessed she had to continue to babysit the duo.

"Aww, damn," Julian said ten minutes later. He held up an empty bag of tortilla chips and shook it dramatically. "We ran out of chips, bae!" He peered over Honey's head at Diamond. "You got any more of these around here, College Girl?"

"Nope. All out," she answered succinctly.

"Shit, what *do* you got? Too busy livin' the rich girl life to do some grocery shoppin'?"

Diamond cut her eyes at him then returned her attention to the television, ignoring his jab. How was she supposed to know they would show up and eat seventy percent of all the leftovers and snacks in her cabinets and refrigerator in one afternoon? It wasn't her job to replenish their supply.

Honey pushed herself up from Julian's chest. "Why don't we head out and get some more food then? We can go around the corner to the—"

"No!" Diamond said, leaping to her feet.

Julian and Honey stared at her in confusion.

"No, what?" Julian asked.

"Uh, no. No, don't go around the corner. Just . . . just stay here," she said, holding up her hands.

They both continued to stare at her. She knew she looked insane and desperate and more importantly, she wasn't being very convincing. She had to keep them here. If they went to get something to eat and the police arrived, or if they were walking back from the store, and saw cop cars waiting downstairs, Diamond's whole plan would be destroyed. And worse, Julian would suspect she was the one behind it; he would rightly conclude that she had snitched on him. And who knew how he would take out his retribution on her before he was caught?

"Don't you want to find out what the judge decides?" Diamond tugged her cellphone from her pocket. "Besides, you don't have to go out to get food. I have an app on my phone where we can order whatever you want, and they can deliver it here."

Julian pointed to her. "See, I knew you were smart, College Girl! Let me see what they got on there."

She ordered them Mexican fast food, specifying extra nachos, and settled back into watching television while she waited for the cops. The court show ended, and a news break flashed onscreen. Cyrus's picture appeared behind two anchors sitting behind the news desk. At the sight of her husband's face, Diamond eagerly leaned forward and grabbed the remote from her leather ottoman to turn up the television's volume.

"*Channel News 11 has received word that the recent victim of a shooting in the Fell's Point area is now on the mend,*" the grinning female broadcaster said. "*Cyrus Grey, who was shot Monday at his home on Fells Street, has now emerged from his coma.*"

"Hey!" Julian shouted, pointing at the screen. "Ain't that your husband?"

"Ssshhh!" Diamond cried, waving off Julian.

"Don't 'Ssshhh' me!" he grumbled.

Honey shook her head and whispered something into his ear.

"Nah, she being rude as fuck," he murmured to Honey. "She forgot who the hell she's talking to!"

Diamond tried her best to ignore him by turning up the volume even more.

"Police are still investigating the shooting and currently have no suspects." The female news anchor then turned to the male anchor sitting beside her. *"But now that he's awake, maybe the police will be able to make some progress in this case."*

"Seems likely. Here's hoping," the male anchor said with a nod before turning back to the screen. *"Today at five, find out what in your house could kill you. Our Consumer Reporter Joel Gonzalez tells us the ugly secret lurking in your household that could be right under your nose. You don't want to miss this one, folks!"*

Diamond stared blankly at the screen as the broadcast segued to a toy commercial.

Cyrus was awake. He was okay. She wanted to burst into tears. She wanted to run from the condo straight to the hospital and wrap her arms around him, but she couldn't. She had to stay here with Julian and Honey until the police came, and it was starting to feel more and more like some cruel punishment.

"Shit, they still ain't figure out who shot that nigga," Julian said, snapping her out of her thoughts. "Bet they're never gonna find out."

"Yes, they will!" Diamond argued, lowering the volume again and tossing her remote back onto the ottoman. "If they'd just focus on what I already told them, instead of running after all these other stupid leads, they would—"

"What did you tell them?" Honey asked.

Diamond slowly exhaled. She was getting tired of telling the same story. Each time, it felt like her words were falling on deaf ears.

"I told them I saw the guy who shot him," she began grudgingly. "I didn't see his face because he was wearing a mask. But the security guard downstairs thinks he saw him too and he saw his face. We both remember him having this tattoo on his arm. It was this fancy nine. It was big. It had to be the same guy!"

"Did you say a nine?" Julian asked.

Diamond nodded.

"Shit!" Julian chuckled and took another drink from his beer bottle. "I haven't heard about them niggas in a minute."

Now Diamond was the one squinting. "What are you talking about? What niggas?"

"The Nine Crew," Julian explained. "They used to be pretty big around here when I was a little youngun. This was before Dolla Dolla and the Latins took over and took out most of their people about ten years ago. They were big in the drug trade. You couldn't buy coke or bud in D.C. without it coming through them. And they protected what was theirs. Those niggas did drive-bys on the regular."

"If they were so big, why haven't I heard of them before?" Diamond asked, cocking an eyebrow.

"Because you ain't from here, College Girl! Your ass just came here for school. But trust me—those were some hard niggas back in the day. All the other crews and street mobs answered to them. If you were with the Nine Crew, nobody . . . and I mean, *nobody* fucked with you! They were brawlers . . . shooters. I'm surprised your man ain't dead. Usually, when one of them niggas came for you, its lights out. Guess they fell off."

Diamond gnawed the inside of her cheek. Noelle had mentioned that Cyrus had business deals with figures in the underworld. She said he'd been stealing from them too. Were these the people who had come after Cyrus in retaliation?

Diamond's musings were cut short when she heard a knock at the door.

"Aww, shit!" Julian said, clapping his hands. "That must be my nachos!"

Diamond rose to her feet, muttering to herself. How was this man still hungry?

She strolled out of the living room and into her foyer, listening as another court show came on television. When Diamond approached the door, she stood on the balls of her feet and gazed out the peephole. Instead of seeing the DoorDash guy standing in the hall with their food order, she saw five uniformed police officers.

Diamond breathed an inward sigh of relief. *Oh, thank God! They're finally here!*

And they had brought more than enough officers to handle Julian in case he decided to make a run for it.

After they arrested Julian, she could still make a quick drive to the hospital to see her husband. She would hold him tight and give him a big fat kiss. She didn't want to hear any explanations for why he had lied to her and not told her that he was already married to two other women. They had time for that later. For now, she just wanted to be with her man.

She glanced at Honey and Julian who were still lounging on her sofa sectional, blissfully unaware of what was about to happen next. She then unlocked the door and opened it. As soon as she did, the cops came rushing in like a powerful stream and she had to go flat against the wall to keep from getting knocked over and taken with the current.

"Hands up!" the white one who stood in front shouted. He'd already drawn his weapon. All the cops had. "Put your goddamn hands up! Do it now!"

Julian and Honey jumped to their feet and turned to the door. Julian raised his hands, looking shocked at first to see the cops there. But as two of the officers rounded the sofa and grabbed his hands, twisting them behind his back, his eyes settled on Diamond who still stood beside the door.

"You bitch!" he yelled. "You shady ass bitch! You called them, didn't you?"

"I told you I'm not going to jail for you, Julian!" she shouted back.

He tried to tug his arms out of the officers' grasp, but they shoved him onto the couch cushions, even as he yelled. They then began to put on his handcuffs.

"Stop! Don't touch him!" Honey cried, reaching out for her man, but one of the cops yanked her back and tugged an arm behind her as well. He began to put her in handcuffs, too—to Diamond's alarm and dismay.

She hadn't told them Honey had been the one to help him escape from the halfway house. She hadn't even breathed her name. The goal was to get Julian back to prison and Honey from under his corrupt influence. Not to send her to jail *with* him.

"Wait! Wait!" Diamond shouted. "You didn't say anything about arresting her, too! He's the one who violated his parole. She hasn't even gone to jail before! Why are you taking her in?"

The cops didn't answer her. She watched instead as Honey burst into tears as they placed her under arrest.

"Turn around and face the wall," Diamond heard someone say behind her.

She turned to find one of the uniformed officers lingering in the doorway. He looked to be in his early fifties with thin lips and glacial blue eyes.

"What?"

"I said turn around and face the wall. I'm not going to say it again," he answered in a low voice that was harder than granite.

"*Excuse me?*" She dropped her hand to her hip. "You must be confused, officer. I was the one who called you guys in the first damn place! I was the one who told the executive director that—"

She didn't get the chance to finish. He whipped her around and shoved her against the wall—hard.

"I'm warning you not to resist, ma'am," he said as he wrenched her arms behind her back and she felt the steel cuffs clamp tightly around her wrists. "I don't want to have to get rough with you, and you don't want me to get rough with you either. *Comprende?*"

If this was him being gentle, she hated to see what rough was. Hot tears burned her eyes as her face was smashed against the textured wallpaper, as the muscles in her arms began to burn from being twisted at such an awkward angle.

She was taken into the hallway first. Julian and Honey were taken out after her. While Julian screamed, kicked, cursed, and had to be controlled by two officers along the way, she and Honey remained silent as they were read their Miranda rights while they walked. Diamond stumbled a few times as she was led to the elevators that would take them downstairs to the first floor. She felt like she was in a daze, like she was stuck in a bad dream. She glanced over her shoulder and saw that Honey had the same shell-shocked look on her face.

The trio were led past the front desk where the security guard Richard sat. His pale face went even paler while he watched them, making his freckles stand out like brown polka dots on his cheeks.

"Mrs. Grey," he said, slowly rising to his feet. "What . . . what's happening?"

She tried to answer him, but the cops kept a fast clip, taking her with them.

"Should I call someone? Is there anyone you want me to call for you?" he shouted after her.

"Try to get in touch with my husband at the hospital," she called back over her shoulder. "Tell him what happened! Please?"

"What hospital? *What hospital?*" he shouted back as they stepped through her building's glass doors into the afternoon sunshine. Several people walking along the sidewalks stopped to turn and look at their little parade.

She found the cop cars waiting as she'd expected, except she hadn't anticipated she'd be climbing into one.

"Watch your head," the cop said as he eased her into the back of one of the squad cars.

Diamond blinked back tears and prayed that this was all a big misunderstanding and she would be released almost as soon as she arrived in jail. But part of her suspected that was pure fantasy.

Chapter 27

Noelle

Noelle stood in front of her bathroom mirror, gazing at her reflection, adding the last finishing touches before Tariq arrived at her home.

She adjusted the silk lace robe around her shoulders. It was open just enough to reveal the new plum-colored bustier, thong, and black thigh-highs underneath that she'd purchased today. She'd done it during a clandestine shopping trip while on break at work. Noelle had left the shopping bag in the trunk of her car, not wanting to have to explain to Miranda, who was familiar with the lingerie shop's signature red bag, why she was purchasing sexy underwear when her husband was in the hospital in a coma.

Noelle reached for the lipstick on her counter, adding another layer that was a few shades darker than her bustier. She definitely looked sexy, almost enticing enough to eat.

"Tariq will like it," she muttered, fluffing her bob so that it looked more tousled.

So why didn't she *feel* sexy? Why did she feel so uncomfortable?

It wasn't misgivings about "breaking her wedding vows" and starting an affair with Tariq. She had already surmounted that mental obstacle. She knew now that her marriage to Cyrus wasn't and had never been real, and why deny herself something good and pleasurable with Tariq out of misguided guilt?

No, the truth was that she still felt ill-at-ease from meeting Big El that morning at Tariq's house. She'd texted Tariq about Big El's message and told him to contact him. Tariq had responded within minutes.

"Thanks. I'll hit him up later today," he'd texted back.

Ideally, that should have been the end of it. She had relayed the message. She could have pushed Big El and everything he'd said out of her mind, leaving Tariq to handle whatever issue the two men had—but she hadn't been able to do that. Her conversation with Big El lingered with her like bad indigestion. She replayed it over and over, and was left with lots of questions. For instance, who the hell was Big El and how did Tariq know him? He did not seem like a guy Tariq would be friends with. And why did they have the same tattoo? The style of the number seemed so distinct, it couldn't be a coincidence. What had Big El done for Tariq that he refused to pay him in full because "he didn't get all that he asked for"?

She didn't know if Cyrus's lies were making her paranoid and suspicious of all men in general, but she felt like Tariq had something questionable going on with Big El. She just couldn't put her finger on what. And now secrets raised alarm bells for her. She just couldn't dismiss them anymore, no matter how inconsequential they may seem on the surface. For all those reasons, she needed her questions about Tariq's relationship with Big El answered before she and Tariq did anything tonight. There was no getting around it.

The doorbell rang and Noelle turned away from her mirror. She walked downstairs and strolled to her front door. She unlocked it and walked back toward her living room. "It's open!" she called out.

Tariq eased the door open farther and poked his head around the frame. He found her sitting on the sofa arm with her legs crossed and her robe dangling off one shoulder seductively. He stepped inside and shut her front door behind him.

"Well, damn! I bought sushi," he said, holding a plastic bag aloft as he strolled into the living room. He sat the bag on her console. "But I'll be honest." She watched as he slowly tugged off his suit jacket before tossing it onto one of her armchairs. He then walked toward her, unbuttoning his cuffs and rolling up his sleeves along the way. "I'd much rather be nibbling on you right now than some California roll. Bet you taste a lot better, too."

"Guess there's only one way to find out," she whispered, gazing up at him.

Tariq cocked an eyebrow, leaned down, cupped her face, and brought his lips to hers.

The kiss was good as all the previous ones. The same butterflies fluttered in her stomach. The same tingling erupted between her thighs. As their tongues danced, he spread her legs and stood between them. Noelle could feel him trying to open the belt of her robe, tugging eagerly at the knot with one hand while the other went for the waistband of her thong. That's when she knew she had to slow this down or she'd never accomplish anything tonight but a roll in the sheets.

"Wait. Wait, Tariq," she said, leaning her head back, tugging his hands away.

"But why, baby?" he asked. "I'm ready. Trust! You just

gotta look down and see," he whispered into her ear before kissing her neck then her bare shoulder.

She eased away from him again. "But *I'm* not ready."

He lowered his hands and took a step back. His lazy grin disappeared. "Okay, umm, then I guess I'm getting mixed signals because I thought all this," he said, gesturing to her lingerie, "was saying you were ready. Not just ready, but you were already off the starting block! So you're telling me you don't want to hook up tonight?"

"I do . . . I mean, I did."

"You did . . . but not anymore?"

"Not right at this very moment!"

He ran his hand over his head. "Again, I'm not up for the guessing games, Noelle. Just tell me what's wrong. What happened in the last twenty seconds that changed your mind?"

"Something . . ." She licked her lips and took a shaky breath. "Something happened today that we need to talk about."

"Okay . . . what is it?"

She didn't know where to begin. How could she ask these questions without offending him, not to mention the fact that the answers were essentially none of her business. Still, Noelle couldn't pursue any relationship with Tariq—serious or strictly sexual—if she felt this awkward around him.

"Shit! Just spit it out, girl," Tariq urged jokingly when she went silent.

Noelle rose from the sofa arm and sat down on one of the cushions instead. She patted the empty spot beside her, motioning for Tariq to sit down too. He looked mildly annoyed, but did as she asked. She reached out and took his hand within her own.

"That guy . . . that guy who came by your house today, Big El. Who . . . who was he?"

Tariq tilted his head. "What do you mean who was he?"

"I mean who was he to you? A friend? Did he work for you?"

"I paid him to do job a while back, if that's what you mean. He did a shitty job though. I would've been better off doing it myself, but you live and you learn."

"So he *is* a contractor then? Like a . . . a handyman or something?"

"Why?" Tariq chuckled. "Were you thinking about hiring him?"

"No, it's just . . ." Her voice faded.

"Just what? Why are you so concerned with Big El? What's the issue? Why are we even talking about him at all? I don't get it."

She decided to just spit it out. "Look, when I was talking to Big El, I noticed he had a tattoo. A nine on his arm. It was the same number, done in the same style as the tattoo on your chest. I wondered . . . I wondered why you guys had the same tattoo. Did you know him some other way? Was he a friend from your old neighborhood?"

Tariq didn't immediately answer her. After a few agonizing seconds of silence, she wondered if he was going to answer her at all.

"Yeah," he finally said, "we knew each other from back in the day. We didn't grow up in the same neighborhood, but we ran with the same crew. We all got that tat. That's how you showed you were down . . . that you were one of them."

He'd mentioned his crew before, last night to be exact, while they were in bed together. But she'd assumed it was just a generic term for his group of childhood friends. She hadn't suspected anything more serious than that. Now Noelle realized that Big El had raised her suspicions for a good reason.

"So you mean you got the tattoo in like a . . . a what? Gang initiation?"

"I mean that my past isn't perfect, Noelle. *Just* like yours. But it's in the past! I did things . . . I ran with a crowd when I was younger . . . when I was a teenager and I got into some trouble. I'm not proud of it, but I'm not that person anymore."

She loosened her hold on his hand and stared at him. "What things, Tariq?"

"What difference does it make if it happened a long time ago?"

"If it happened a long time ago, then why can't you just tell me what you did?"

"I gotta give you my rap sheet now? You want me to print out all the charges? Would that help? Would that make you feel better?"

"Oh, come on!" she cried. "You just told me that you used to be in a gang! You said you committed crimes! You never mentioned any of this shit before, and now you're pissed off that I'm asking for more details? I asked you where you got that tattoo and you were intentionally evasive the first time. You didn't tell me the truth, Tariq!"

"Because none of it mattered!" he bellowed as he shot to his feet, catching her by surprise. "What matters is the here and now. I came here to make love you, to spend the night with the woman I'm in love with. Not to talk about that lame ass nigga Big El or old shit that has nothing to do with the man I am today!"

She stilled. Her mouth fell open in shock. "You're in love with me?"

He gazed back at her in exasperation. "Yes, I'm in love with you! Why else would I be here? Why else would I do half the shit I do for you?"

She had always thought Tariq had done things for her, befriended and encouraged her, at first out of obligation to Cyrus and then because they had developed their own genuine friendship. She had never thought his feelings had run deeper than that.

He grimaced, like it pained him to admit it. "I'm in love with you, Noelle. I have been for a while now."

She rose to her feet and walked toward him. "I'm falling in love with you too," she confessed, letting the words sink in even as she said them. "That's why I asked you what I asked tonight, because if I'm going to give my heart to another man, I have to know who I'm dealing with! I'm not gonna judge you for what you did almost two decades ago, but I need to know the truth. You understand me?" She rested her hands on his shoulders then began to stroke the taut muscles in his arms, wanting to ease whatever anxiety he now felt. He gradually relaxed and she wrapped her arms around him. "You can't hide anything from me. That's not what people who love and respect each other do to one another, and I won't put up with that shit again!"

"It won't happen, baby. I swear it won't." He wrapped his arms around her, too, and drew her closer so that she was pressed flat against him. He then kissed her long and hard, taking her breath away. "I will never treat you the way he did," he whispered against her now kiss-swollen lips. "I'll do everything in my power to protect you, Noelle. I made you that promise, and I meant it. I swear on my mama!"

"And you won't lie to me," she repeated, because his vows of love and protection were important, but not as much as his honesty. "You promise from now on that you won't hide anything from me? I'm not gonna find out you're married to someone else or . . . or you're wanted in another country, am I?"

"Of course not, baby. I promise."

Noelle stared at his face then into his eyes. She tried to detect a blink or twitch that might reveal any subterfuge, but she didn't see any signs of deceit—to her great relief. Noelle believed him. She was finally with a man she could trust.

"So did I answer all your questions? Do you feel better now?" Tariq asked.

She nodded. "I do."

She felt his hands slowly slide from her back to her bottom. He cupped both cheeks and leaned down to kiss her bare shoulder, making her laugh.

"So can we get back to what we started when I came in?"

"After you give me what you owe me," she said, linking her arms around his neck.

"*What I owe you?*"

"Yes! I believe you took something of mine and I want it back."

"Oh!" He reached into his pants pocket and pulled out her lace thong. "You mean this?"

"Exactly," she said with a giggle before snatching it out of his hand and bringing her mouth back to his.

But within minutes, she ended up trading one pair of panties for the other, wearing neither all night.

Saturday

Chapter 28

Diamond

They'll realize they made a mistake and they'll let me go.

Diamond had been telling herself that since yesterday when the cop car pulled away from the curb in front of her building with her handcuffed in the back. From there, the cops had taken her to the Baltimore Detention Center where they took her fingerprints and mugshot. The entire time, she'd felt like a steer being blindly led along.

When they said hold out your hand, she did it. When they told her to stand in front of the line, or turn to her left or right, she followed orders like she was told.

They made her strip off her clothes. Diamond had stood naked and shivering in a chilly room that looked like it was in a school basement. She'd nearly burst into tears as she watched the female officer, who looked like she could be someone's grandmother, snap on blue latex gloves to do her full cavity search.

"Bend over," the officer had ordered as dispassionately as one would if they were reciting their ABCs.

Once again, Diamond had closed her eyes and did as she was told.

"Spread your legs! More . . . *More!*" the officer had shouted, and Diamond's legs began to shake. She'd felt close to toppling over. The officer then shoved her fingers inside her, groping for something that wasn't there.

This was worse than when she'd been with one of her tricks in the old days. At least then, it had been on her terms. She'd rarely enjoyed being manhandled by strangers, but she had done it willingly back then knowing she was still getting something in the end for her efforts. But she knew nothing would come of this besides humiliation and regret. There would be no three hundred dollars waiting for her on the night table when this was over.

After that, she couldn't hold in her tears anymore. She began to cry, biting on her lower lip to hold in her sobs.

The humiliation continued during her health screening with a doctor that had stinky breath, cold hands, and a wooden bedside manner. He took a blood sample. He made her pee in a cup. He gave her a pelvic exam. She'd guessed he was making sure she wouldn't infect the other inmates with the Bubonic Plague or tuberculosis or herpes. Diamond was issued a khaki-colored uniform and taken back to a crowded holding cell filled with several other inmates who were either furious at being there, apathetic, or just as bemused as she was. While there, she was reunited with Honey.

They'd removed Honey's signature golden weave, revealing the matted cornrows underneath. It made Honey look different. She seemed to have aged at least fifteen years in one day.

"Honey," she'd called to her.

"Don't say shit to me," Honey had mumbled stubbornly in return, staring forward, refusing to look at Diamond.

"Honey, I'm sorry," she'd continued anyway. "I didn't know they were gonna arrest you . . . arrest us. I thought they were just gonna arrest Julian. I swear!"

At that, Honey had finally turned to her. The look in her eyes was almost murderous. "I don't know what they're charging you with, but whatever it is, I hope they keep your ass in here for a long time, bitch! I hope you never get out!"

She then got up and walked to the other side of the holding cell and sat down next to a large woman who was snoring loudly.

They didn't speak to each other again after that.

One hour passed, then another, then another hour after that. The whole time, Diamond sat huddled in her corner of the room with her back flat against the cinderblock wall, waiting patiently for the moment when another cop would appear in the doorway, call her name, and tell her she could make a phone call, though she didn't know to who. She didn't know Cy's number and no one else could rescue her from this predicament.

Her stomach rumbled. She was hungry, but didn't know who to ask for food or even if they would give it to her. She nodded off. She only woke up when she heard a guard shout her name and roughly shove her shoulder.

"Rise and shine, princess!" the officer shouted.

Diamond slowly raised her head and gazed up at the woman, groggy-eyed.

"Come with me, inmate."

They're finally going to let me go, Diamond thought with relief.

She tried to hop to her feet and rush to the door, but she was sore all over from sitting up so long. Instead, she staggered across the room and stepped through the holding cell door, only for the officer to tell her to turn around so she could be placed back in handcuffs.

They were not going to release her after all, she realized with dismay as the officer led her down one hall then another. She passed a window along the corridor that showed bright morning light. Diamond had spent an entire night in this place. She hoped she wouldn't have to spend another. The officer led her to another room with bare white walls. Two men stood inside waiting for her. She instantly recognized them as the detectives who had come to the hospital to question her the day Cyrus was shot.

What were they doing here?

"Hey, Diamond! Good to see you again," the black detective said, smiling as he stood near the table in the center of the room. His partner sat in a seat facing her, sipping from a Styrofoam cup of coffee. "You remember us, don't you? Detective Turner," he said pointing to himself, "and Detective Macy." He pointed to his companion as he sat down beside him.

"Y-yes," she whispered, still gazing at them hesitantly at the room's threshold. "I-I do."

"You can have a seat," Macy said, pointing to the empty chair on the opposite side of the table. "We'd like to talk to you."

Diamond did as he ordered, lowering herself into the chair.

"Guess you're sad you and your man's reunion got cut short, huh?" Turner asked, eyeing her.

"My man? You mean Julian?"

"Of course, I mean Julian," Turner said. "Who else would I be talking about?"

"Julian isn't my man. Not anymore. He hasn't been for years! I'm with Cyrus now. He's my husband. *He's* my man!"

Turner cocked an eyebrow. "Is that so? Well, if that's the case, then why have you been spending so much time with Julian lately?"

"What do you mean?" she asked.

"The guys at the halfway house where he lives said you

came by to pick him up Wednesday," Macy chimed in before taking another sip of coffee. "We heard you took him to the mall that day and bought him a nice gold chain."

"I only bought it for him because I was trying to get him to tell me if he had anything to do with what happened to Cyrus! I wasn't sure if he was behind it, and he told me that he'd tell me the truth if I got him the chain. I wouldn't have done it if that wasn't the case."

"So you were trying to bribe him, you mean?" Turner asked.

"I wouldn't say I was bribing him. I was just . . . I was just . . . giving him a reason to tell the truth. It was just an . . . an incentive."

"Uh-huh," Macy said, sounding incredulous. "And what other incentives were you giving him at your place yesterday when the cops arrived?"

Diamond didn't like the way the detective said the word "incentives." She didn't find his sarcasm amusing or appreciate what he was implying about her relationship with Julian.

"None," she said through clenched teeth. "He and his girl Honey had just shown up out of nowhere. They said they needed a place to hide before they went on the run . . . before they left the state. Julian knew the cops would come looking for him after he missed curfew. He asked if he could stay with me for a day or two. I told him yes, but I didn't mean it. I was the one who called the halfway house to tell them he was there! I was the reason the cops showed up in the first place! If it wasn't for me, he could still be walking around out—"

"So did he ever answer your question?" Turner interrupted. "Did he ever tell you if he was the one who tried to kill Mr. Grey?"

She nodded. "He said he didn't do it. He said he didn't have anything to do with it at all. And I believe him."

The two detectives exchanged a look.

"What?" she asked.

"Well, that ain't what he told us," Turner said, leaning his elbows on the table. "He told us that *you* asked him to kill your husband."

Her mouth fell open in shock. Her stomach dropped.

"And he said the gold chain was the payment for what he did for you," Turner continued, making her furiously shake her head.

"That's a lie! He's lying! I never asked him to kill Cy!"

"Diamond, you can save the Oscar performance, baby," Turner muttered. "Just come clean and admit what you did. No more bullshit."

"I'm not pretending! I'm not lying either. *He* is! I never asked him to kill my husband. He knows why I bought him that chain!"

"Besides his confession, we've got plenty of circumstantial evidence, too," Macy explained. "We've got records of about a dozen phone calls between you two, showing you've been in contact almost every day since the shooting. You've been seen together by multiple people. For Chrissake, he was at your home, lounging on the couch when the cops showed up, according to the police report. None of this looks good, Diamond! You aren't fooling us, and you aren't going to fool any judge or jury once they see all the evidence against you! Fess up now and maybe . . . *maybe* you can work out a plea deal later or—"

"But I didn't try to kill Cy! Julian is lying. I swear!" she cried. "I don't care how it looks, because I know the truth! Julian's just saying all of this now because he's pissed that I turned him in, and he knows he's probably going back to jail for a long time. He's got nothing to lose. He's just trying to drag me down with him!"

But she could tell from the looks on their faces, her pleas were falling on deaf ears. They didn't believe her.

"What about the man with the nine tattoo that I told you about? The tattoo on his arm right here," she said, pointing to her forearm. "Did you ever find him? Did you even look?"

Turner loudly sighed and slumped back in his chair. "We're not even convinced he exists. For all we know, he's just a figment of your imagination. Some shit you made up!"

"But he's not! Richard, the security guard at the front desk in my building, saw him, too! He saw the tattoo. He told me! If you question him, he'll prove I'm not lying. He can give you a description of what the guy looked like. He wasn't wearing a mask when he saw him. Maybe that way you can find him!"

Turner laughed. "So now you're dragging the security guard into this mess? Did you seduce him too so that he'd lie for you?"

"Enough of this! Just confess, Diamond," Macy urged. "Tell us the truth. Make it easier on yourself!"

She lowered her eyes to the tabletop and sniffed, on the verge of tears again. "I can't confess to something I didn't do! I didn't try to kill my husband. I didn't do it!"

The room went silent. "Fine," Turner said. "Have it your way."

Out of the corner of her eye, she saw Turner rise from his chair and walk across the room to the door. He opened it and murmured something to someone waiting in the hall. A minute later, another female cop appeared.

"You can take her back to her cell for now," Turner said.

The officer nodded, stepped forward, and grabbed her arm. "To your feet," the woman ordered.

Diamond stood up with her head still bowed.

"I guess she can wait there until her bail hearing for her attempted murder charge," Macy said.

At those words, Diamond felt her knees go weak again. She felt lightheaded. She took one step then another before crumpling to the ground in a faint.

Chapter 29

Noelle

Noelle sat on one of her stools at her kitchen island, sipping coffee and watching as Tariq cooked her breakfast. He'd said he was doing it to give her the romantic morning-after that he couldn't give her yesterday, but she suspected it was really because he didn't want to risk eating her cooking.

He stood at the oven burner, bare-chested with a towel wrapped around his waist, flipping pancakes and frying bacon. He absently chewed a slice as he did it. A few droplets of water still lingered on his back and shoulders from the shower they'd taken together a half hour earlier. They'd made love against the wet tiles and glass, laughing as they almost slipped and fell to the shower floor. She'd gotten her hair wet in the process and now wore it in a towel that she'd wrapped like a turban. She'd worry about the mess on her head later; Noelle was too distracted to toil with a comb and flat iron right now.

Watching Tariq as he cooked and how the sun brightened her kitchen, filling it with light that played on the island's surface and warmed her skin, Noelle felt at peace. Tariq loved her and she can honestly say she was falling head over heels in love with him, too. It was amazing how her life had done a complete one-eighty in one week. She'd been devastated by Cyrus's lies and his various betrayals, but now they were the furthest thing from her mind. She felt mushier than a marshmallow. She was happy and floating in the stratosphere on a natural high of passion and love—and she didn't want to ever come down.

Tariq turned off the burners and added pancakes and bacon to the ceramic plates sitting beside him. When he turned around, ready to serve her breakfast, he narrowed his eyes at her and grinned.

"Why are looking at me like that?" he asked.

"Like what?"

"Like you know somethin' that I don't."

"I'm afraid I have no idea what you're talking about," she whispered before batting her eyes and raising her coffee cup back to her lips. She took a sip.

"I thought we agreed no secrets. Or does that rule only apply to me?" he asked playfully before leaning over the island to give her a kiss that tasted of mint toothpaste and bacon.

Just then the phone rang, making her lean back her head and reluctantly pull her lips away from his. "I'll get it." She rose from her stool and walked across the kitchen. "I don't know who's calling this early on a Saturday though."

She grabbed the cordless phone and glanced at the Caller ID screen where the words, "Johns Hopkins Hospital" appeared. She hesitated for only a second before clicking the button to answer.

"Hello?" she said, expecting to hear a doctor's or a nurse's voice.

"Hey, baby," she heard her husband's rumbling baritone answer instead.

Noelle almost dropped the phone from her ear to the kitchen's tiled floor. She breathed in sharply; it felt like all the air was sucked out of the room.

When Tariq turned from the refrigerator, closed the stainless-steel door, and sat a bottle of OJ on the counter, he must have seen the mood change play out on her face because he paused and frowned.

"What's wrong?" he mouthed.

She quickly shook her head in response, unable to articulate words or even a sound. She was so overcome.

"Noelle, baby?" Cyrus said. "You still there?"

"Y-y-yeah," she stuttered, licking her lips which had suddenly gone dry. She was breathing so hard.

"I'm awake now. I'm at the hospital in the recovery ward. Can you come up here so we can talk? I'd like to see you . . . to talk to you in person. When can you come?"

Her rapid breathing halted. Her brows knitted together. "*When can I come?*" she repeated. "When can I come? Are you kidding, Cy?"

"No, baby, I'm not—"

"Don't 'baby' me! Don't you ever fuckin' 'baby' me again!" she shouted as her grip tightened on her phone. "You lied to me! You've been lying to me our entire relationship . . . since the beginning . . . since day one!"

"I can explain," he began.

"No, you can't. No, you can't fuckin' explain this away! You can't explain away being married to two other women!"

"Baby," he tried to interrupt, but she wouldn't let him.

"You can't explain away that every time you told me you were going on a business trip, you were really going home to Vanessa and your three kids or . . . or Diamond and your fuckin' high-rise condo! You can't explain away the fact that you never told me that you had a vasectomy and you can't have any more children!"

At that, he went silent.

"Yeah. Yeah, I know, Cy," she said as her eyes lit with tears and she wiped her nose with the back of her hand. "Vanessa told me. You had me waste my time for almost two years and would have had me waste my time two years more and maybe even more than that rather than tell me the goddamn truth, you piece of shit! You made me think I was the problem. That I was too crazy to raise a baby, when it was really you! You fucking sociopath!"

"Noelle, just hang up on him," Tariq urged, shaking his head. "It's not worth it. *He's* not worth."

"Who is that in the background?" Cyrus asked. "Is . . . is that Tariq?"

"It's none of your damn business who it is!"

"It *is* him, isn't it? Why can't you tell me?"

"Because I don't have to, Cy! You're not my fucking husband! You never were. And even the fake marriage we had wasn't good anymore. You knew that shit yourself. That's why you up and married someone else in February. You knew it was over!"

"Just tell me. Is it him?" he asked again, like he hadn't heard a word she'd said.

"Yes!" She gazed at Tariq who was looking at her grimly. "Yes, it's Tariq!"

"What is he doing there?" Cyrus asked, having the nerve to sound outraged. "What the hell is that son of a bitch doing over there at *my* house at nine a.m. on a Saturday, Noelle?"

She crossed an arm over her chest and sniffed, still fighting back her tears. "You have no right to ask me that."

"Just hang up, baby," Tariq urged again. "You don't need him."

"*Baby?*" Cyrus squeaked. "Since when did he start calling you baby? Are you fuckin' him now? Is that what all this 'you're not my husband' shit is about? You think you've found yourself a new man?"

"Goodbye, Cy. I'm hanging up now," she said, pulling the phone away from her ear.

"No, wait!" he called out, just as she about to press the red button on her cordless, making her pause. "Wait! Don't hang up! You have to hear me out. Listen to me because its important. You cannot trust Tariq. I'm warning you, baby. Don't trust that nigga. He isn't who he says he is."

"Why should I listen to one goddamn word you have to say?"

"Because I know him. I know him a lot better than you, and I know how he betrays people. He probably planned this shit all along. He probably wanted you all along. That's why he betrayed me."

She watched out the corner of her eye as Tariq walked around the kitchen island and stood beside her.

"What is he saying?" he mouthed.

"He lies, Noelle. He's even better at it than I am," Cyrus continued. "And he's a criminal. He used to be—"

"In a gang a long time ago. He already told me that. You're going to have to try harder, Cy!"

"All right. Fine. Did you know that motherfucka has killed people, too? He's ruthless, sweetheart. I only kept him around because I had to, but you don't want to mess with a man like that. Trust me! It's like letting a wild animal into your home. You may love them and want to help them, but they'll turn on you. He turned on me. He tried to have me killed!"

Her eyes met Tariq's as Cyrus spoke. She tried to reconcile the man Cyrus was describing on the phone with the one who stood before her, who had cooked her breakfast, made love to her, cracked jokes, and given her honest, loving advice. She didn't see it. She didn't see any resemblance to the monster he was describing.

It felt like yet another lie, yet another elaborate story Cyrus was telling her to manipulate her and ruin the one genuine thing she had left.

Fool me once, shame one you. Fool me twice, shame on me, she thought.

She wouldn't give Cyrus a chance to do this to her again.

"You know what, Cy. It's bad enough that you lied to me for five years . . . that you made a fool out of me and an absolute farce of our marriage. But you actually think I'm gullible enough to believe your bullshit all over again," she said as the tears finally spilled over. "If Tariq is such a criminal and killer, then why is he your business partner? Why did you call him your right-hand man and invite him to our house for dinner? Why did you trust him *at all?* If he's so goddamn horrible, then what the fuck does that say about you, you lying, manipulative, sadistic son of a bitch?" she asked, but she didn't give him the chance to answer.

She hung up before he could, then slammed the phone down on the counter. When she did, she broke down into sobs, letting all the anger flood out of her.

"It's okay," Tariq said, as he wrapped her in his arms. She rested her head on his shoulder. "It's okay."

They stood there as he let her cry. He comforted her, rubbing her back and whispering consoling words into her ear for several minutes. Finally, Noelle raised her head to look up at him with bloodshot eyes.

"Cy . . . Cy tried to ruin this, too," she said between sniffs. "The *one* thing that made me happy for once. He tried to ruin it, but I wouldn't let him!"

"No, you didn't, and I'm proud of you. I know it wasn't easy." He placed a finger under her chin and tilted her head up to meet his gaze. "We won't let him do it—no matter what."

"No matter what," she vowed.

He then lowered his mouth to hers for another kiss.

Chapter 30

Vanessa

Vanessa shut the door to her Mercedes and strolled across the asphalt and then the wet grass, swatting at bugs and cursing under her breath as she went. She had to ignore everything—the fruit flies and mosquitoes, the scorching heat, and her poor choice in footwear that meant her heels were sinking faster than the Titanic into the grass and dirt. She had to focus; she was on a crucial mission today.

She'd left the kids at the hospital with their father almost an hour ago, watching as her children ran across the hospital room to hug and kiss him like they hadn't seen him in years, not a week.

"Daddy! Daddy!" they cried before leaping onto the bed, crying and squealing as they did it.

Even Cy Jr. had run to his father, ignoring his usual "I'm ten years old now. I'm not a kid anymore" façade.

She'd watched the scene from the hospital room's doorway, refusing to walk inside. Something seemed off with Cyrus. She'd expected him to be happier when he saw the children. Instead, he'd been quiet. He looked almost troubled.

Oh, well, not my concern anymore, she'd thought. *If the son of a bitch is depressed, he deserves it.*

"I'll pick you guys up in a couple of hours, okay?" Vanessa had called to them, making her children and husband turn to her.

"You aren't staying, Mom?" Cy Jr. had asked, looking perplexed by her announcement.

"No, honey," Vanessa had replied before putting back on her sunglasses. "Mommy has an errand to do."

Which is what brought her here today to Woodley Park where several ten-, eleven-, and twelve-year-old boys scrambled around the soccer field, chasing after the ball while Bilal stood on the sidelines, blowing his whistle and barking commands like some drill sergeant.

She knew she would find Bilal here.

Cy Jr. would have been at today's practice, too, if it hadn't been for Cyrus's shooting. Cy Jr. would be running up and down the field, building up a sweat with his friends while she stood in the stands, shouting encouraging words to her son and his teammates. Meanwhile, she'd be staring at Bilal and pretending not to fantasize about what she and he would do in the backseat of his car later that day or week.

Ah, the good old days, she now thought flippantly.

"Vanessa?" she heard someone call from behind her.

Vanessa turned to find Reanne and Helen, mothers of two of the boys on Cy Jr.'s soccer team, strolling toward her. Reanne was a single mom with wide hips, a jiggly tummy, and a big mouth. Helen was recently divorced and had the build of a lamp post, but tried to accentuate what little she *did* have by always wearing short shorts and midriff baring tops. Both flirted shamelessly with Bilal on the regular—to Vanessa's great annoyance. Bilal said Helen had even asked him to come over so that she could give him a "home cooked meal with her own special dessert."

"We heard about what happened to your husband!" Reanne cried before stepping forward and enveloping Vanessa in a hug, smothering Vanessa in her bountiful bosom. "You poor thing! You must be devastated!"

"How are you doing with the kids?" Helen asked. "Do you need anything, sweetheart? Anything at all?"

"Just ask!" Reanne chimed in, releasing Vanessa and stepping back. "We'd be happy to help. We know what it's like to struggle on your own, honey. Us moms have to stick together!"

"That's so kind of you both to offer, but really, we're doing fine!" Vanessa said.

She looked over her shoulder at Bilal who had just blown the whistle, which meant practice was coming to an end. She wanted to catch him, to pull him aside before he left. The boys started to huddle up along the goal line and he walked toward them. If only she could get his attention and signal him to wait.

"Are you sure, Vanessa? Don't try to put up a brave front for our sakes!" Reanne insisted, snapping her attention and making her turn back around.

"I'm not putting up a front. My mom has been helping out with the kids," Vanessa explained, "and besides, Cyrus woke up. It looks like he's going to be okay."

"That's great to hear, girl!" Helen exclaimed.

"Praise God!" Reanne said, clasping her hands together like she was in prayer. "Won't He do it?"

"So what on earth are you doing here then?" Helen asked, looking her up and down. "Shouldn't you be at the hospital checking up on your man . . . making sure he's recovering okay? I know if something like that happened to my husband, I wouldn't leave his side!"

Vanessa's fixed smile was starting to wobble.

Not only were Reanne and Helen keeping her from speaking with Bilal, they were also getting into her business and riding on her last nerve. It was on the tip of her tongue to remind Helen that she didn't have a husband. In fact, she hadn't had one in three years, but she kept that response to herself and decided to go with a more neutral one.

"I was there this morning. The kids are with Cy now."

Vanessa watched out of the corner of her eye as Bilal said a few words to the team then made them stack hands in the center of their huddle and chant their team name.

"I just . . . I just came here to ask Coach Bilal about the . . . the game schedule."

"The game schedule?" Helen repeated.

Reanne reached into her tote bag. "Well, I got a copy of it right here if you need to—"

"No, that's okay. I'd rather ask Coach. It's a very . . . uh . . . specific question." She turned away from the two women. "It was nice seeing you two. But I really have to go. Bye!"

She didn't give them a chance to respond before she walked off. She went from a fast clip to a near run to catch Bilal's attention.

"Coach Bilal!" she shouted, making Bilal turn and look at her. "Coach Bilal, do you have a few minutes?"

"Oh, hey, Mrs. Grey," Bilal said casually, keeping up the pretense. "How can I help you?"

They usually didn't talk at practices or games any-more—not in front of everyone else and certainly nothing beyond a greeting or bland conversations that were always soccer related. They didn't want to trip up and blurt out anything that could make anyone catch wind of their affair.

But things are different now, Vanessa thought.

Now she knew an investigator had been following them all those times they had gone off for secret rendezvous together. And who knew what else that bastard Cyrus had been tracking, maybe their phone calls or text messages. Now it seemed the only privacy they had was in public, where a sea of yelling kids and chattering parents offered a wall of sound protection, allowing them to fade into the background. And they needed that mask of privacy today if she was going to ask Bilal to do what her mother had suggested. She didn't want any phone calls, text messages, or photos that could lead police back to the day she'd set her plan into motion to murder her husband.

"Walk with me back to my car," she whispered as she began to walk across the field. Bilal followed her, catching up within seconds.

"What's wrong? I didn't expect you here today," he whispered back to her as they strolled past the bleachers. He nodded at parents and kids who shouted their good-byes at him as they walked by. The noise was so loud she could barely hear him.

Good. That meant other people couldn't hear him either.

"Cy is doing better. He woke up."

Bilal paused and stared at her in shock. "*What? When?*"

"*When* doesn't matter." She motioned for him to keep walking. "What does matter is that he's awake and he knows . . . he knows everything."

"What the hell does that mean?" Bilal whispered.

"What do you think it means?" she asked, still smiling. It felt glued painfully to her face. "He *knows*. He hired an investigator. He has pictures."

"*Pictures?* You mean of . . ."

She nodded. "And now he's holding it over my head. He said he'll show them if I try to leave him. He'll use them in court."

"That motha . . . So what are you gonna do? You aren't sticking with that bastard, are you?"

"Absolutely not! I have a plan, but it would mean—"

"Hey, Coach!" a white guy with a beard and a beer-gut called out as he ambled over to them, sweating even more than Vanessa was at that moment. "Can I be Butt-in-ski for a sec? I've been meaning to ask you something."

So much for them having their conversation out in the open.

"Meet me in the Target parking lot down the road. I'll be parked near the entrance," Vanessa quickly whispered.

Bilal nodded as she walked off and Mr. Butt-in-ski started asking about the new formation that the team had been using lately.

Vanessa drove to Target alone. As she waited with the AC turned up full blast, she practiced her words over and over again, rephrasing them each time. She still hadn't settled on a speech by the time Bilal arrived after twenty minutes of waiting. He knocked on the driver's side window of her Mercedes, startling her. She motioned for him to come to the passenger side and hop in.

"So what's the plan?" he asked, glancing over his shoulder to make sure no one was watching them. "And why the fuck are we talking about it here? Why not meet at our usual spot?"

"I didn't even want to meet here, but I didn't have much of a choice. Honestly, I don't think we can do meet-ups at your place anymore. And no more long drives either. It's too risky! And no texts," she said when he opened his mouth to ask another question. "We don't want anything that the cops could trace later."

"*Cops?* Why the hell would the cops want to trace our text messages?"

"Because when Cy turns up dead, they'll question and investigate everyone all over again, and we don't want to give them any paper trail to use against us."

He squinted at her like he still didn't understand what she was saying, making her roll her eyes and loudly grumble in exasperation.

"We have to kill my husband!"

The instant she said those words, Bilal's face changed. It went from shock to outrage. "I ain't killin' that man!" he yelled, making her furiously wave her hand, motioning for him to quiet down.

"We're inside a car, but people can still hear us if we're shouting, Bilal."

"Shit, why can't you just leave him?" he asked, dropping his voice again. "End it with his ass once and for all, Nessa!"

"Because if I leave him now, he'll show pictures of what we did to everyone. My friends. The kids' teachers. The—"

"So what? That's not a reason to kill someone!"

"And what if he uses those pictures of us in court to fight the divorce?" she argued. "The case could drag on and on. We'd end up spending all the money on lawyers. I might get half as much as I was expecting to get from Cy—or maybe I won't get any money at all outside of child support."

"So *that's* what this is about? *Money?*"

"It's not just about money! But I'm a mother of three kids. I have a reputation to uphold. And those kids need to be taken care of. I haven't worked a day job in more than a decade. I need money for myself and my children! You know that!"

"Well, if that's the case, I can get you a job at my gym."

"As what? One of the trainers? Get serious, Bilal!"

"I *am* being serious! My uncle will let me put you on staff. Maybe you can work at the front desk or in the back office."

She loudly groused.

"Shit, it's something, bae! It sure hell is better than killing your damn husband! You can still get a divorce. Even if all his money's gone in the end, I can take care of you and the kids, too, if . . . if I gotta. You can move into my place. It may mean downsizing for a while. But we can put your stuff in storage. It's only temporary anyway. I'm supposed to get promoted to manager at the gym when my uncle retires in three years. Then I'll make more money."

Vanessa closed her eyes and lowered her head to the steering wheel, now beyond frustrated.

This conversation was not going as she'd planned. She had come here to convince Bilal to join her in her murder plot. Instead, he was trying to convince her to just leave Cyrus and her life as a trophy wife behind. He was trying to argue that she could be just as happy greeting people from the front desk at Get-It-In Gym during the day, and spending her nights sleeping on his bare mattress and box spring in his one-bedroom apartment. Such a life would be her version of hell on earth.

She had to bring Bilal to her side. She had to get him to understand there was no other option but to get rid of Cyrus.

An idea came to mind. She had to be convincing though. A lie like this was too big to do half-heartedly. She bit the inside of her cheek until the pain was so intense that her eyes flooded with tears. When she raised her head and opened her eyes, Bilal saw them.

"Damn, don't cry, Nessa! I swear we'll be okay, bae," he said, placing a comforting hand on her shoulder.

"No, we won't," she sniffed. "I'm . . . I'm pregnant."

Bilal yanked his hand back from her like he'd been zapped with an electric volt.

"I took the test a few days ago," she continued, trying to look vulnerable and scared. "I'm pregnant, Bilal. We're gonna have a baby." She dropped her hand to her waist and rubbed her stomach.

"So it's . . . it's mine?" he asked, looking down where her hand now rested.

"Of course, it's yours! It can't be Cy's. He can't even have kids anymore."

"But I always wore a condom! You always made me. I—"

"And condoms break!" She sniffed again. "When Cy finds out that I'm pregnant, he's going to make my life miserable. He doesn't want me to leave him. He'll probably pressure me to get rid of it because he'll know the baby isn't his."

"But you won't get rid of it," Bilal said firmly.

"I don't want to, but what choice do I have? How do we make this work? It will be hard enough starting over with no money, no job, and three children. Now we'll have to do it with a baby, too? And they need lots of things, honey. A baby isn't going to wait three years for you to get your promotion."

Bilal grimaced.

"Killing Cy is our only option," she insisted, reaching out to touch his forearm. She gazed into eyes. "With him gone, we'd have all the money we needed. We wouldn't have to sneak around anymore. You could be my man. We could be a *real* family, Bilal!"

Bilal stared back at her, not saying anything for several seconds. Finally, he licked his lips and took a deep breath. "How would we even do it? How would we kill him?"

Now I've got him, she thought, fighting back a smile.

"I don't know. Maybe we could use one of your uncle's guns to shoot him. He's already weak from the last attempt on his life. It should be easier this time."

"But if I do it, won't I get arrested?"

"You'll wear a mask like the last guy. The cops might think it's the same guy who came back to finish the job."

"That . . . that makes sense," he muttered, now nodding.

"Doesn't it?"

"So when would we do it?"

"I don't know. Let's wait until he gets out of the hospital and comes home. But we can't wait too long." She rubbed her stomach again. "You have to kill him before I start showing."

"Good point." He slumped back into his chair. "Goddamn! We're really going to do this, huh?"

"We've got no choice but to. He's practically forcing our hand!"

"You're right. You're right!"

"So you'll do it?"

Bilal gradually nodded. "Like you said. We've got no choice but to do it."

This time, she did smile.

Sunday

Chapter 31

Cyrus

"You haven't taken a bite to eat, Mr. Grey," the nurse said as she stood at the edge of his bed, speaking loudly and slowly like he was deaf or like English wasn't his first language. She motioned to his tray and stared down at him over the plastic rims of her glasses. Her lips puckered with distaste as she spoke. "It's important that you finish your meals. You won't recover any faster by refusing to eat."

Cyrus glanced down at the plastic tray perched in front of him—the applesauce, mushy peas, mashed potatoes that looked like a pile of wet tissues, and meat that he wasn't sure whether it was supposed to be Salisbury steak or meatloaf with gravy—and curled his lip in revulsion. He suddenly felt sympathy for his children when Vanessa served lima beans or squash with dinner and they refused to eat it.

"None of you can get up from that table before you clean your plates," Vanessa would say. "Do you hear me?"

Now the nurse was insisting that he'd be stuck in this hospital if he didn't do the same, if he didn't clean his plate. And Cyrus had to get out of here. He had to get his life back in order. It had taken him more than a decade to build everything he had—and it had taken less than a week for it all to fall apart in his absence.

Now his cheating bitch of a first wife Vanessa was screaming for a divorce, and his second wife Noelle wasn't much better. Not only was she leaving him, too, but she had also hooked up with the very man who'd tried to have him killed. Cyrus was still trying to wrap his head around that one. And he'd just received word from the police that his third wife, Diamond—the one he trusted would remain loyal to him despite all that happened—was now in jail facing charges for his attempted murder. Not to mention the fact that he would probably face charges himself for bigamy.

How did it all go wrong so quickly?

He'd like to blame his own personal Judas . . . that son of a bitch Tariq for all his troubles, but the truth was that Cy's life had always been a delicate balancing act.

He would sometimes envision himself as one of those high-wire performers rolling across the Big Top on a unicycle. Or maybe he was the one in the pit, juggling bowling pins or swords, adding more and more until the audience was stunned by his feat. Those death-defying acts had gotten addictive. He'd loved the challenge . . . the thrill of living on the edge, telling and juggling so many different stories and lies. But perhaps, Cyrus had gone too far. He'd finally pushed his luck.

To be honest, Vanessa had been a handful by herself. He didn't know why he'd gotten it into his head to date, let alone marry, Noelle. Sure, he'd had girlfriends on the side for years with Vanessa none the wiser, but Noelle had been the first that he'd decided to give his last name. And after he managed to juggle two wives for so long with neither of them knowing of the other's existence, Cyrus had figured what could be the harm in adding a third? Diamond was such a sweet girl. She needed someone to take care of her and guide her. He thought he was the right man for the job.

But after a while the cracks in the complicated house he'd built started to show. Cyrus found out that Vanessa was having an affair with Cy Jr.'s kiddie soccer coach. Noelle was pressuring him to give her the baby he couldn't give her, and he knew it could mean the end of their marriage if she found out about his vasectomy. And taking care of three women . . . three households was starting to become more than just an emotional strain. It was a financial burden as well. Money was leaving his accounts much faster than it was coming in. He was up to his ears in debt. He had enlisted Tariq for help, and instead, the bastard had betrayed him.

I never should have trusted his ass, he now thought as he glared down at his lunch that the nurse was still waiting patiently for him to eat. *No honor among thieves, and he's the biggest damn thief of them all!*

But Cyrus was wiser now. And all was not lost. Vanessa wouldn't leave him. Not with the threat he had hanging over her head. He'd figure out a way to convince the cops that Diamond had nothing to do with what happened to him without pointing the finger at the real mastermind, who he'd take care of on his own. And somehow . . . somehow, he would get through to Noelle. She didn't believe him now, but maybe if he could see her face-to-face, she would. He didn't trust Tariq around her. He didn't trust his motivations or what he would tell her. But he couldn't handle any of his problems while stuck in a hospital bed. He had to get out of here.

Cyrus opened the bag on his tray that contained a plastic knife and spork. He took out the spork and shoved it into his peas. He then brought the peas in his mouth, took a deep breath and ate, cringing as he did it.

"Very good, Mr. Grey!" the nurse exclaimed. "Keep this up and you'll be out of here faster than you know it!" She then turned and glanced over her shoulder into the corridor. "Well, look at that! I think you have another visitor. This should cheer you up!"

Had Vanessa brought the kids back today, he wondered.

Cyrus swallowed his peas and was just about to swallow another spoonful when the nurse stepped aside to make room for his visitor. When Cyrus saw who it was, he almost choked on his food.

"Hey, Cy," Tariq said, smiling ear-to-ear. "Glad to see you're awake!"

"Aww, isn't that sweet?" the nurse gushed, pointing to the oversized teddy bear Tariq held in one arm. A vase filled with red roses and white lilies were in the other. "That is so adorable. What a cute gift!"

"Blame our assistant Kelsey for this one. She bought it. I'm just delivering it."

Cyrus didn't respond. Instead, he looked at Tariq warily, like Tariq was a waiting wolf, about to pounce.

What the hell was Tariq doing here? How could the bastard be so bold?

"Well, I'll leave you to your visit," the nurse said, beaming. She then playfully wagged her finger at Tariq. "You make sure he eats his lunch. Every single bite, you hear me?"

"I will, ma'am," Tariq said with a wink. "Don't worry."

When she walked out, Tariq slowly made his way to the other side of the hospital room. He sat the teddy bear on the windowsill and the vase beside it. The whole time,

Cyrus tracked him, watching for any sudden moves, anticipating the moment when his business partner would reach for a weapon. He should have asked the nurse to stay. He should have told her he didn't want Tariq in here, but he didn't want to make a scene. He didn't know what Tariq would say or do if he did.

"How you doin', Cy?" Tariq said, turning to look at him and walking to the end of the bed.

"How you think I'm doin'?" Cyrus snarled.

Tariq tilted his head. "Not good, but you're still alive so . . . hey, at least there's that!"

"No, thanks to you, motherfucka."

Tariq chuckled, making Cyrus want to knock that smug expression off his face. If he weren't in such a weakened state, he probably would have hit him.

"I never should've trusted your ass."

"Same," Tariq said, bracing his hands on the bracket at the end of the bed. "But we all make mistakes, right?"

"So you couldn't take my life, so you'll take my wife instead."

"I don't know what you're talkin' about, Cy," Tariq said, feigning innocence. "You're being paranoid, bruh. I didn't do a damn thing to you, and if you're referring to Noelle, you and I both know she ain't your wife. Not legally, anyway. And it's not like wedding vows ever meant much to a dude like you to begin with."

"She's mine. They *all* are mine! You think I'm just gonna let you take her away from me? You think I'm just gonna accept what you did to me?"

"I think you have no choice but to accept your circumstances. Look, don't worry about Noelle. I've got her handled. She's all taken care of. You've got bigger issues right now . . . more important shit to deal with, like your recovery and avoiding jail time. I suggest you use what little money you have left to hire a good lawyer so maybe you'll luck out and get less than a year behind bars, or maybe even house arrest. I knew a dude who had it for two years. You might not like that little ankle bracelet, but it's better than being cooped up in a cell. Trust!"

"You should be the one worried about jail time. All I gotta do is make one phone call to the police and your ass could—"

"So do it," Tariq challenged, motioning to the hospital phone on the night table beside Cy's bed. "Do that shit right now. Go ahead and call them."

Cyrus's eyes shifted to the phone, but he didn't move an inch, making Tariq laugh again.

"I thought so. You ain't gonna call them. If you were going to, you would've done it by now. And we both know why you haven't." He leaned over the bedrail to glower at him. "Don't try to bullshit a bullshitter, Cy. It won't work, bruh! You know if I go down, you go down with me, because I'm tellin' *every*thing—especially that last little favor you asked me to do for you. And I've got the proof to show them."

At that, Cy clamped his mouth shut. He felt the peas he'd just ingested rise back into his throat.

He'd forgotten how much he and Tariq were alike when it came to these things. They were both grand masters at the chess game of plotting, lying, and manipulation. That's why he had taken him under his wing in the first place. He had liked the young man's street smarts and natural cunning. He saw the potential. He'd just had no idea Tariq would later turn on him.

"I know all your shit," Tariq continued. "I know where all the bodies are buried. I know how you really built your company and made your money. Don't fuck with me, Cy. You'll regret it."

"I already regret it! I regret the day I met you, you ungrateful piece of shit! I helped you. I made you into what you are today. When I met you, you were nothin' but a nigga with sweat-stained shirts and two hundred dollars to your name, sleeping on couches and doing small-time hustles, robberies, shakedowns, and whatever other shady shit they asked you to do. With that baby-face, I wouldn't be surprised if you were your crew's bitch, too. Probably sucked a few dicks, didn't you?"

"You know dick suckin' wasn't my specialty. We had girls for that. I was there for somethin' else."

"Yeah, you were. I bet you had plenty of blood on your hands even then."

Again, Tariq didn't respond. He wasn't one to boast, but Cyrus knew his deadly reputation.

"I cleaned you up. Made you legit. I brought you into a real business as a favor to a friend. I taught you everything you know. And this is how you repay me?"

Tariq blew air through his inflated cheeks and pushed himself away from the bed. He waved his hand dismissively. "Man, fuck you! You brought me in because you wanted a connect with my crew. You wanted our money. And you used me, like I used you. Yeah, you taught me a lot, but I was your one-man cleanup crew. I took care of a lot of your messes, Cy. So don't act like you're Mother Teresa, nigga, because you ain't." He looked him up and down. "I wasn't a charity case. And I don't feel bad about any of this shit, so don't bother with the guilt trips. I have no idea who shot you—"

"Don't insult my intelligence."

"—but as far as I'm concerned . . . you got what was coming to you."

That's what the gunman had said when he shot him:

"*You deserve this shit.*" Cyrus figured it had to be a message from Tariq, his last parting words to his mentor.

"So even if you felt I deserved it, why leave Diamond swinging in the wind?"

Tariq raised an eyebrow. "What do you mean?"

"I mean she's being charged with my attempted murder. They think she was the one who set me up. She's gonna take the fall for you!"

"Shit," Tariq muttered. His shoulders fell as he loudly exhaled. "I swear cops are so fuckin' stupid." He sucked his teeth. "I guess I've gotta work on that one. I'll figure it out. Don't worry."

"Don't worry," Cyrus repeated with a cold laugh. "You're just Mr. Fix-It, aren't you?"

"Always have been, always will be." He tugged up his shirt cuff and glanced down at his wristwatch. "I better get going. I'm supposed to meet up with Noelle later. I'm taking her out to dinner."

Cyrus's jaw tightened as he watched Tariq stroll back to the hospital doorway. The bastard was actually gloating about stealing his wife.

"She's not as stupid as you think, you know!" he called after Tariq, making him halt and turn to face him again.

"I don't think she's stupid," he said, genuinely looking offended.

"Could've fooled me from all the shit you've probably been feeding her. You've convinced yourself that you're in love with her. That's part of the reason you did all of this, I bet. But you're no different than me, Tariq. The person you love most is yourself, and she's gonna figure that shit out. She's gonna figure out who you really are. And when she does find out the truth, that's the end of it. I know her. She isn't gonna stay with any man she doesn't respect. And I'll be the one laughing in *your* face! I'll be laughing at how you fucked me, yourself, and our partnership over for a woman who doesn't even want your ass!"

For the first time, Tariq's nonchalant mask slipped. His features hardened for a few seconds, showing the real anger and hatred for Cyrus that bubbled underneath, as hot as magma.

So that was his trigger now. Noelle was his weak point, Cyrus realized. He may be able to use that to his advantage in the future.

But in a few seconds, Tariq got himself back under control. His licked his lips. His face went placid again. His mask was firmly back in place.

"See you later, Cy," he said casually before stepping through the doorway into the corridor, but he paused to look at him once more. "Oh, I almost forgot. Don't call the house anymore, okay? It upsets Noelle. If you do call her again, I'll tell her to just block your number or I'll do it myself."

"You can't block my number! *To my own goddamn house?*" Cyrus sputtered with fury. "I'll call her whenever I goddamn want to! Who the fuck do you think you—"

"And if you so as much come within three feet of her," Tariq said, speaking over him, "I'll make sure the little errand I sent a fool to do, I'll take care of myself next time. And you know when I takeover a job, I get it done, Cy. Don't test me." He then adjusted his suit jacket and strolled into the hallway and out of the hospital room.

When he left, Cyrus glared at the oversized teddy bear that Tariq had left sitting on his windowsill, at its big dumb face, and he was flooded with wrath. He wanted to hurl it across the room. He wanted to stab it with his spork. He started pounding his fist on the table in front of him over and over again instead. His tray flipped over onto the floor, splattering the linoleum tiles with yellow, brown, green and white, making it look like a Jackson Pollock painting.

"Mr. Grey! What did you do?" the nurse cried as she came running into the room. She looked down at his be-spattered lunch and clucked her tongue. She dropped to her knees and picked up the tray. "I hope that was an accident, sir. If not, this is a major setback."

It certainly was. Tariq may have won this round, but Cyrus was already lining up his pieces on the chessboard again, plotting out all the moves that were necessary to take the queen and win the game.

Can't wait to see what happens next?
Keep reading for a sneak peek at
the next action-packed entry in the series
coming soon from
Shelly Ellis
and
Dafina Books!

Chapter 1

Vanessa

"Nessa! *Nessaaaaa!*" Cyrus Grey yelled from upstairs.

His voice ricocheted like a sonic boom out their bedroom door, down the hall, and then down the stairs to Vanessa as she stood at the kitchen counter, assembling his lunch—a club sandwich with tomato bisque and chips—on a serving tray.

Her husband may still be mostly bedridden from the gunshot wounds he'd suffered almost two months ago, but nothing seemed to be hampering his mouth. He was as loud and demanding as ever.

"What?" she shouted back irritably over her shoulder as she poured pomegranate juice into a glass.

"What the hell is taking you so long, woman? I'm starvin'!"

She sucked her teeth. "Well, you can starve to death for all I care, you son of a bitch," she muttered before slamming the glass onto the wooden tray, making juice slosh over the side.

Vanessa had been catering to Cyrus since he'd arrived home from the hospital—feeding him, washing him, clothing him, disinfecting his wounds, and changing the bandages. And she'd hated every minute of it. It was bad enough that he had cheated on her for years, even marrying two other women behind her back while he was still married to her. It was bad enough that he was now blackmailing her to stay in their farce of a marriage by holding evidence of her affair with her eldest son's soccer coach over her head. (He'd threatened to email that photographic evidence to everyone, from the other soccer moms from their son's team to their children's stuffy school principal.) But now, Cyrus was making Vanessa cater to him like some handmaiden and nurse all rolled into one. It was a slow torture that she endured daily. She just wished it would end.

Vanessa opened one of the kitchen drawers to retrieve a spoon. As she did, her eyes landed on a bottle of Clorox spray she'd left sitting on the counter yesterday after she'd scrubbed down the kitchen. Her eyes then shifted back to Cyrus's glass of pomegranate juice. Maybe she could pour a little into his drink. Not too much that he would taste it, but just enough to kill him. If he died, this whole ordeal would be over. No more Nurse Vanessa. No more pain-in-the-ass Cyrus. She reached for the bottle.

"Nessa! Did you hear me?" Cyrus shouted again, making her jump in alarm and snatch back her hand. "Where the hell is my food?"

Vanessa grumbled. Instead of grabbing the bottle of cleaning fluid, she grabbed a spoon and slammed the kitchen drawer shut.

She wouldn't poison her husband—not today, anyway. It was too risky; a coroner might find traces of the bleach in his system. She'd have to stick to the plan and let her lover, Bilal, kill him for her. She just hoped Bilal did it soon. Though she had to admit Cyrus being laid up in his

bed at home most of the time didn't make carrying out
their murder plot any easier.

"I'm coming, damn it! Stop yelling!" she shouted back
before grabbing the tray and trudging out of the kitchen
and later up the stairs to their bedroom.

Vanessa eased the bedroom door open with her shoulder and found Cyrus sitting up in the center of their
California king in maroon silk pajamas.

Though the bed was easily big enough for two, Vanessa
hadn't slept in here with her husband since he'd arrived
home. Instead, she slept in one of the guest rooms two
doors down the hall. She'd told their three children she'd
made the move to the other room because she wanted to
give their father space to spread out and get comfortable,
anything to expedite his full, healthy recovery from the
shooting. But the truth was, the less time she had to stay in
the same room with Cyrus, the better. And she suspected
Cy knew the truth and hadn't asked her to stay in here
with him because of that reason.

Besides, if they slept in the same bedroom, she couldn't
vouch that she wouldn't try to strangle or smother the bastard in his sleep.

"Lunch is served," she now announced dryly as she carried the tray to his bed.

"Took you long enough," he muttered.

She sat the tray on his lap. "Even if I didn't come up at
all, you would've been fine. You could skip a meal or two,
honey." She poked his growing paunch through his shirt,
making him swat her hand away.

Cyrus had never been a man with sculpted muscle, but
he'd always been solidly built—her own John Henry with
a bald head, big arms, and tree-trunk thighs, like the folk
hero. That is, until recently. Cy had gone from frail when
he first returned from the hospital, to now almost doughy

after being in bed and stuffing his face for so long. He even worked from his bed now, grazing on snacks as he typed emails and made business calls.

Vanessa glanced at the opened bags of nacho chips, chocolate chip cookies, and trail mix that sat on his night table. If she didn't kill him, all the food he was eating certainly would.

"Don't worry about me. I'll be up and around sooner or later and get back to my old fighting weight," he assured before taking a bite from his sandwich.

She turned away. "Let's hope its sooner rather than later," she tossed over her shoulder with a withering glance as she strolled out of the bedroom.

A half hour later, Vanessa was finishing up her own lunch when her doorbell rang. She rose to her feet and walked out of the kitchen through the living room and into her foyer. When she swung the front door open, she saw her mother Carol standing on her welcome mat in a tank top, capris, and kitten-heeled sandals.

"Hey, Mama," she said tiredly.

"Hey! How's the patient?" her mother asked as she cocked a finely-arched eyebrow over her sunglasses. "Still alive, I assume?"

"Unfortunately," Vanessa whispered before cutting her eyes at the stairs. "Let's go outside to the deck and talk."

Her mother nodded as she stepped inside and shut the front door behind her.

"You don't look too good, sweetheart," her mother said as she trailed behind her across the house. They wound their way through the spacious living room and sunroom.

"Oh, thanks," Vanessa replied sarcastically.

"I mean it, baby! Are you getting a good night's rest? When's the last time you got a facial or at least an exfoliation treatment? You can't neglect yourself, Nessa. You're a woman of thirty-seven. You have to maintain what you have, my dear!"

As Vanessa neared the French doors leading to the rear of her home, she caught her reflection in the window-panes. Her mother was right. She didn't look like herself. She was wearing a wrinkled, nondescript sheath dress rather than the clingy designer dresses and outfits she usually wore that showed off her petite, curvy figure. Her glossy dark curls were haphazardly pulled into a bun at her nape because she hadn't been in the mood to style her hair in days. There were bags bigger than Birkins under her eyes. And worst of all, she was starting to look pale, especially next to her mother, whose soft, brown skin had taken on the warm radiance it always did this time of year. Vanessa hated it when her own skin lost its healthy, golden glow. She had Cyrus to blame for all of this as well as the stress she was under.

"I've just been down lately," she mumbled to her mother. She swung open one of the doors and stepped onto the two-story deck.

Her mother closed the French doors behind them. Both women headed to one of the patio tables, squinting at the blinding afternoon sun that now hovered in a cloudless sky.

"I haven't had much energy for self-care thanks to Cyrus," Vanessa continued. "Taking care of his big lazy ass is a twenty-four-hour job."

Carol pulled out one of the table chairs, looked over her shoulder at the overhead windows, searching for the man himself. When she didn't see Cyrus and was reasonably sure he wasn't eavesdropping, she sat down. "Well, hopefully you won't be taking care of him too much longer, honey," her mother whispered. "Any progress on that little project of yours?"

Vanessa shook her head as she sat in one of the chairs

on the opposite side of the table. "Nope. Bilal can't really do anything while Cyrus is staying home all day." She inclined her head. "I guess we could try to do it while I'm out on errands and the kids are away at day camp. Maybe he could break-in, do a fake robbery, and . . . you know . . . get the job done, but I really don't want him to do it here at the house." She grimaced. "It could get messy, and it might creep out the kids."

"Hmm, I see your point," her mother said, pursing her lips. "Now explain to me again why you two decided not to do it as he was leaving the hospital."

Vanessa groaned. It was still a touchy subject for her. She and Bilal had discussed the plan about a dozen times, then had to abruptly abort the mission only hours before it was supposed to take place.

"He was supposed to walk up and shoot Cy as he was being wheeled out to our car," she said, dropping her voice to a whisper again. "He was supposed to wear a ski mask . . . you know . . . so his face would be covered, and everyone would think it was the same guy who tried to kill Cy the first time. But the night before, I found out that Diamond and her pimp boyfriend were charged with Cy's attempted murder. If the cops already have the guy who says he did it, Bilal couldn't very well pretend to be him, could he?"

"I guess not." Her mother slumped back in her chair, removed her sunglasses, and tossed them onto the patio table. "Too bad that other wife of his didn't succeed the first time! All your problems would be taken care of."

"Maybe," Vanessa said, though she still wasn't convinced the cops had arrested the right person.

She wasn't fond of Diamond, Cyrus's third wife, by any estimation, but she found it hard to believe the young woman would try to have Cyrus killed. Diamond had defended him fiercely to both Vanessa and Noelle, Cyrus's second wife, the last time they were all together—the *only* time all three women had agreed to meet once they learned of each other's existence. Vanessa grudgingly had to admit that Diamond seemed firmly smitten with Cyrus. And Cyrus was equally convinced of her innocence, insisting to Vanessa that Diamond wasn't the culprit and he knew who really was behind his attempted murder—though he refused to name names. But still, the cops said Diamond's boyfriend had confessed to the shooting, claiming that he'd received a gold chain as payment. And the cops wouldn't charge her with the crime unless they had credible evidence against her, would they?

"So, what are you gonna do?" Carol now asked. "Just hope your husband heals faster and finally gets off his ass and out the house? I thought you had a deadline with this. Didn't you tell that boytoy of yours that you were pregnant months ago? Won't he start wondering why you aren't showing?"

"I gave him a copy of one of my old printouts of Zoe's ultrasounds to buy some time. I altered the dates on my computer, so it looks like I took it a couple of weeks ago."

"How inventive! I guess he believed it then?"

Vanessa nodded. "He started crying. He keeps the printout on his refrigerator."

"Oh, my goodness!" Her mother threw back her head and cackled. "The dumb pretty ones never cease to amaze me!"

Vanessa didn't join Carol in her laughter. The truth was she was starting to feel a bit guilty for lying to Bilal about being pregnant. He was so excited at the prospect of becoming a father, musing about what the baby would look like and how he hoped they were having a boy.

"But I'd be okay with a girl too, bae," he had assured her just yesterday over the phone. "I'll be happy either way!"

She didn't enjoy lying to him about something like this,

but she didn't know what alternative she had. He wouldn't have agreed to murder Cyrus if she hadn't told him about having a baby on the way.

"Well, hopefully," her mother said as her laughter tapered off, "he's finally able to take care of your husband for you in the next month or so. Or you'll have to dig up another ultrasound photo, I suppose, or maybe start wearing a damn pillow underneath your clothes when you see him."

"Let's hope it doesn't get that ridiculous," Vanessa muttered.

Though she had another printout saved on her computer, just in case, *and* a pillow on standby.